RITUAL OF BLOOD

RITUAL OF BLOOD

Book One
Wizards of the Vactican

Penny Pearson

Cover design: Stephen Zimmer

Cover design in this book copyright © 2020 Stephen Zimmer & Seventh Star Press, LLC.

Editor: Holly Phillippe

Published by Seventh Star Press, LLC.

ISBN Number: 978-1-948042-97-0

Seventh Star Press

www.seventhstarpress.com

info@seventhstarpress.com

Publisher's Note:

Ritual of Blood is a work of fiction. All names, characters, and places are the product of the author's imagination, used in fictitious manner. Any resemblances to actual persons, places, locales, events, etc. are purely coincidental.

Printed in the United States of America

First Edition

Chapter 1

"**W**e're going to have to split and go separate ways."

The statement shocked Zoe. "What?" They were in the middle of nowhere.

Her friend Susie nodded as she folded the map while juggling a flashlight under her chin. "Yes, Zoe. Only twenty-five minutes left until the deadline passes. We need three more items from the list. We are so close. Imagine," she cajoled, "how nice it would be to spend some of your vacation time in Las Vegas. It would be such a nice break from work."

Zoe moaned at her friend's tone. "It doesn't seem safe to go separate ways. It's dark. We can barely see." Twirling a lock of short, black hair, she glanced into the darkness. It had felt like a bad idea to get on a chartered bus and go on a Halloween night scavenger hunt, but here she was, doing exactly that.

Tiffany, the third wheel of the adventure, sidled next to Susie. "Come on, Zoe, don't be a downer. I am going on my own, too. We are so close to winning this scavenger hunt."

"I didn't know we would be splitting up in the middle of the woods," Zoe snapped. She realized she sounded as if she was whining, but didn't care. She was whining. "It can't be safe."

Susie held out an extra map to Zoe while she shone her flashlight on the surface. She pointed a painted fingertip toward the middle. "Here is the Boston Cemetery, and it is only five minutes away down that walking path. You need to go there and make a tombstone rubbing from the year 1864. I will go up to Johnson's barn to find a pitchfork. Tiffany, you go to the gas station near the bus. It says to get coffin nails, which means cigarettes."

"This is the worst list," Zoe complained. "Who asks people to walk around at midnight to find pitchforks, coffin nails, and tombstones?"

"Where is your sense of adventure?"

"At home in bed."

"We don't have time," Susie huffed. "We can win if we do this. We did so well on the other items. If we all hurry, we'll meet back at the bus in less than ten minutes. We'll be done before everyone else, and we'll win!"

"Fine, but I'll have you know, I don't appreciate being the one to go to an abandoned cemetery." Zoe gazed at the two women with narrowed eyes.

"You'll be fine. Now, go! Remember Las Vegas and how awesome it's gonna to be. Come on, Tiffany, let's get moving." With that, the two other women started jogging away from Zoe, their flashlights jumping with each stride.

"*Remember Las Vegas*," Zoe mimicked sarcastically as she pulled her lightweight jacket tighter around her. Nearing almost thirty years old, she wondered why she still couldn't tell Susie that sometimes her ideas were ridiculous.

She'd run up the trail and find the damn grave. Then she'd give Susie and Tiffany a piece of her mind, and she would claim ownership of the biggest bedroom in their Vegas hotel. Shining her flashlight in front of her, she set out toward the cemetery.

The Ohio cemetery wasn't overly large, due to the fact that Boston Township was nonexistent now. The government had bought out the entire village more than forty years ago and declared it a natural park. Rumor had it that the buyout was due to some sort of chemical spill, but it was urban legend. Eventually all the houses were demolished, and the last lingering soul moved from the city years ago. So, out went the townsfolk and in came the ghost hunters and paranormal weirdos.

Now you're one of the weirdos, her brain teased.

Ritual Of Blood

"Shut up, Brain," Zoe mumbled and continued to shine her flashlight on the tractor path leading to the graveyard. Two minutes later, she illuminated the trail in front of her with her slim flashlight and stared at the paths that veered away from each other. She'd been here a time or two before, but didn't remember the path splintering off. Taking the path on the right, she walked a few feet, but grew confused when she came to another fork.

In front of her, a broken fence rose eerily in the moonlight, and she startled when she thought she saw a shape move in the darkness. Zoe picked up her pace, but soon realized she didn't see the cemetery that should have been right in front of her. Quickly bringing out her cell phone, she pulled up her map app and set the cemetery as her destination. The phone stated she was three minutes away from her destination.

Shining the flashlight in front of her, she stared at the screen and followed its directions. Finally spotting the raised area that protected the old cemetery plots, she picked up her pace. She put her cell phone in her jacket pocket as she took in the deserted town's cemetery. A twig snapping somewhere beside her caused her to squeak in fright. She stopped and listened, but only the leaves overhead rustled and brushed against scratchy bark.

She told herself it was simply her imagination. She had plenty of it. It also didn't help that urban legend said the cemetery had been home to an odd satanic cult or two. Her heart beat faster. "1864," she repeated to herself. "Find the grave and get out of here." She quickly shined her light on the waist high gravestones. All the years were wrong, so she kept walking in search of the elusive 1864.

Another sound, a groan, floated through the cemetery. She whirled and scanned her surroundings for some sign of a person or animal, but she could see nothing in the utter blackness outside her feeble light. She took a deep breath to calm her nerves. Circling to shine her flashlight around her, she searched the gravestones for the needed year. Off to her right side, she spotted a potential candidate. Quickly walking to the grave, she spied the date.

She hit the jackpot! She pulled a piece of paper out of her

purse and scratched a pencil across the engraved date. It wasn't a professional gravestone rubbing, but she wasn't about to take time out to tape up her paper, get rubbing wax, and create art. She needed a date to verify she was in a cemetery in the middle of the night, by herself.

She was a fool.

As she berated herself, another sound drifted from behind her. What was that? A strange gurgle emanated somewhere outside her field of vision. Her flashlight beam jumped from gravestone to gravestone.

A chanting voice rose from the graveyard and her heart jumped into her throat. Zoe pulled her cell phone out of her pocket and typed the name of the bus stop. She needed to get out of the cemetery as fast as possible. She didn't care about winning the contest.

Her fingers fumbled over the small keyboard while she spun around to get her bearings. A strange fog rose, and she could barely see in front of her.

The chanting grew louder and more feverish. The smell of something vile and rotten permeated her senses. Suddenly Zoe found herself facing a pair of men, one prone on the ground, the other kneeling at his side. Leaves shifted around the pair. Without thought, she pressed her finger on the picture button. The area lit up with the camera's flash the same moment the kneeling man raised a long knife and brought it forcefully down.

Zoe screamed. The man's hand jerked at the sound of Zoe's voice, but the knife was still buried to the hilt. The victim writhed and gasped. Horror gripped Zoe, holding her immobile.

The kneeling man closed his eyes against the glare of the camera flash with a snarl curling on his lips. Long, dark hair fell over his brow and plastered across his gaunt face. Dark clothes hid his shape.

Zoe pulled her gaze from the man to gawk at the body. The light from the moon illuminated a young man with bright blond hair who stared sightless into space.

He was dead.

Ritual Of Blood

Her brain barely registered the thought before her body's flight response kicked in. She spun around to run and instantly slammed headfirst into the outstretched arm of a praying angel. She stumbled backward and cried out, as pain sliced across her cheekbone. Lights sparkled across her vision.

Grasping her cell phone, she sprinted as fast as she could out of the cemetery. Zoe pumped her arms and legs and flew over the tractor path. Her flashlight had been dropped in the cemetery, but the full moon illuminated the path. She ran past the spot where Tiffany and Susie argued with her, and past the beaten down sign declaring the road closed to Boston Township.

As Zoe ran, fear nearly choked her with every stride. *Oh my God, I just saw someone killed!* Disbelief clouded her brain. Blood dripped down the side of her face from her run-in with the cemetery statue, but she continued her flight to safety. She didn't want to die, and she had no idea if the man followed her. She didn't look back for fear of stumbling on the rocky terrain, as she concentrated on the ground in front of her. Her ears strained to listen for chasing footsteps, but the pounding of her heart made it impossible.

She tripped over a rock, and her phone flew out of her hands, but she wasn't about to stop and search for it. She continued to run. She pictured the murderer running behind her, sinking his knife in her back. Steering her mind away from the horrible images, she forced herself to concentrate on the path ahead, not the possibility of the monster behind her.

The lights of the awaiting tour bus came into view. Zoe used one last burst of speed to get to safety. The man wouldn't be idiotic enough to chase her into a crowded bus, would he? Her side ached, and she knew she was nearing the end of her endurance.

"Help me!" she screamed as she ran closer. "Please! Call the police!"

Chapter 2

5 minutes ago....

Dale Hicks fought down his rage. If this ritual didn't work, his debts would come due, and he wasn't ready to pay up. How had the woman stumbled across him unnoticed? His finely orchestrated ritual could have been ruined by the intrusion. He stared in the direction the girl had run. She could be of help. Her youth would buy him many more years before his obligations caught up with him.

He forced his thoughts back to his ritual spell. At the moment, he was collecting more life, more time, to his life bank. The body before him grew colder by the minute. He needed to capture the essence of his victim before it dissipated. Carefully reciting the spell needed to seize the unused life of his young sacrifice, he completed the necessary motions. A sharp wail ripped through the air. He smiled as the body's soul shrieked as the ritual devoured it. A few minutes later, the spell was complete. The body wasn't needed any longer.

It had been a relative success, with the exception of the interruption. There wouldn't be much time to cover his tracks, not with a witness on the loose. She was probably screaming bloody murder at the moment. With any luck, the authorities would assume someone pranked the girl and be slow to respond. The smell of gasoline cleared his sinuses, while he squirted the strong-smelling liquid over the body. Glancing through the darkness, he caught a glimpse of a nearby coyote. He scowled at the creature as it moved closer.

"You didn't warn me," the necromancer hissed at the animal.

The coyote stared at him through unblinking eyes, and then turned his head to look at the statue of an angel with outstretched arms.

Walking to the monument, an unholy glee spread through him. Dark red glistened in the moonlight; the faint glow of life was still present and visible now that he was out of the ritual circle. The girl had cut herself.

Perfect! He held up his index finger and opened the top of his potion ring. He recited a spell, calling the liquid into the small container. He carefully shut the ring, making sure it was secure. He would find the girl, then he would use her for the next ritual. As a necromancer, his power was to communicate with the dead, to control and shape it. He would find this woman.

He pulled out a matchbook from his pants pocket. Quickly striking, he tossed the match and instantly flames engulfed the body. There wasn't much time. He needed to be well away from the area when the police responded. Once again, anger simmered in the pit of his stomach. How had the woman gotten past his shields and the deterrent spell? He'd taken great pains to ensure they were strong. She shouldn't have been able to stroll up to him unnoticed. *Unless she was a sorceress.*

Unease travelled down his spine at the thought. He couldn't afford to have someone messing with his ritual. They had no idea what they were dealing with, but he swore he would make them regret their decision to meddle in his business.

***

"What are you talking about?" Susie cried after Zoe made her declaration. "Holy shit, are you bleeding?" Susie slowly pulled her phone out of her purse, dialed 9-1-1, and handed the phone to Zoe.

Zoe took the phone with shaking, blood-smeared hands. Her

face hurt from her not-so-graceful attempt to escape. Her fingers gingerly touched her cheek as she waited for the operator to answer. Her fingers came away dripping with blood. She grew light-headed, but stayed focused.

"9-1-1, what's your emergency?" The voice was calm and matter of fact.

"There's been a murder," Zoe choked out. Anxiety and adrenalin played their game on her, leaving her feeling weak and adrift in a strange sea of confusion. Tremors began to rack her body in great waves.

Gasps sounded from the others at the mention of murder. She lifted her eyes to stare at Susie. Even in the darkness, she could see the faces of the others that had come on this scavenger hunt. Their evening should have consisted of silly fun and spooky haunts.

"What is your name?" The voice prompted her to rejoin the present.

"Zoe Hunt." Her voice shook, she couldn't seem to control her reaction.

"Where are you located?" the dispatcher asked in a level voice.

Panic shot through Zoe. "Uh, the bus … Oh God, I don't know." She turned and frantically questioned, "Where are we?" Hysteria laced her voice, but she couldn't tamp it down.

"We are on Snowville Road, about two miles east of Brecksville Road," the bus driver answered. His eyes were wide, and his gaze shifted around him. "You saw a murder out there?"

Zoe turned her back on the bus driver to ignore his query. She needed to concentrate on delivering the facts as clearly as possible. "We are on Snowville Road east of Brecksville Road." She repeated the directions back to the 9-1-1 dispatcher.

"Are you hurt?" Once again, the female voice was calm, as if she'd taken a million of these calls already.

"N-no, but I saw a man murdered."

"Are you somewhere safe?"

"Yes," Zoe answered. She sank down onto the cold ground because her knees wouldn't hold her. "I think so. I ran, but I don't think he followed me."

"Can you describe what you saw?"

In a shaky voice, Zoe related all the details.

"Stay where you are. The police will be there. Can you please hand the phone to the bus driver?"

"Okay," she told the dispatcher as she located the driver. She handed the phone to him. "They would like to speak with you."

The man nodded and took the phone from her. He proceeded to give his own accounting of the events to the dispatcher.

Zoe sat on the seat in the first row and stared out into the darkness. Numbness settled inside her. However, it didn't deter the tremors; her limbs continued to shake violently.

Susie crouched down beside her and put her hand on Zoe's knees. "What happened, Zoe?"

Tears gathered in her vision, but she quickly wiped them away. She told herself she was strong and could get through this. "I told you going to the cemetery was a bad idea."

"What happened?" Susie persisted like a terrier with a rat.

"I saw someone die."

"Really? It's so dark out. Are you sure you weren't seeing things? Maybe some kids are playing games."

Disbelief cut through Zoe's terror. "Are you kidding me? Why would I make this up? I wouldn't kid around about this!"

Police sirens in the distance quieted everyone. The impact of what possibly occurred was a buzz kill for all. Zoe remained sitting until uniformed officers walked toward her in the shadow of their parked squad car's headlights. They stopped and asked for Zoe by name. She rose and walked over to them.

"I'm Zoe Hunt." Their flashlights traveled over her, and she shielded her eyes from the bright beams.

"I am Officer Murdock, and this is Detective Williams," the man stated and gestured to his female partner. "Can you tell us what happened?"

The uniformed man pulled at his button-up jacket that fit too tightly around his paunchy middle. He was of average height, but made up for it in bulky muscle. He reminded Zoe of a bulldog. He held a small pocket notebook in his hand.

Ritual Of Blood

"I was walking through Boston Cemetery to find a scavenger hunt item. While there, I saw someone get stabbed." That, she admitted, sounded lame to her ears.

The officer looked at his partner to his right. Her dark skin glistened in the light of the cars, and she scowled at Zoe's words.

Zoe drew in a breath. "I promise; this isn't some Halloween prank. I saw someone murdered in that cemetery." She pointed a shaky finger in the direction of the cemetery. "He could still be there."

"You realize that cemetery is closed. It is against the law to trespass," Officer Murdock declared with disapproval ringing in his tone

Somehow, the tables had turned on her, and the officers stared at her as if she was a suspect. Never mind that some killer was probably getting away as they spoke. Then, she remembered her phone. "I dropped my phone as I was running to the bus, but I took a picture of him. If we can find my phone, you can see what he looks like. I ran down the path right in front of us. It leads to the cemetery."

The officer clicked a radio button on his shoulder and called for more back up. It seemed others must have been curious about the situation, for two more squad cars pulled up beside them. Two men got out of their cars. "Murdock, Williams, what's the story here?" one of the newcomers asked. Tall and broad-shouldered with a military buzz cut, he looked as if he could pick up five of her with ease.

Officer Murdock looked at his partner before stating, "She says a man was murdered up in the cemetery."

Everyone stared up the hill, but none appeared inclined to investigate.

In frustration, Zoe declared, "It's been less than ten minutes." Surely, that would prompt them to go up the hill and do some detective work, yet they continued to stand still, seemingly not in a hurry to examine the lead she'd given them. Zoe didn't want to go either, but this was their job. They *had* to go.

"We should go up there," Officer Murdock spoke in an

uninspired tone, a tone that spoke of doing the opposite of his words.

Zoe looked at Susie in disbelief. What was going on? Susie only shrugged. Deciding to take the lead because she could think of nothing other to do, she started walking. "Let me show you where it was."

Detective Williams stepped up and put a slender hand on Zoe's sleeve. "No," she commanded. "We will go. Officer Murdock, will you stay with Miss Hunt."

At Williams' words, all the officers came out of their lassitude. All clicked on their flashlights and strode up the darkened road toward the cemetery.

Zoe watched the officer's flashlights bob in the distance. Suddenly she heard shouts, and Officer William's voice came from Murdock's radio.

"Control, we've got a 904 at the cemetery. We're going to need fire trucks."

Chapter 3

"**I** found something that might interest you."

Erik Vardan stopped stalking down the hallway and turned to stare at the grinning girl. In his opinion, her peppiness at such an early hour on a Saturday morning was unacceptable. Her bright blue pigtails bounced. She rocked back and forth on her booted heels and hummed some sort of annoying tune. "What did you find?" he asked. Jenny was the resident Goth figure, and she fit the label well. He wasn't sure if she modeled herself after Abby from *NCIS*, or if was serendipity.

She waved at him to follow her and spoke over her shoulder, "Something in Ohio caught my attention."

Erik was intrigued. Jenny had a knack at finding work for him. He joined her in the tight closet of a space she called an office and waited expectantly for more details.

Jenny sat at her computer and clicked the mouse with a flourish, bringing up a police file. A report bearing the proud logo of the "Village of Peninsula Police Department" lit the screen.

"There is evidence of a ritual murder in Boston Township, Ohio. The police were able to obtain a good picture of the murderer. Well, not a good picture of the *man*," Jenny admitted, "but an excellent picture of the murder weapon." She pointed to the screen with painted black fingernails. Erik noted the swirls on her nails were the same blue tone as her hair.

Erik squeezed farther into the office to lean over Jenny's

shoulder where he could better view the photo. She had been correct; the photo was a disappointment if one wanted to capture the likeness of the suspect, but the view of the murder weapon was perfect. The ceremonial knife gleamed in the picture, a single blade athame. The ancient knife originated in the middle ages and was one he had seen many times. A simple design, the versatile knife could carve symbols into candles, as well as carve out a heart.

"Where was this again?"

"A small town outside of Cleveland."

"Is the witness alive?"

"Yes," Jenny answered.

He looked at her with a smile. "You keep finding things like this and I'll see if I can get you a bigger office."

Jenny scowled as she looked around her workspace. "Don't you dare threaten me with another office. I love my home!" She narrowed her eyes at him and asked slyly, "So, is this something you want to investigate, or do you want me to send it to the monsignor? Because if you want this, you better not bring up the subject of another office again."

Erik didn't even pause in his decision. He wanted this. All the leads he had explored on these black wizards led to nowhere, and he wasn't good with down time. He felt like going to Village of the Peninsula, Ohio.

***

Zoe gently touched the side of her bandaged face. Five stitches graced her cheek, and the covering itched. She couldn't wait for Tuesday when the stitches would be removed. Forcing herself to lower her hand before she did damage, she sat at her kitchen table to stare out the window. It was a sunny day, too sunny for the day after a murder in her opinion. The water of Lake Erie glinted like diamonds. Her fifteenth story apartment had the most wonderful view of the lake, and she lamented the cold weather that neared. She missed her cozy deck chair with its accompanying warm summer breeze on the balcony.

Ritual Of Blood

Her tiny, yet comfortable, studio apartment was on the far eastern edge of Cleveland, overlooking Lake Erie. She might not have a proper bedroom with a door that closed, but work and friends were nearby. She'd lived in the apartment for five years and always felt safe before. Even when the summer tourists from all over the world swarmed the beaches, she never felt threatened.

Zoe yawned and rubbed her tired eyes. She arrived home late after the police finished questioning her, only to fall asleep. Her nightmares didn't yield a killer's face. No, they somehow were worse, because it wasn't the visions of the dreams that haunted her. It was the smell of the cemetery, cloying and rotten.

In the morning, the foulest smell lingered in her room, wafting from her clothes from the night before. If death had a scent, she imagined that would be it.

She shivered and shook her head, trying to be done with the remnants of the dream. Instead, the face of the dead boy filled her mind. She tried to block out the horrid images of the night before, but her mind wouldn't stop. She continued to see the dead man's sightless eyes, and the killer's cold stare. It haunted her.

What if he came after her?

Her blood ran cold. It worried her when she thought of the murderer trying to find her. What would he do if he did? Other than, you know, stab her to death.

It had been dark last night, even with the full moon high overhead. She never expected to stumble across anyone in the cemetery. Zoe told the police officer she and the killer might have gazed at each other a split second before she snapped the picture. Shortly a police sketch artist sat down beside her, hopeful she could provide some sort of positive ID on the killer. She gave the best description of the murderer as possible, but it was hard to describe any part of him. She only remembered dark hair against pale skin that shone in the moonlight.

When she took the picture, her cell phone's flash potentially could have blinded the man. He probably had not been able to get a good look at her. It probably also aided Zoe in her escape. With his vision impacted, he hadn't been able to pursue. That's what

Officer Murdock told her after the burned body of the victim had been recovered.

Zoe couldn't help being a little worried. If she could remember things about the man from a brief glance, there was a huge chance he would remember something about her. The idea that he could possibly be hunting for her was terrifying. She didn't have a security system, but maybe she should get one. She had limited means to protect herself since she refused to own a gun.

The officers found no trace of the murderer, in or near the cemetery, when they finally got around to searching. She still couldn't believe all the officers stalled so long before looking for the suspect. Disappointment flooded her when the local news channel reported no suspect in the murder of nineteen-year old, Caleb Brown. Internet searches yielded the same results. The man had disappeared with no sign.

How am I supposed to deal with this?

Somehow, she would not let this affect her. People dealt with many worse things on a daily basis. She would not fall apart. She only needed to be on the lookout for any danger. She wouldn't overreact. The police would find the murderer. It was their job. The man would go to jail and never get out.

Her cell began to play the *Doctor Who* theme, and Zoe spied Susie's name and picture on the screen. "Hi, Susie," she answered on the second ring.

"Hi, Zoe," Susie spoke in a hushed voice. "I wasn't sure if you'd gotten your phone back from the police. I'm checking to make sure you're okay."

Zoe smiled into the phone at her friend's thoughtfulness. It was evident Susie was feeling guilty for not believing her last night. "Yeah, the police didn't have to keep it. They downloaded an electronic copy of the picture I took. Nothing else on my phone was any help. I'm glad they could find it after I dropped it."

"It's terrible," Susie remarked. "Did you get a look at the killer?"

"No, not really, it was too dark." Not for the first time did Zoe wonder at her bad luck. The universe lined up exactly in the wrong place last night. The young man who died probably didn't expect it, the killer certainly didn't expect to have a visitor, and she didn't know when they set out on the scavenger hunt that she would wind up witnessing a murder.

"Do you want to come and eat lunch with Tiffany and me?"

Zoe's first instinct was to refuse her friend. She loved to go out to eat, but she was scared. It was a stupid emotion. There was no reason to be frightened. If the police thought she was in danger, they would have said something, or they would have found her somewhere safe to stay.

At least, that is what she thought would happen.

In reality, she had no idea how police procedure worked, and she wasn't stupid enough to think everything went down exactly like on the TV shows. Besides, how many times did women get restraining orders on someone, only to wind up dead anyway? Sometimes the police can't help. But she wasn't going to end up dead, so she told Susie, "Sure. I think I need to get out for a while to clear my head."

"Great. Do you want to meet us, or should we come get you?"

Zoe decided to drive herself. That way, if things got too uncomfortable, she could leave whenever she wanted. Restaurant chosen and a promise to see each other in an hour, she headed to her bedroom. She quickly put on nicer clothes because she didn't think people wanted to see her in her old cocker spaniel t-shirt and baggy gym shorts that doubled as pajamas. She wondered if she was still single at twenty-eight due to her choice in bedclothes. Not exactly conducive to sexy time, but comfort was becoming more and more important to her.

She pulled on a pair of dark jeans, a t-shirt with a grey cardigan for warmth. Her black hair was long enough to put in a tiny ponytail, and she styled her bangs to lie straight. Remnants of her long-lost Goth days were hard to let go, so she continued to cut her bangs straight and wear black as often as she could.

Casting one last look around her apartment, she grabbed her car keys and purse and set out for her lunch date. The wind bit at her cheeks as soon as she stepped out the doors, and she was glad for her cardigan to provide a little extra warmth. She smiled at one of her neighbors walking their black Labrador. She bent and petted his large head. The dog smiled up at Zoe, and she felt a little better. Dog smiles tended to do that. With one last pat, she continued to her car.

Tick Tock Tavern was a local favorite and one of Zoe's usual go-to eateries. The chicken was to die for, and the drink specials kept the girls happy on many a late night. The green and tan décor eased Zoe's jangled nerves. Susie and Tiffany waved her to their table as soon as she walked through the door.

"Over here!" Susie called.

Zoe raised her hand and walked toward the shared booth. Tiffany smiled sympathetically, while Susie grabbed her in a bear hug that lasted a little too long for Zoe's taste. She pulled back from Susie with a tight smile.

"We're so glad you are okay."

"I'm fine," Zoe insisted. She looked at Susie, "How is your mom today?" Susie had been the primary caregiver to her terminally ill mother for almost a year. That was one of the reasons Susie had been excited about the scavenger hunt. The idea of getting out of town and forgetting her troubles for a while was a dream to her.

"She's resting comfortably. We're still holding out hope for a new drug, but the doctors don't know if a test will be conducted near us. Oh, gosh, look at your face," Susie breathed dramatically, effectively changing the subject from her dying mother.

Zoe went with it. "Yeah, but it could have been worse. Only a few stitches and some bruises." The bruise around her eye began to pulse, as if sensing it was being talked about.

Tiffany clucked as if she were a mother hen. "Did they give you ice to put on it?"

Zoe nodded. "Yes. The hospital did a really good job taking care of me."

"Well, let's order our food. Then you can fill us in on all the details."

Startled at Susie's declaration, Zoe shifted uncomfortably. "I'd rather not. I've been trying not to think about it; otherwise, it consumes my every thought. I keep seeing the boy's face."

"I've heard it's better if you talk about it," Susie offered. Her eyes sparkled in curiosity.

Tiffany followed with, "It might help you remember something about your encounter with the murderer that you forgot."

And that was how Zoe's lunch proceeded. She dodged their pointed questions and offers of help and provided no details. She didn't want to talk about what she saw. She relived it constantly for the last twelve hours. She didn't need more reminders.

Erik Vardan walked the murder scene. His plane had landed a few hours ago, but he lost time when he stopped by the police station to announce his arrival. He moved as quickly as possible to get to the cemetery, but the small roads and weak GPS signal didn't help.

He bent to touch the cold ground under his fingers. The wind picked up, sending chills through him. Ignoring everything but the energy flowing up from the earth, he wrapped his free hand around his wooden staff and felt power slide into his arm and up to his shoulder. While saying the words of a divining spell, he observed the area for signs of dark magic.

Fine wisps rose from several locations and Erik easily identified the trail of magic. He pulled shields to protect himself from the onslaught of hateful energy. Old power festered beneath the new necromancer's and the power signature was familiar.

Mammon.

Hundreds of years ago, he remembered first encountering this particular demon's helpers. It took the help of the Grimm brothers to dispatch the necromancers. He shook his head at the memory of the outrageous brothers. Of course, their tales made them famous, but reality made them legends.

Concentrating on the task at hand, he glanced around to find further clues. Animal tracks glowed briefly. Rising, Erik peered at the impressions in the ground. A set of tracks resembling a dog's paw prints appeared in a circle near human footprints. He guessed the necromancer worked up enough power through various rituals to call upon nearby animals. His ministrations revealed the sacrifice's exact location, and echoes of the necromancer's power rolled over him.

Chapter 4

Someone knocked on Zoe's door. Her stomach plummeted. She didn't get many visitors, and none of her friends said they were stopping by this afternoon. Glancing around, she spied an electric fly swatter laying on her desk that she hadn't had a chance to pack away for the winter yet. She picked it up.

Apparently, she tarried too long because another series of abrupt knocks began. She tiptoed to the door and looked out the peephole. A lump of fear sat in her throat, causing her to take short breaths.

A man stood on the other side. A man she didn't recognize. He had dark hair and a dark coat. In fact, everything about him seemed to be dark. Her fear level ratcheted up to high as her brain screamed that the killer had found her.

"Hello?" she called through the door as she gripped her fly swatter more tightly. She forced herself to calm down. Maybe he was selling magazines or offering to save souls and not wanting to stab her to death and do who-knew-what with her body.

"Miss Hunt?" the man questioned.

Zoe remained silent. It worried her that he knew her name.

The man continued with an unfamiliar accent, "My name is Agent Allen. I am from Interpol. May I come in?"

Interpol? What in the world? "Can I see your badge please?" she asked through the solid wood door. She glanced through the peephole again. He instantly held out his badge and ID card for her to view through the tiny opening. Zoe had no idea what an Interpol ID card should look like, but this looked like what she'd seen in the movies. She unlocked, then opened the door.

Zoe continued clutching the big yellow electric fly swatter. The man's green eyes fastened on her unusual weapon, and he sent her a wry grin.

"May I come in?" Erik decided instantly that he liked this woman. Okay, her choice in protection was highly questionable, but at least she was on the defense. He'd never touched an electric fly swatter. Who knew? Maybe it packed more of a wallop than what the bright plastic frame would imply. She might prove worthwhile after all.

This man was created for me, Zoe's brain declared brashly as she took in his form. His black hair glinted under the hallway lights, and his cheekbones were sculpted enough to make anyone swoon. His tan skin contrasted with his bright eyes. He even smelled heavenly, like old wood, mixed with leather and some strange spice.

The insane thought came out of nowhere. When had she become so man-hungry? Would that be considered "mangry?" She wanted to shake her head and tell herself she was deluded. Maybe she was experiencing some form of PTSD, and her brain wasn't functioning at its normal capacity. Her body had other ideas, though. It reacted instantly to the man. He was beautiful in a way no one had a right to be, she admitted. His broad shoulders filled out the long, black coat he wore, and his deep green eyes sparkled at her. Maybe it was the cologne, or the accent.

Realizing her mouth might be gaping open, she clenched her jaw and stepped out of the way for the man to enter. "I'm sorry. What did you say your name was again?"

"Agent Jordan Allen, ma'am."

Zoe cringed. She'd just been ma'am-ed by the man of her dreams. In fact, he was beautiful, so beautiful that he was almost painful to look at. He was not too big, yet a sense of power rolled off him in waves. Her body tightened. Apparently, it didn't have any trouble with the man's looks.

Erik stepped through the door to Miss Hunt's apartment

and instantly assessed his surroundings. At first glance, everything appeared normal. Nevertheless, he knew from experience, deception wasn't easily detected. Her declaration of seeing a murder could be a planned distraction. He really didn't know. "I am here to ask you more questions about Friday night's murder."

Zoe had a few questions of her own. "You said you were from Interpol. Why would an international police agency be involved in a local murder?" Wasn't Interpol a spy agency? No, wait that might be the CIA. She wasn't sure, but she knew he wasn't an ordinary sheriff or police officer.

Erik understood her skepticism. He encountered the same reaction when he visited the Peninsula Police Department earlier in the day. They weren't happy to hear another organization edged in on their case. He explained that Interpol was only observing at the moment and offering him as assistance with their investigation. That set them more at ease, and they brought him up to speed on their research into the murder case.

Sending her a calming look, he explained, "Sometimes our organization steps in to assist with certain cases. We have offices located nearby. The local officers filled me in on the details of this case, but I wanted to get your account in person. Sometimes another recount of the occurrence brings up new memories."

Zoe nodded reluctantly in acceptance. The police informed her that more people from the police force might need to question her as the case progressed, surely someone would have mentioned Interpol.

Agent Allen stood in the middle of her apartment and assessed her belongings, as if he were looking for something. His eyes travelled over every nook and cranny, and she wondered at the man's interest in her things. She waited for him to continue.

"Why don't you have a seat?" he asked, still perusing her tiny apartment, as he motioned toward her worn, blue couch.

Zoe nodded and sat, still clutching the fly swatter. She stared at the agent and wondered what he was looking for. Was she a suspect? It should have been enough that she provided the picture of the murderer to the police, but this man acted as if he was investigating her. "How can I help you, Agent Allen?"

She hoped this man might be able to provide more information about the murder. Her grip on the electric flyswatter tightened. She didn't know if the police would keep her in the loop or if they would investigate and let her find out about any happenings in the local newspaper. She'd had no previous run-ins with the law before.

Dragging in a kitchen chair, Agent Allen sat and casually stretched his long legs in front of him. His black hair glistened blue tones in the morning light. "Can you tell me what happened Friday night? Start from the moment you left your apartment that morning."

Zoe took a breath and prepared to retell, for the fifth time – at least, what happened. It was all pretty simple: walk through a condemned town's cemetery, stumble across murderer, run from said murderer, and call police.

"How did you hurt your face?" he questioned. In the middle of her explanation, he'd taken out a notepad and pen to jot down comments.

The bandage on her cheek felt large and bulky. Grimacing, she raised her hand to her cheek and admitted, "When I turned to run, I smashed face first into an angel statue. It was so dark, I didn't even see it."

"Bet that hurt," he said wryly. Alarm bells went off in his head. His ritual earlier should have turned up her blood.

Zoe couldn't help but smile. "Yeah, a little."

"Can you think of anything else that happened?"

She shook her head. She'd told the story so many times, she felt as if she could recite it in her sleep. Then she remembered the arriving police officers' reactions. "You know, this is going to sound crazy, but after the police arrived, no one acted as if they wanted to go investigate the cemetery. They all stood around, hemming and hawing, but no one really took the initiative to look for the murderer. It's possible they could have caught him if they only would have hurried."

Erik knew why the police didn't want to go to the cemetery. The murderer probably put an avoidance spell over the area. He wondered how this woman got through such a spell. "What were you doing as you were walking to the cemetery? You said your friends left you to find the other scavenger hunt items."

"Well, I had to pull the GPS up on my phone. I got lost for some reason, which was weird because I'd been there several times when I was younger. I'd never gotten lost before, but this time I did. I was following the app when I heard chanting."

"So, you heard the suspect chanting?"

Zoe nodded again. "Yes." She couldn't take her gaze off his wonderfully shaped hands. A few scars graced the tanned skin. *What would those hands feel like when they touched her?* She became lost in the daydream of what this man would actually do with his hands and where he would put them.

Erik wasn't so strait-laced that he didn't enjoy Miss Hunt's obvious attraction to him. He'd been alive a long time and was beginning to feel tired and out of sorts, almost adrift in time. Her stare pleased him more than he was willing to admit. He cleared his throat to bring her back to the present, and he knew instantly when that happened.

A brightening slowly crept along her uninjured cheek, and her mouth opened in the sexiest expression of shock he'd ever seen. "Did you happen to understand anything he was saying?" Erik asked as he straightened in the wooden kitchen chair.

Zoe had no idea what came over her. She had caught daydreaming like a silly character in romantic comedies. Chanting, yes, chanting. She grabbed onto the logical train of thought and let it carry her to normal town. "No, I couldn't make out really anything he said." She stopped, trying to think back. One word stuck in the corner of her brain. "Vitae!" A memory triggered, and she recalled the word.

"Vitae," Erik said slowly. *Life.* Therefore, the necromancer, whoever he was, was conducting a ritual spell to give power to something or someone. He'd finally hit on the right lead. "Did you see anything else when you were facing the suspect? Any objects?"

"No. It was so dark, and I never expected to stumble across a murder scene. I just wanted to get out of there alive."

Erik knew from the police reports that nothing had been left behind, other than the burning body of a teenager. Zoe managed to get into and out of the cemetery relatively undetected. On the way in, she was able to avoid the avoidance spell because she had concentrated only on her phone. It was possible on the way out she might have left behind something the killer could use to find her – her blood. He would have to keep an eye on her to ensure that the man didn't try to come for her. "Have you seen anything else out of the ordinary?"

The question caught Zoe off-guard. "What do you mean?"

The man brought his bright green eyes up to stare at her. "Have you seen anyone watching you or following with their car?"

Fear clogged her brain, making her slow to reply. "N-no. Why would you ask that?" He couldn't be suggesting the killer might have found her. "No," she told him with more confidence.

Erik nodded. "I am simply covering all aspects of this investigation. I am not inferring that the man will be attempting to follow you." He stood and pulled out a business card. "I have no further questions at this time, but may I check back if something arises?"

You can check back as often as you want.

She tamped down that voice again. "Yes. That would be fine." She'd never reacted to anyone this way. She'd had crushes and boyfriends before, but nothing quite compared to the feelings that arose as he sat across from her. She reached out to take the business card, and their fingers brushed.

His fingertips were hot, and she caught the scent of spice again. Maybe she'd imagined the heat, but she desperately wanted to know what cologne he wore. She glanced at the business card and the name at the top: Agent Jordan Allen. Her stomach flipped, and her body grew hot. What in the world was wrong with her? It was a normal name, and he was a normal guy. She had to get out more often.

"Thank you for your time, Miss Hunt."

"You're welcome, Agent Allen." Zoe walked him to her door and said her goodbyes. She stared at the closed door, still reeling from her shaky reaction to him. Her body refused to give up the jittery, excited feeling. For the first time, she thought about something other than a murderer on the loose.

Erik stood outside Zoe Hunt's door and contemplated the spell he would work around her apartment. She had seen the necromancer mid-murder. The necromancer possibly would come back for her to ensure she couldn't tell any more about him. He didn't want to assume the woman would be safe, so he needed to act fast to perform something that would alert him to the necromancer's approach.

Pushing open the doorway to the staircase, he jogged down the stairs while sorting through potential spells in his head. Time kept his options limited, but he managed to work a quick spell that would trip if dark magic entered the area surrounding Zoe's apartment.

The police wouldn't worry the necromancer, but Erik didn't know what the man would do if he detected white magic.

Chapter 5

Twenty minutes later, another knock on the door snapped Zoe out of her man-dreams. Maybe Agent Allen had more questions, maybe he wanted to ask her out to dinner, or maybe ... Her hopes flittered away when she peered through the viewer and spotted Susie. Pasting on a smile, she opened the door and invited her friend inside.

"I was in the neighborhood and wanted to stop by to make sure you are still doing okay." Susie bounced through the door, her ponytail in time with her motions.

Surprised by her friend's concerned words, Zoe closed the door and glanced at Susie. "Yes, thanks. It's nice of you to check on me, but I'm fine. Still rattled, but who wouldn't be, right?" She cringed at the almost manic sound of her voice. At least she didn't follow it up with a high-pitched cackle.

Susie didn't notice Zoe's stressed tone; she was too busy being nosy. She stared at the papers on the table and moved to pick up the business card the agent left. "Agent Jordan Allen. Hmm. I don't remember that name from Friday night."

Zoe stared at the business card and wished to pull it from her friend's grasp. "No, he came about an hour ago. He had more questions. He's from *Interpol*."

"Was he cute?" Susie asked, completely unaffected by Zoe's announcement of the police organization.

Zoe nodded reluctantly. She should have told Susie he was

old and fat. That would have been the end of twenty questions.

"What did he look like?"

Zoe shrugged and looked out her window, at the choppy waters of Lake Erie. A slight chill filtered through the window, and she shivered. *Really gorgeous.* She kept that fact to herself. "Black hair, tall." She attempted to sound casual; as if she hadn't been thinking how incredibly handsome he was, only fifteen minutes ago.

"Is he married?"

Sputtering in laughter, Zoe cried, "I don't know! We were talking about a murderer. The subject of marital status never came up."

"You should have checked for a wedding ring."

"No," Zoe disagreed in exasperation. "I don't need to check for a wedding ring. He's a police officer doing his job. He doesn't want needy women hitting on him."

"You're not needy," Susie defended.

Zoe turned to stare at Susie. "You're right. I don't *need* a man, and I definitely don't need Agent Allen."

"When's the last time you went out on a date? Or got laid for that matter?" Susie flicked the business card between her fingers, and watched it slide across the marble countertop.

"I don't know," she said truthfully, as she reached to catch it before it slid off the counter. Zoe set the card back down on her table, next to the other officers' cards she'd collected since Friday. "But I'm not looking for a man. I'm concentrating on me."

Susie moaned loudly. "What's gotten into you? You used to be so much fun. Now, you hardly go out."

Incredulously, Zoe looked at Susie. "We went out Friday night!" She narrowed her eyes at her friend. "What's going on, Susie? We still go out, maybe not all the clubbing, but we have our girls' movie nights and our dinner nights."

Susie shook her head, clearly frustrated. "I don't know. I'm just stressed with all that's going on with Mom."

"I understand," Zoe said, but the words sounded false to her own ears. She really couldn't understand what Susie was going through. She never had to take care of a terminally ill loved one before.

"It's so much. The paperwork for insurance is piling up. The doctors need more tests. The care manager wants to move Mom to a facility." Her eyes met Zoe's. "I don't want to do that. I don't want to ship her off, and then go on my merry way while she's dying." Susie covered her face and cried softly.

Zoe hugged her gently. "I'm sorry that you are going through this. You are doing the best you can, and I will do anything I can for you and your mom."

Sniffling, Susie looked at Zoe through tear-filled eyes. "Thank you. I needed to get that off my chest."

Zoe squeezed her hand.

"Well, why don't you hang out here? We'll order a pizza for lunch. We can veg out and watch some movies. It might help a little." Zoe knew her friend was on board with the offer because her face brightened.

***

The pizza arrived a half hour later, and the movie marathon began. Both decided it should be a '80s tribute afternoon, so they started with *Top Gun*. Zoe's crush on Tom Cruise hadn't lessened throughout the years, and she thoroughly enjoyed the movie again, for the millionth time.

When the movie ended, Zoe hunted Netflix for another. Susie stood up and stretched her back. "I have to run out to my car. I forgot to show you what I bought at Target."

"Okay," Zoe said, as she narrowed her eyes to read the description of a movie on the television. "Hmm, do you remember *Very Bad Things*? It has Christian Slater in it." She turned to look at Susie.

"No, but I do love me some Christian Slater." This was said with a Slater-esqsue arched brow and a wide smile.

"Okay, we'll give this one a chance when you get back." Zoe selected it and put it on pause, waiting for Susie's return.

Susie shut the door behind her and was back in two minutes

with a Target bag in tow. "Look at this cute sweater I bought." She pulled a dark green sweater coat out of the bag and held it up for Zoe to see.

Zoe rose and turned on the kitchen light to get a better view. It was almost completely dark outside, but not nearly six yet. Hooray for fall in Cleveland. "That's pretty," Zoe remarked, because really, she couldn't think of anything else to say. It was a sweater. It was green.

"Oh! I almost forgot to tell you the weird thing I saw outside. Some man was driving around with a weird Halloween decoration in his car. It was a hand with flames coming from its fingertips. It was so creepy." She shivered dramatically.

Zoe frowned. "Really? That is weird. It can't be very safe to be driving with a lit candle, though." Geez, she sounded like a grandma. When had she lost her sense of adventure? Maybe Susie had been right. Maybe she did need to get out more and loosen up.

Susie shrugged at Zoe's cautious words. "I'm sure it wasn't a real candle, and he was probably pulling some left-over Halloween prank."

"You're right. Wow, Halloween was a couple of days ago." Since the murder, time didn't operate normally. Zoe shook her head to clear it. "Let's watch this movie. I'll make some popcorn." Zoe walked to her pantry and pulled out her Whirley Pop and bag of popcorn. "Do you want butter in it?"

"Yeah, that would be great. Oh, darn it! I forgot one more thing! I'll be right back. Can I borrow your coat? It's getting cold out there." Susie gestured to Zoe's gray wool coat.

"Yeah, sure." Zoe wasn't sure why she'd want to wear it; the cemetery funk made Zoe's stomach churn and she had no idea how she was going to get the bloodstain off the collar.

Susie slipped on the coat and turned to jog out the door.

Zoe wondered what Susie could have forgotten this time. Five minutes went by, occupied by cranking the stirring handle and lots of popping, and still she hadn't returned. Pouring the popcorn in a big bowl, Zoe helped herself to a handful before going to the window to peer outside.

Ritual Of Blood

The parking lot sat in almost complete darkness. The weak streetlights did nothing; she couldn't see a thing. Beginning to worry, she pulled on her shoes and grabbed her keys. Maybe something happened to Susie. She could have decided to take the stairs and fallen down, or she could have taken the elevator and become trapped.

The stairway was empty, and the elevator appeared to be in working order. So Zoe continued to the parking lot. Susie's black Honda Pilot sat under a streetlight, but there was no trace of her. A faint scent of leather filled her nostrils. It reminded her of Agent Allen, but she shook her head at her silliness. She was imagining things. After one last check around the parking lot, she wondered if maybe she and Susie had missed each other somehow. Susie probably took the elevator as she took the stairs.

Back inside the main entrance of her apartment, warm air greeted Zoe, and she quickly pushed the up arrow on the elevator. She smiled at one of her elderly neighbors as they stepped out. Once inside, she pressed the button for the fifteenth floor. Tapping her fingers on the handrail, she waited for the elevator to stop and the doors to open to her hallway. She walked into her apartment, fully expecting Susie to be munching on freshly popped popcorn and complaining about Zoe's whereabouts.

Her apartment sat empty.

A strange feeling shivered through her. She didn't want to panic, but her mind shouted *Susie had been taken!* She glanced one more time down at the parking lot in hopes of spotting Susie. But the facts pointed to something nefarious. Susie was missing. Zoe picked up one of the cards from various police officials.

She called Agent Allen.

He answered on the first ring.

"My friend has been abducted." She didn't beat around the bush.

"Miss Hunt?"

"Yes!" Zoe said in exasperation. He should know exactly who was calling. He'd just seen her a few hours before to question her further on the murder investigation.

"Where are you?" His voice was calm and steady.

"At my apartment. My friend Susie went to her car to get something, and she never came back. Her car is still in the parking lot. I can't find her."

"Could she have stopped to visit someone in your apartment building?"

"No," Zoe told him urgently. "She doesn't know anybody; at least, not well enough to go inside and sit down to have an unannounced chat."

"Could she have made a run into a nearby convenience store?"

"No, not without her car."

"How long has she been gone?"

Zoe looked at her watch. "Almost thirty minutes now."

There was a pause.

Erik quickly processed Miss Hunt's words. The necromancer found her sooner than he expected, he admitted. Zoe wouldn't be safe at her current location, especially once it became evident that the necromancer took the wrong woman. The killer would be back. "You need to get out of your apartment. I'm going to text an address of a safe place to stay. It's a nearby hotel. I will also include the keypad code to get you into the building and into the room. Do not talk to anyone as you leave, and do *not* open the door for anyone."

Fear scrambled up to Zoe's throat. "What?" she asked numbly, not quite registering his urgent words.

"I am not close enough to your place to get to you quickly," Erik explained slowly. "You need to get out of your apartment as soon as you can. I cannot guarantee your safety if you stay there." Silently he cursed himself for not seeing this.

"Should I call 9-1-1?"

"No. I will take care of things on this end. You need to concentrate on getting out of your apartment in the next five minutes." He wanted Zoe to be focused on packing her things and not calling the police. They would get in the way for they had no idea what they were dealing with.

"Is Susie dead?"

"I can't answer that question. My priority right now is keeping you safe. That means you need to get packing now and go to the location I just texted you."

She put him on speakerphone and ran to her bedroom. "Okay. I'm packing." Grabbing a small rolling tote, she threw shirts, pants, pajamas, and bathroom items inside, not caring if things got wrinkly or ruined. She didn't know how long she would be gone, so she shoved more things than she probably needed.

"What kind of car does Susie drive?" he asked.

"A black Honda Pilot. It's in the main lot in front of my building."

"What is she wearing?"

"My gray wool coat," she related and then gasped. Susie had Zoe's coat on when she went out the second time. With the hood pulled over her head, anyone could have assumed it was Zoe walking to the car. Her stomach roiled, but before she could panic, the agent spoke.

"I'm going to let you pack. Get out as quickly as you can, and I will meet you at the hotel as soon as I am able. If anyone tries to approach you, make as much noise as possible."

She would be on the lookout for anything strange, and she would raise the roof if anyone tried to come after her. "Okay. Thank you," she told him in a trembling breath. For some reason, she added, "Be careful."

She wanted to take the words back the instant they left her mouth. She didn't know him well enough to offer that kind of sentiment. He was going to think she was crazy, but she was under a lot of pressure. Her mind had been through a lot.

He must not have thought her request of him was out of line because he said, "You be careful, too. Remember what I said, talk to no one."

"Okay."

After he hung up, Zoe stared around her room, at a loss. Frankly, she was at a loss for what had happened these last few days. Then she thought of Susie's story about the person driving with a candle in their car. Could that have anything to do with her friend's disappearance?

She redialed Agent Allen. When he answered, Zoe said in a rush, "I remembered that Susie mentioned seeing a man driving in a car with a burning candle, a weird hand shaped candle I know this sounds crazy, but it happened right after Susie went outside the first time. I thought it might be important." It sounded lame to her ears.

"That is helpful. Thank you, Miss Hunt." He hung up again without another word.

Zoe wasted no time worrying about the short conversation. She needed to leave. Grabbing her purse, a bag of Twizzlers from the counter, and her work laptop, she rolled her tote out of her apartment and headed for the elevator. Worry for Susie caused the stitches in her cheek to twinge and her head to ache.

The navigation directions on her cell phone were easy to follow and, twenty minutes later, she pulled into a crowded parking lot belonging to a local hotel that Zoe could never afford. She pulled into an empty, well-lit parking spot as close to the door as she could get, grabbed her bag, and made her way to the entrance. She punched in the security code that he had provided. The door opened without trouble.

The luxurious, red-hued hallway was empty. Checking the room number on a nearby door, she turned down the hall and headed toward the correct room as directed through the text message. Another keypad decorated the room door, as well, and Zoe wondered about it. She'd never seen keypads on hotel rooms before. She punched the code in, and the light on the box glowed green.

Zoe hesitantly opened the door and walked inside Agent Allen's hotel suite. She turned on the light, and the room brightened to a comforting level. Warm air circled her, inviting her in further. She closed the door quietly behind her and set her bags on the soft carpet. Light creams and brighter brown shades colored the walls in pleasing tones. Textured wallpaper tied in the flooring and the furniture. A large TV sat atop an armoire.

Glancing around, she spied three adjoining doors, and Zoe

investigated each in an effort to find where she would put her bags. The first door led to a large restroom. The expansive tile shower was the size of her entire apartment bathroom, and the garden tub made it embarrassing to compare spaces. The second door led to a bedroom. She peeked inside before going to the third door. Another bedroom.

Upon closer inspection, Zoe deduced the first bedroom belonged to the agent. There was a hint of the cologne, deep and dark, that he wore, lingering in the air. She stepped further inside and noticed a small leather zipper bag sat on the connecting bathroom counter. He must not have had time to unpack or he was a Type A personality because she didn't spot a razor, or soap, or deodorant on the marble surface, save a toothbrush still in its packaging.

Trying not to be creepy, she quickly backed out and closed the door. It would not be a good idea to snoop in a police officer's personal sanctuary. She turned back to the second door, hoping to find it empty of enticing smells. It was. She rolled her bag inside and got to work unpacking her things. Happy to discover her own personal *en suite* bathroom, she lined up her bathroom items on the grey-flecked marble counter. If she was going to stay here for a while, she might as well be comfortable.

Realizing she'd done as much busy work as she could, she glanced at her watch and wondered when she would hear anything back about Susie.

Chapter 6

Erik frowned in the darkness, as he slid his cell phone back into his coat pocket. Zoe Hunt's words echoed in his head. The necromancer must have detected his magical wards around the apartment and avoided them, enabling the man to kidnap who he thought was Zoe.

Picking up his wooden staff, Erik moved from the murder site and made his way quickly to his car. His second visit to the murder site had proven successful, as he was able to ascertain what ritual spell the necromancer utilized. In the past, he hadn't quite been able to arrive at the ritual murder site so quickly. Today, the magic lingered, still fresh in the air, even though it was days old. The necromancer's book contained strong power, and the ritual only built on that power. The problem was, he didn't know where all the power was going, and for what reason.

He knew it was the necromancer, as soon as Zoe told him about Susie spotting someone driving with a "hand shaped" candle. He must have been utilizing a Hand of Glory to find Zoe. Zoe's injury must have been substantial enough for the necromancer to procure enough blood, to fuel his spell. A Hand of Glory, a macabre artifact, combined with a location spell could aid in pinpointing her exact location. It would only give a general area, but the necromancer must have been patient, or lucky enough for his prey to surface.

Where did the necromancer take Zoe's friend, and what

would happen, once he figured out he'd taken the wrong woman? He didn't hold out much hope for the friend, though there was a small chance she would make it out alive. He'd never met the man who'd taken the girl, but he knew his type. Erik knew what they were going through, and what they'd do to survive. He'd hunted the necromancer's kind for centuries. There was never a fairy tale ending. Well, not a modern fairy tale, it was very likely to resemble the stories recorded by the Grimms.

Born Hurik Vardanyan, he was an orphan from a small Armenian town in the year 1302, when an ex-Knight Templar took him in as his own. His adoptive father had seen how he learned and set to make him his apprentice. Erik learned how to sword fight and balance financial matters, but it wasn't until his mastery of the Latin language become evident, that he captured the attention of the Vatican.

From then on, his training involved magic and the wizardry. At first, he'd been skeptical, but after a few minor spells managed to set nearby books on fire, he became an exemplary student. His belief in God guided his hand and instincts, and it protected him when he met the creatures from other realms.

Throughout the years, his given name evolved into Erik Vardan. It paid homage to his rightful moniker, but with twenty-first century normality. He had hundreds of aliases as his job warranted, and Agent Allen from Interpol wasn't on his first case chasing ritual murders.

It took forty minutes to get from Boston Township's cemetery to Zoe's apartment in Lakewood, Ohio. During the drive, he called and left a message with the local police station and checked in with Jenny. He told her to notify him if anything out of the ordinary came out of the Cleveland area on police or hospital channels.

Erik outlined in his head what he would do if he were the necromancer. A hideout must be found, and depending on where it was located, it would be a questionable amount of time before he discovered, that he had kidnapped the wrong woman.

Zoe's apartment came in sight, and Erik pulled into the almost full parking lot. Spotting the black Honda that Zoe described, he parked next to it. Before opening his door, he scanned the area visually and magically. No trace of dark magic lingered, so he set out to work.

With a quiet incantation, he set up a spell to hide his form, while he searched Susie's car for what he needed. The woman was a hoarder, and her car was her suitcase. Clothes littered the backseat and piled on the floorboards. The passenger seat fared no better. Makeup bags and loose nail polish in various bright colors lay haphazardly on the cloth seat. A stray French fry peeked up between two face brushes of some sort. He spotted a hairbrush wedged between the parking brake and the driver's seat. Even in the dim light, he could see bright blonde strands wrapped around the bristles. He could use the hairs to track the woman.

He pocketed the item as he closed the car's door and scanned lot for Zoe's car. Jenny researched Zoe's information before he left, so he knew she owned a dark blue Ford Focus. Her car was gone. She had better follow his instructions.

He thought of her breathy request for him to be careful, and something tilted inside. He didn't know what possessed him to answer her back. Somehow, she called to him. Her attitude and her motions acted as a beacon. It was dangerous. He continued to relive the moment he realized she was daydreaming about him in her apartment. She seemed embarrassed at her reaction. Maybe that would keep her at arm's length. He couldn't afford the distraction, not when so much was at stake.

Back in his rental car, Erik lowered his shields to conserve his energy. He didn't know what the night would bring. There was a chance a confrontation with the necromancer and his helpers would occur, and he needed to be on top of his game. He stared at the hairbrush and tried to decide where to do the tracking spell. The Hand of Glory the necromancer used was black magic, but what he had in mind was similar. The spell would give him a general idea of Susie's location, but nothing exact. At the moment, it was all he had, so he mentally sorted the tracking spell in his head.

Erik decided on conducting the spell in the parking lot, for the sake of lost time. Murmuring the concealment incantation again, he pulled out a map of the area and reached for the spool of thread, which poked out of his open worn brown leather bag, that sat in his passenger seat. He wrapped the thread around Susie's hairbrush and held it over the map.

"*Teghadrek' ays eut'yuny*," he ordered in Armenian. The hairbrush began to inch back and forth, pendulum-like. He knew what to look, for when the answer was ready to be found. The light from outside his car illuminated the map, and the hairbrush gently swayed over the same area. Susie had been taken due south, about seven miles away. She was somewhere along Rocky River. He couldn't pinpoint her exact location, but it was better than nothing. He started his car and headed south.

His phone rang while he was driving. He answered when he saw it was Jenny. "What's going on?" he asked, as he squinted at the poorly lit road sign in front of him. He had four more miles to go.

"Are you having fun in Ohio?" Jenny said in a cheerful tone.

"Mediocre." He grimaced and swore as he missed his turn.

"Well, your local PD got a GPS ping from a woman's phone with an urgent help message ten minutes ago. The number registers to a Susan Monroe. They are headed to the location."

"Zoe's friend, Susie," Erik breathed.

"Also known as," Jenny supplied with a teasing lilt in her voice. "Spill it, what's going on? First a murder, and now a kidnapping. Is something serious going on there? Do you need me to supply backup? We can get someone on a plane in thirty minutes. You know, Merrick is in your neck of the woods. I'm sure he would be willing to help."

"No. Merrick is in the middle of the Bathory case." He knew Merrick would be furious at being called away. He'd been hunting Elizabeth Bathory's spirit for centuries. He couldn't pick up and leave and expect to have the Blood Countess waiting for him to get back to continue the merry chase. No. That would never happen. Erik had things under control. "Send the coordinates of the 9-1-1 call to my cell. I am good here."

"Okay. I will be in contact when I hear any helpful news from the police." The line went dead.

Ritual Of Blood

During the call, the pendulum had grown still over the map, its job done. The magic dissipated without a trace. Susie was nearby, along with his quarry, he needed to get to her and the necromancer before the police did. He glanced at the car's clock. More than an hour had gone by since the necromancer took Susie. Selecting the location Jenny texted on his phone, he followed the directions. As Erik drove, he opened up his senses for any usual movement in the wood. Off to his left, he could see bright police lights.

A coyote ran in front of him, and Erik slammed on his breaks, dodging the animal. His car skidded but stayed on the road. The creature held its ground in the middle of the road, staring at him. Its eyes sparked in his car's headlights, daring him to continue his trek. Erik felt the hint of magic.

This was one of the necromancer's creatures. He knew from his first visit to the cemetery, that the man had night creatures to call. Their tracks were all over the area near the body. The animal lowered its head and narrowed its eyes, almost appearing to glare at him. As if growing bored, the wild dog turned and trotted away. The wail of sirens drew his attention away from the retreating creature.

Chapter 7

A dozen Boston Township police cars – marked and unmarked – parked haphazardly in the front lawn. If lawn was the correct term. Scraggly trees and tall weeds completely engulfed the space around the property. Gas generators roared on the perimeter, powering large floodlights that illuminated the area. An old, dilapidated house rose before him, spewing overgrowth out its windows. The police cars cast red and blue light across the white house, causing a macabre dance routine.

Parking his car out of the way, closer to the woods, Erik grabbed his badge. Bits of the officers' conversations drifted to him, as he approached the house.

"This is the craziest thing," one officer commented, as he removed his hat to scratch his baldhead, his voice floated across the night. "Should have known something like this would happen, sooner or later."

A taller officer beside him said something unintelligible, and both turned to walk to the house.

Erik feared the worse, as he examined the area for Zoe's friend. An ambulance sat empty off to his right. His phone vibrated in his coat pocket. He reached inside and pulled out the device, tapping it to read Jenny's text message.

"The suspect is dead. Details unknown."

"Damn," Erik swore under his breath. He wanted the necromancer alive. This complicated matters. If the police hadn't been so trigger-happy, it would have made things a lot easier. As he ducked under the yellow tape, he had his badge at the ready. He flipped the cover open as he passed an officer guarding the crime scene.

The outside neglect carried to the inside of the house. Paint on the kitchen cabinets peeled to reveal rotting wood underneath, and blackish mold patterned up a wall beside a gray refrigerator. The floorboards were soft, as Erik stepped lightly on the waterlogged planks. There was no electricity; therefore, the police had brought generators and floodlights to aid in the recovery process.

He stepped up to one officer whose badge read, Officer Clark. "I'm Agent Allen from Interpol. What are the details?"

Taken aback by the casual mention of the revered anti-crime organization, the officer's eyes grew round, and he stuttered, "I-Interpol?"

Erik looked him dead in the eyes and held up his identification. "Yes. I need details." He found short, terse sentences worked best when he communicated with police officers. They respected each other's time, and it didn't matter if he was in Germany, Asia, or the United States, all expected him to get to the point.

"Let me get the sergeant for you." The officer clicked the radio strapped to his shoulder. "Sergeant Vega, I have an Agent Allen from Interpol here. He needs to talk to you."

There was no verbal response from the young officer's request, but, thirty seconds later, Sergeant Vega stood before Erik. Tall and wiry, the sergeant had the air of a military man about him.

"Agent Allen, nice to meet you. We heard Interpol was assisting in the investigation." He put obvious emphasis on the assisting part.

Erik sent the sergeant an easy, low-key smile to put him at ease. "At this point, Interpol is happy to assist. Up until now, it seemed a pretty routine investigation."

Sergeant Vega snorted. "Nothing routine happens around Halloween. If it were up to me, we'd cancel all Halloween activities. Nothing but trouble and violence. Then we have this case. Someone playing at Satanism, or something, before things go wrong for them."

Ritual Of Blood

The sentiments voiced by the sergeant were common. He understood certain persons took advantage of the pagan holiday, and it became hard for the police to protect and serve. "Can you tell me what occurred here?"

Vega nodded and lifted a hand, motioning for him to follow. "Yes, but hold on a second." He turned slightly to face two officers walking past, toward the door.

Erik spotted a third figure in between the two men. A large blanket covered the person from head to foot. Frightened eyes met his, from inside the darkened folds. The slight figure froze, and her eyes widened.

"Officers, escort Miss Monroe to the hospital right away. We can get her statement once she's safely entrusted in the hospital's care."

Erik tried to catch Susie Monroe's gaze, but she refused to look at him again. The officers gently guided her out the door and into the night. He stared after them, wanting to question her on her ordeal. That would have to wait until later.

The sergeant headed to the back of the house, and Erik followed him down to the basement. Another set of portable lights illuminated the sprawling floor plan under the house. The basement floor was dirt, and the corners of the walls trickled with tiny streams of running water. The smell of mold grew more pronounced the farther into the room they proceeded.

"The suspect's body is over there," the sergeant informed Erik. He pointed to a wide area in the middle of the room.

Erik continued forward, until he stood over the body of the necromancer. Magic, power, and anger swirled in the air. Turning, he surveyed the dark room, and searched for the necromancer's instruction grimoire. He had to find it. Only after it was safely ensconced in the Vatican's vault, would he be able to rest easy, at least until another demon's artifact popped up. The grimoire contained instructions on gaining and giving power. Most of it involved death in one way or another.

At this point, he didn't know if the book was on the premises. The necromancer would have a concealment spell protecting it, rendering it nearly impossible to find. The necromancer's corpse still had a story to tell, though. "I'd like to examine the body."

Sergeant Vega shook his head. "Not until the M.E. releases the body to the morgue. We can meet up at the hospital once we are complete with our documentation." He looked at Erik to reiterate his point.

Erik shrugged. It would have been better to view the body first, but he could start his research at the house instead. The body could wait. He would be patient. Because what he looked for couldn't be washed off or removed. He'd spent so much time tracking this particular demon, Mammon, and his necromancers, that he could wait a few more hours.

"Did your men attempt to take the suspect alive?" he asked the sergeant a moment later. His gaze drifted to the dead man on the floor.

"My men had no part in the suspect's death. He was dead by the time we arrived. According to the victim, Susan Monroe, the man tripped and fell, striking his head on a rock."

Erik glanced at the body lying on the ground a few feet off to his right. A large rock with a bloodied edge lay nearby. A small number marker displayed the number 36. A forensic officer knelt, swabbing the item for DNA. From the looks of it, she hit the jackpot. A large pool of dark blood spread across the floor. The liquid had begun to seep into the dirt floor. The necromancer must have bled out quickly.

"One unlucky step brought him down," Erik said, mostly to himself. "What is the suspect's name?"

"The photo I.D. in his wallet reads Dale Hicks. We're checking the database to see if he had any hits in our system." The sergeant shook his head. "This is going to be a nightmare to catalog." His eyes travelled over the stacks of papers, haphazard piles of books, and various unknown paraphernalia.

Most of the manuscripts were originals, from what Erik could tell simply from looking at them. Dale Hicks has served the demon for quite some time, based on the size of the pile of magical books that decorated the bookshelves. This was not Mr. Hicks's first rodeo. And, if Erik didn't act fast, Mr. Hicks was going to transition from living necromancer to undead revenant soon. Then, he'd have a completely new set of problems to deal with.

"I must have the results of the autopsy as soon as possible." Erik held the man's eyes, to communicate the seriousness of his request. The procedure should prevent the necromancer from rising, ending the connection to the demon.

"Sergeant Vega! Over here! We have more bodies." A female dressed in coveralls with dark hair, waved to them.

"Bodies? Christ, this keeps getting better and better." Vega grumbled. He lifted his chin and shouted to the nearby officers, "Everyone, keep your eyes open. With the potential of multiple victims, the subject may not have acted alone."

The sergeant turned to walk toward the other bodies discovered, and Erik regarded the wall of books. With whispered words, he conjured a concealment spell. At that moment, the books vanished from sight. This would buy him time to come back and inspect the manuscripts. It was possible the necromancer's spell book was in the stack.

Erik turned casually and stepped toward the necromancer's body. He wouldn't be able to do anything to stop the necromancer's change to a revenant, not with all the police around, but he did need something that belonged to the man to assist with future spells.

He glanced down at the wide pool of blood at his feet. Pulling a rubber glove as inconspicuously as possible from his jacket, he slipped it on, crouched down, and purposely lost his balance. He ran his fingers through the drying blood as he caught himself.

"Hey!" cried the criminologist who worked near the body. In the process of unfolding the body bag, she glared at Erik with a frown.

"Sorry," Erik said, pasting on a contrite smile, "I lost my balance."

Vega stepped back into the scene. "Agent Allen, I think you've seen enough. We will contact you once the M.E. releases the body."

And, as quickly as that, he'd been kicked out of the murder scene.

Chapter 8

Zoe couldn't help it.

Curiosity got the best of her. She knew she shouldn't snoop, but what harm would a little peek do? It was almost one-thirty in the morning. Almost five agonizing hours passed since she arrived at the hotel, and she was going crazy. Her mind swirled in conspiracy theories. Every noise outside had her panicked, thinking the killer had come to finish his job. She couldn't sleep, and her cell phone was charging, so she couldn't read or play solitaire to calm her nerves. Instead, she did the only thing she could think of while she waited to hear if her friend was okay.

She tiptoed into Agent Allen's suite.

Once again, the scent of wood, leather and spice assailed her senses. It had to be some cologne he wore. Whatever it was, it smelled delicious. Her body tingled. She forced herself to concentrate on listening to the front door, in case Detective Allen walked in. She didn't need distractions when she was set to snoop around the bedroom of an international police officer.

What the heck was wrong with her? Was she acting out due to the stress of the last few days? Because in a court of law, she would be found guilty of trespassing. Oh, and add the little fact that the victim of the crime happened to be an Interpol agent.

The room was dark, but she didn't want to turn on the light. She pushed open his bedroom door to filter in more light from the main room. Duffle bags stacked along the wall captured her interest. Creeping quietly forward, she bent down to stare at the worn zipper. Agent Allen must have had the bags for years. The leather was worn and soft to the touch. The zipper moved easily and barely made any noise.

In the middle, the zipper caught on something, and Zoe pulled harder. Something snapped, but everything seemed okay, so she kept unzipping the bag.

Once she reached the end and could open the bag up, she leaned down to peek inside.

Small and large books filled the bag. She ran her finger along one of the spines, and she felt the worn paper. Some appeared positively ancient. Old books were strange things to be in a police officer's bag. It was possible he was an international agent with a voracious reading habit. She continued digging around the large bag. A small cooper pot nestled on one side of the duffle, and on the other side there was a large glass orb. Her fingers trailed over the cool surface.

The scent from earlier called to her, and she turned to search for its source. Rising to her feet, she literally followed her nose to the closet. As she opened the door, the aroma wafted toward her. She lightly traced her fingertips over one of the agent's jackets.

Did she become a stalker or something creepy like the woman from *Single White Female?*

Zoe knew she should back away, but she didn't. Something was in the closet. The strong smell caused her eyes to water. A sneeze rushed up on her, but nothing would deter her. She moved his hanging trousers out of the way and spotted another duffle bag. She sniffed another sneeze away, as she pulled the bag out into the open.

The bag wasn't as full as the ones by the wall, but it contained several items wrapped carefully in a cloth. She picked up the longest object and peeked underneath the cover. She gasped when she spied the sharp edge of a knife. Laying the object on the ground, she carefully unwrapped it. Its intricately carved handle was worn smooth with age. Zoe gingerly touched the bare handle. A sharp snap and an arch of electricity caused her to gasp loudly, and she pulled her hand away.

"Okay," she whispered shakily to herself. "He has a very old, pointy knife. Every Interpol agent probably has one. Nothing strange about that."

But there were many strange things about that.

Who carried around a knife that looked as if it belonged in a museum? Were the Persians missing an ancient relic? What kind of government agent carried around such a weapon? Was he an arms smuggler?

Her mind froze. She'd unwrapped a knife from his luggage. With shaking hands, she wound the fabric around the knife and shoved it back in the duffle. Her hasty actions caused glass bottles lining the end of his bag to clank loudly together. Liquids of various colors sloshed up against their sides.

It is a bomb. Her brain declared instantly. *He's making a bomb.*

Her hands froze over the bag and wondered if she managed to stumble across some terrorist plot disguised as a rescue. What if she'd blindly believed Agent Jordan Allen was a good guy? The thought made her sick.

Pulling the sides of the duffle bag together, she zipped it closed and shoved it back in the closet. She swung the trousers in front of the bag to disguise it from view. She ran from the room as quickly as possible. She wouldn't have a good excuse if he walked in and saw her snooping in his belongings.

Zoe picked up her mostly charged cell phone and opened the internet. She would see if she could find any information on Agent Allen. As she was scrolling through the Interpol website, her phone rang, nearly causing a heart attack.

Clearing her throat, she answered as calmly as possible.

"Zoe, this is Agent Allen. We've found Susie. She is fine."

Zoe's legs went weak, and she sank into a nearby chair. "Really?" she asked in disbelief. "She's okay?"

"Yes, she was a little shaken, which is to be understood, but otherwise she appeared unharmed. The police have taken her to the hospital."

"The hospital? Oh, my God," she breathed. "Is she hurt?"

Zoe grew lightheaded at the thought of Susie injured because of her.

"No, she is fine from what I can tell. This is routine due to the circumstances. They will take blood work and any samples needed to help put the story together."

Zoe breathed a sigh of relief, all ill thoughts of the agent chased away. "Thank you."

"Now that you know your friend is okay, I suggest you get some rest."

"Is it safe to go home?"

"Stay where you are. I have more work to do, so you have the place to yourself. Try to get some sleep. Sometime tomorrow morning you should be able to see Susie."

His logic for her to stay overnight made sense. She did bring all her things. It was well past midnight, and the drive home would take a while. It made more sense to spend the night, especially since she would have the place to herself. "Okay," she agreed. "I'll stay."

"Good. I will be in touch with you tomorrow once I find out more information. Good night."

The line went dead.

Scowling, Zoe stared at her phone. The entire conversation took thirty-five seconds. She wished he had told her what happened, but the police were involved in an investigation. Various laws probably limited what he could say and couldn't say, but it would have been nice to get a little more information.

She followed her bedtime routine and pulled the covers up to her chin twenty minutes later. The sooner she fell asleep, the sooner she could get up and be ready to help Susie.

How quickly the tables turned, she mused as she settled into the middle of the big empty bed. She wasn't the one in danger. Now it was Susie. Susie was in the spotlight, and Zoe was more than willing to step down from that madhouse. With any luck, Susie suffered no lasting damage from her ordeal.

But any injury or damage occurred, because Susie wore *her* coat.

Zoe had been the intended target. The coincidence was too

great to ignore. Zoe fell asleep with the realization that she should have been the one kidnapped.

Chapter 9

The next morning, Zoe woke in a strange bed. That *never* happened. In all her twenty-eight years, she'd never once woken up in a strange bed with no recollection of how she got there.

Then, the recollecting began.

She was in Agent Allen's hotel room, without Agent Allen. He hadn't come in at any point during the night. It was possible he was still working the case, but the man must need rest at some point. The alarm clock beside the bed read 7:30 a.m., so she moved her legs over the side and got up to prepare for the day. Fifteen minutes later, she pulled on jeans and a sweater and headed to the door.

Zoe slung her purse over her shoulder, as she closed the hotel room door. The stillness of the long, dark hotel hallway added a sense of spookiness that Zoe didn't need. She expected ghosts to shimmer to life directly in front of her eyes. Halloween was over, yet here she was, fancying herself in a haunted house. "It's November. Time to stop thinking about ghouls and goblins. Now we have Santa and sugar plum fairies," she whispered to herself. She wouldn't think about the goat-man, Krampus, the opposite of Father Christmas, and his pack full of beating sticks. That would only start the nightmares again.

Outside, the cold air took her breath, but she tucked her chin and jogged to her car. She needed to stop by her apartment to find some spare clothes for Susie and grab her friend's purse. Zoe wasn't sure if police procedure called for tests to be run on clothes, but she wanted to be safe and bring Susie something new to wear, if needed. Being taller than Susie, Zoe tried her best to find clothing items that would somewhat fit her friend. At least, her things would cover the important bits, and that was all that mattered.

Surely it would be fine going to her apartment for a few minutes, she assumed. After all, Susie had been rescued and was safe now. That would mean she was safe, as well. As soon as she sat down, after gathering a selection of clothes for Susie from her apartment, her phone rang. She didn't recognize the number. "Hello?" She tentatively answered.

"Miss Hunt? This is Detective Williams. Am I catching you at a good time?"

"Ah, yes. I was going to see my friend Susie Monroe. I was told I could visit with her."

"Yes, she should be released later today. The hospital kept her overnight for observation, I am told. I would like to ask you to come into the station this morning. We have a few more questions for you."

"Okay," Zoe said in agreement. Her nerves jangled at the woman's words. "I can be there in a little bit. Is it the main station off of Detroit?"

"Yes. Go to the front desk and ask for me."

"That sounds fine. I will see you soon." Zoe hit the red button, and the phone call ended.

Minutes later, Zoe turned left on Detroit Road and spotted the police station. A few people walked from the building while she parked, so she knew the building was open. She'd never been to Lakewood's police station. She'd driven by it plenty of times, but never had a reason to stop and look around. The big stone building sat back from the main road, surrounded by mature maple trees and projected power and security.

She pulled into a parking spot and tucked Susie's purse under her car seat. The odds of someone breaking into her car, in the middle of a police station parking lot, were probably slim to none, but she didn't want to take any chances. Taking a deep breath to calm her nerves, she walked through the main doors.

The front desk officer, a sleepy-eyed Asian woman, looked up and asked how she could help.

"Detective Williams requested I stop by to see her."

"What's your name?" The woman asked in a slightly bored tone, which was surprising for so early in the workday. It was possible the woman's day didn't just start, though. She could be at the end of a twelve-hour shift, for all Zoe knew.

"Zoe Hunt," she answered.

Without another glance at Zoe, the woman spoke into the phone receiver, "Hello, I have Zoe Hunt in the main entrance." The woman stared into space as she listened to the other speaker. "Ah, yes, yes. Okay. I will." The desk attendant hung up the phone with a gentle click and glanced at Zoe. "Now sign here and we'll get you a visitor badge."

A laminated card was slid across the desk and the woman supplied, "Someone will be out shortly to escort you back."

Zoe took the offered pen and provided the needed signature. "Thank you."

A row of chairs on the other side of the room caught her attention, and she made her way toward them. Sitting down in the surprisingly comfortable seat, she waited. A short while later, a uniformed woman walked through a door, beckoning for Zoe to follow her into another room.

Several card swipes through various doors brought her face to face with Detective Williams.

"Hello, Miss Hunt. Thanks for coming by."

The detective offered her hand, and Zoe shook it awkwardly. Handshakes were never her strong suit.

Detective Williams continued, "I would like you to look at some pictures of the suspect from Friday night."

Zoe should have guessed the police would want some sort of positive ID of the murderer, if possible. That must mean they caught the man. Relief flooded through her. The detective pointed to a nearby, empty desk. "Please have a seat. I will be right back."

Watching the woman walk away, Zoe scanned the room. At least ten other officers were sitting at their desks. Some were on the phone, others on their computers, and a handful chatted with their fellow desk mates.

After a moment, Detective Williams returned with a folder in her hand. She spread it out on the desk and slid a picture toward Zoe. "Do you recognize this man?"

Leaning forward on her seat, Zoe studied the photo. The picture was of a man with closed eyes and a slack expression. He looked dead.

Zoe's mind reeled and her stomach lurched. In disbelief, she realized she was looking at a picture of a dead man. As in, no longer living. Her eyes sought Detective Williams. "Is he dead?" She fought the bile in the back of her throat.

"Try to concentrate on the facial features. Does he look familiar to you?"

Zoe knew what the officer wanted. Her eyes flicked to the picture again. Dark hair. Yes, that could be the man in the cemetery, but she truthfully didn't get a good look at him. It had been too dark, she'd been too surprised, and it happened too quickly. She wouldn't have been able to pick him out in a line-up of live men; she definitely couldn't be sure about a picture showing few details of a dead man. "I'm really sorry, but I don't know for sure. It *might* be the man from the cemetery, but I didn't get a good view of him that night."

Nodding, Detective Williams patted Zoe on the shoulder. "That's okay. We wanted to see if a picture sparked anything from your memory of Friday night."

"I am sorry." Disappointment filtered through her. She wished she could have been more help. "What is his name? The man from the cemetery? The one who kidnapped my friend?"

"At this time, we are not ready to release that information. It's an ongoing investigation."

"If you don't have any further questions for me, I am going to head to the hospital to see Susie now."

"That will be fine. The hospital should be done with

everything for your friend. Her release time should be scheduled for later this morning."

"Oh, good. I have her purse that she left at my apartment. Her car is parked there, too, so I'll give her a ride."

"Ah, yes. Agent Allen said something as much."

Zoe's ears perked up at the mention of Agent Allen's name. "You've talked to Agent Allen?"

"He is assisting with the investigation. He mentioned he stopped by to interview you."

So, he is legitimate. Guilt resurfaced at her snooping through his things, but she ruthlessly pushed it aside. "Yes, we did meet." For some reason, she didn't mention his invitation for her to stay at the hotel.

Detective Williams said cryptically, "Though, not sure he's going to be around much longer, not with that European attitude."

Zoe remained silent on the officer's point of view. She didn't know the agent well enough to agree or disagree, never mind the very suspicious items he kept in the closet of his hotel room. She didn't want to open *that* can of worms at the moment.

"I believe we are done here, but, once again, please let us know if you have anything else to add or discuss." Detective Williams ushered Zoe into the main lobby.

Chapter 10

As Zoe walked into the main entrance of the hospital, a door banged loudly, startling her. Agent Allen walked through the other side of the large room. A grim, determined expression was written on his face. Uniformed police officers strode behind him. He glanced up, and his gaze caught hers. Zoe's stomach set loose a million butterflies, at his intense stare.

Oh my God, he looked at me! Zoe's brain shrieked in the most unfortunate voice. She couldn't look away from the agent, and she felt her face flush in embarrassment. In her defense, he seemed to be having the same trouble, too. Finally tearing her eyes from his, she stared down at her shoes, her boring, black, comfortable shoes. Was she making up for lost time in high school? Was this some sort of punishment for not having some unrequited school crush years ago?

She absolutely should not have a crush on some unknown man who sashayed in her life a day ago. There was still a chance he was some sleeper cell terrorist, at worse, and at best, he was some weirdo that kept pointy knives and strange bottles of liquid in his luggage.

And she'd stupidly stayed over in his hotel room last night. It was one thing to take his word that she'd be safe, and that he'd be working the entire time, but that was the problem. She took the word of someone she'd just met! He could have come in and killed her in the middle of the night, and she'd have no one to blame but herself.

Really, she was the worst case for Darwinism – at its best. She shook her head, trying to get her thoughts back on track.

"Miss Hunt," his deep voice called.

She lifted her eyes to travel over Agent Allen's incredibly fit form. He wore no coat and stood before her, dressed in a light blue button-up shirt and darker blue pants. She noticed mud splattered on the bottom of his pant legs and his brown boots.

"I see you made it in to see Miss Monroe."

"Y-Yes," Zoe stammered, unable to look away from his sculpted cheekbones and luscious lips. *Oh, no! Not in the middle of the hospital!* She forced her body to obey and flashed the agent a quick smile. "Thank you for offering up your hotel room last night."

"It seemed the safest course of action, until the suspect was caught."

She could only nod wordlessly. His spice laden cologne hit her senses again, and she bit her lip, in order to prevent herself from telling him how much she liked the way he smelled. Her brain told her to move away, but her legs stood firmly planted before him.

His eyes flashed, and he leaned down to say, "Next time I invite you into my room, please do not snoop through my belongings."

Zoe's heart stilled, and her stomach dropped at his words. Her eyes met his. "I-I didn't mean- How did-" No words could absolve her of her guilt. She didn't even try to come up with an excuse. "I'm sorry," she finally said, with a hint of defiance. She wouldn't question him on the strange items in the bags. It was his business, not hers, and now was not the time.

"I have my ways," he told her. "Did you find what you were looking for?" Erik resisted the urge to smile as the color drained from her face. He wouldn't explain about the magical booby traps, that he'd set in each of his bags. His belongings were secured by an unseen alarm system, and he knew instantly when someone disturbed the bags. Her curious snooping didn't concern him, so there was no need for retaliatory action on his part.

Choosing to ignore his pointed question, she told him, "I am going to the help desk to get Susie's room number." To Zoe's relief, he let the subject of trespassing drop. He nodded in response to her words and scanned the area behind her. Zoe resisted the urge to peer over her shoulder and instead continued, "I'm hoping to give her a ride home when she is ready."

"She might be soon," he told her absently. "I have to get back to work."

As he passed by, Zoe noted the dark circles under his eyes. He looked tired. His gaze never left hers, and she grew lightheaded under his penetrating stare. "Okay." She waved at him as he strode down a connecting hall.

***

Erik quickly walked down the empty corridor toward the morgue. His tired legs cramped, and he took a moment to kick out the sensation. Exhaustion began to creep in. He hadn't slept in three days, and the magic spells he worked had begun to take their toll. The medical examiner hadn't granted him access to the necromancer yet, so he could only patrol the thirty-some exits of the hospital in an attempt to prevent the dead man's escape.

He was tired and hungry. Running into Zoe hadn't helped matters, either. Visits with her left him with an entirely different kind of hunger. A kind of hunger he couldn't indulge in. If he kept his interactions with her short, he would be able to keep her at a distance, and he'd be able to think straight.

The expected rise of the deceased necromancer kept his mind on the job, and away from Miss Hunt. The revenant would seek out Dale's apprentice, that is now the new necromancer, or if Dale didn't have an apprentice, seek out a suitable candidate. Erik would be there to track down all the players. Then, he might get his hands on the demon's book, so he can destroy it and all the future evil it would have caused.

Penny Pearson

***

Zoe gently pushed the door open to Susie's room. She spied her friend sitting on the edge of the hospital bed. The sheets were rumbled and nearly sliding to the floor.

Susie glanced up from her hands as Zoe entered the room. Her friend spotted her, and her face crumpled as she cried out, "Oh, Zoe." She held out her hands, demanding Zoe give her the attention she needed. Faint streaks of dirt, tears, and possibly blood marred Susie's pale face. Her blond hair hung in limp strands. She appeared almost child-like in her grey striped hospital gown.

"Susie, are you okay? I am so sorry!" Guilt choked Zoe. If Susie hadn't been wearing her coat, she possibly would have been safe. She bent to envelop Susie in a gentle hug, unsure of her friend's condition. "This is my fault."

Susie's grimy hair touched Zoe's cheek, and a horrible odor wafted around her. She nearly choked on the stench, but concentrated on shallow breathing. The smell reminded her of her recent nightmare. If Susie could survive a kidnapping, she could handle the uncomfortable scent. Holding her breath against the smell, she clung to Susie until her friend pulled away from the embrace. Zoe wanted to ask her so many questions, but decided to let Susie do the talking.

Shaking her head at Zoe's exclamation, Susie scowled, "I'm fine. Everything turned out fine."

"Susie, you were kidnapped from my own parking lot! You could have been killed! Nothing about this is fine."

Susie shrugged as she distanced herself, her eyes not touching on Zoe's gaze. "But it turned out fine. No lasting harm done."

Zoe stared at her friend, unsure what to say. She expected dramatics at some level, but this low-key reaction caught her off guard. "I brought you these." She awkwardly held out the bag to Susie. "I didn't know if the police would need your clothes for evidence. They might not fit perfect, but I thought you'd rather have something clean to wear."

"Thank you." Susie took the bag Zoe offered, and set it on

the bed.

"I brought your purse, as well."

Immediately, Susie took her offered purse and unzipped it.

"Seriously!" Zoe teased in wonder as she watched her friend. "The first thing you do after being kidnapped is put on lip gloss?"

Her eyes, dead serious, met Zoe's surprised gaze. "A girl has to have priorities."

Zoe knew not to come between a girl and her lip-gloss, but still. A minute passed in silence. Susie seemed disinclined to talk about her experience, but Zoe was unable to stand the suspense. "What happened in the parking lot last night?"

Shrugging, Susie related casually, "Someone walked up behind me and asked how to get to the gas station. Then, he blew dust in my face."

"What? Blew dust?" Confusion and shock slowed Zoe's response.

"He must have thrown some sort of sleeping powder, or something, because next thing I know, I'm waking up in the psycho's basement." She shrugged as if she didn't have a care in the world. "But, like I said, everything worked out. Well, for me, at least."

Brows furrowed, Zoe asked in amazement, "How did you get away?"

Susie smiled slyly, as if she had a secret. "I used the emergency button on my phone. I couldn't talk because he was near, but texted that I needed help. A little while later, I heard the police sirens, but didn't really need them, though. The man tripped and hit his head. Splat!" She slapped her hands loudly, causing Zoe to jump. "Down he went, and he didn't get up."

Amazement at Susie's casual explanation of her abduction had Zoe wide eyed. "Did he hurt you?"

Susie shook her head, not offering further explanation.

"Did he say why he took you?"

"No," Susie said in a light tone. She picked up the bag of clothes Zoe brought. "I'm going to change into these now."

The scent of rot crept up on Zoe again as Susie passed on

the way to the restroom. Her friend had to be looking forward to a shower, she thought sympathetically. As Susie changed clothes, Zoe's mind drifted to Agent Allen. She wished she had asked him to give her more details, if he could, about Susie's abduction when she had seen him earlier.

Susie stepped out of the bathroom and handed the empty bag to Zoe. "Thanks for the clothes."

Zoe shot her a quick look. "It's the least I can do. I can give you a ride to your car when you are all finished up here."

Susie waved her away. "No, I don't need a ride. One of the officers will do it."

"But I am going right home after this," Zoe retorted. "It's no trouble. Your car is still in my parking lot."

Susie shook her head. "No, really. I would rather a police officer take me home."

"Okay," Zoe gave in. "I will wait here until someone comes to get you."

Something flashed in Susie's eyes before she turned away to gaze out the window.

The sun shone brightly into the hospital room, causing the cream paint on the walls to glow happily. The effect should have put the room's occupants at ease. It seemed to produce the opposite emotion in Susie.

"I would rather be alone."

Caught off-guard by Susie's blunt reply, Zoe could only stutter, "O-Oh, of course. You've been through a lot." She spread her hands out to her friend. "Do you need me to stop by your house to check on your mom?"

"No. A nurse is with her."

Shot down again. Susie effectively shut her out, and Zoe couldn't think of a way to fix it. "Well, okay," she said uncertainly. "Let me know if you need anything. Are you sure you don't want me to stay?"

"No," Susie replied with an edge of exasperation. "I'm fine."

Realizing she had no other options available to her, Zoe told Susie needlessly, "Well, I guess I will go now." She waited for Susie to say something, but that didn't happen. She had turned away and was rummaging through her purse, effectively dismissing her. "Bye," Zoe said.

There was no reply.

Chapter 11

Heat licked at Dale Hicks's skin, excruciating and throbbing. Pain obscured his thoughts down a never-ending tunnel that twisted and turned, getting narrower and narrower. It burned in the most painful way he'd ever experienced. Opening his eyes, he stared around in terror. What happened? His surroundings sparked no sense of the familiar. He thought back to his last memory, yet it seemed so unattainable. He could almost reach out and touch it, but every time he mentally grabbed at it, the memories floated away, leaving a vast emptiness. The rough ground tore into his back, and he propped himself up against a stone wall behind him.

Red, flickering light illuminated the room. Fear shot down Dale's spine. Something bad had happened.

A large figure came forward. Shadows rippled across the massive frame. Red eyes, sparking fire, focused on Dale. Large scales and protrusions dripped with liquid ooze. "You have arrived sooner than expected," the creature rasped.

The sound travelled across Dale's skin like tiny screams. He looked around him in panic. Oh God, had he died? No! No, it wasn't his time. "How …" His voice trailed off. Still, no memory returned.

The demon spoke, "Your time is up." There was a pause, as it rotated its head to the side, pondering the necromancer. "Your time is mine."

With the demon's words, absolute terror ate at his sanity. "No.

This wasn't supposed to happen. I had time! I gave you sacrifices to buy me more time!" Dale's voice rose in anxiety. He grabbed at his head, willing his brain to show him what happened. Cloudy memories filtered through. There was a woman. He'd taken her for some reason. He rolled the knowledge around his mind. Who was the woman? She must have been a sacrifice. So, how the hell did he end up dead, now indebted to the demon before his time?

"A new necromancer has stepped forward."

A new necromancer. The thought sat idle for a moment.

He was no longer the necromancer, the one working to gain power in trade for extra years on his life. He was now going to be a revenant, back from the dead to serve the whim of the demon and the latest necromancer.

Dale's defiance melted at the demon's words.

He'd been replaced. He would become one of the dreaded lost souls that had once served him. Heat blew out on the demon's breath. The sensation of it distracting him for a moment. The hideous creature crept closer. Leather-like skin slithered and creaked with every stride. It drew to full height before Dale.

"What say you?"

Dale shifted his eyes from Mammon to the floor. Using the demon's name, he offered, "Mammon, I am yours." The words tasted bitter in his mouth, but he knew they were words he had to say. Phase two of his deal with the demon had begun.

"You've always been mine," Mammon sneered. "Once you are back, you are charged with ensuring the necromancer's work is undisturbed. No one interferes. Your folly invited the interest of a white wizard to the area. He must not find the next in line. The revenants and others served you while you were alive. Now you, as a revenant, will serve your new master."

Dale would protect the newcomer at all cost, for he didn't relish meeting the demon anytime soon, especially in failure.

"Do not disappoint me," Mammon ordered. "Or you will regret it with every fiber of your being."

Dale never had a chance to answer.

One minute, he felt as if he were burning alive, while

conversing with an ooze-dripping demon, and the next, he was lying on a cold slab in the darkness. It took a moment to adjust to his new surroundings. A wall was directly beside him. Moving his hand up, he encountered another barrier not a foot above. He pounded once on the surface, and the metal echoed around him. He stilled, but no sound came from outside his metal container. He continued to lie still and wait, yet no noise came from the outside. Nothing. A silence deeper than one he'd ever experienced before. Comprehension dawned, as he realized he didn't hear the pounding of his pulse or the sound of his breathing. He truly was dead.

It didn't take him long to figure out where he had ended up. The only probable outcome was the morgue.

The girl he'd taken must have killed him somehow. Anger speared through him before he remembered his goal of distracting the white wizard. But he couldn't stay where he was. If he was dead, he would be autopsied.

The medical examiner could *not* perform an autopsy on him. He wouldn't survive the procedure, then he would belong to the demon forever. He would be at the beck and call of the creature from Hell, or wherever he was from.

No! He needed more time.

***

Time would be limited, before someone would come for him. He needed to get up, get moving. The urge consumed his entire being. Even in death, he could feel the pull of the demon's will, and he refused to give in.

***

A delicate, screeching noise resonated in his ears. He pushed his bare feet against the metal door, but it wouldn't budge. He twisted around in the drawer, examining the mechanism from the inside. He could see nuts on bolts but nothing else. He swore softly, as he found the nuts torqued down too tightly to move.

Dale had another mild shock, as he suddenly realized he was able to see. This was a sealed morgue drawer, completely lightless. He knew his skeletal minions weren't impacted by the darkness, and that they could see and hear in some fashion, even after their eyes and ears had rotted away. Dale's mind immediately skittered away from that thought, and he kicked the bottom of the drawer in frustration.

Kicking yielded no better results. Dale swore to himself. He needed to get out of the morgue, and he needed to do it unseen. Again, another screech filled the space around him, coming from the other side of the door. He moved his body closer to the edge, ready to create his opening for escape. The door swung open, sending bright light into his small metal box.

A skeleton stood, staring at him through empty sockets. Except the sockets weren't entirely empty now; he could see ghostly eyes, full of fury and madness, peering back at him.

"Well, I'll be damned," Dale muttered. When he died, his helpers must have been nearby, and the police probably rounded up the skeletons. A smile cracked on his stiff face. The bastards had no idea the skeletons were mobile. His helpers proved to be quite handy, when it came to breaking him out of the morgue. "Well, my friends," he muttered. "It seems we have a change of leadership, but let's get this game going."

Dale shuddered as he though he heard faint laughter from the skeleton, as ghostly lips sneered at him.

***

Zoe walked through the hospital hallways, making her way back to her car. Disbelief still battled within her at Susie's words. She would have thought Susie needed a friend to talk to, but that wasn't the case. Then she realized she acted the same way after Friday night's murder. Susie and Tiffany stopped by to help, and all she wanted to do was ignore all their questions, too. She would give Susie some time to process everything that happened.

Ritual Of Blood

If Susie wanted to talk, Zoe would be available.

Heading through the paid parking lot, she closed her coat against the wind and fought her way to the unpaid lot, that sat farther away from the hospital. When would she learn that sometimes it was okay to pay for something, if it made life easier?

Zoe made a list of chores she needed to complete once she got home. The first item on her list would be to log into work to see what she could complete tonight. Not for the first time, Zoe was thankful for her work-at-home job. She was good with computers and had a knack at running reports, which landed her a great job for a nearby hospital in their records department.

After work, cleaning the bathroom and doing laundry would be the highlights of her Monday evening. She couldn't wait to get back to her own place. The agent's hotel room was very nice, but she liked her comfortable apartment with its nice lake views. She also wouldn't have reminders of her unlawful entry, staring at her in the form of duffle bags.

A familiar, rotten smell floated through the air, causing Zoe to stop in her tracks. The area surrounding her appeared empty, but the smell grew stronger. Wondering if it were something to do with a sewer mishap, she veered to her left to follow the odor. She experienced the strange smell in too many unrelated places. She needed to get down to the bottom of the scent.

A loud bang and the sound of breaking glass startled her. A man wearing a baseball cap opened a truck door. When he closed the door, glass cubes fell from the shattered safety glass and bounced across the parking lot. Zoe peered around to see if anybody else saw the break-in, but the parking lot was strangely empty.

The revving engine didn't register, as she ran in front of the truck in an attempt to stop the car thief. She looked through the windshield and froze at the sight of the man in the driver's seat. The man from the cemetery snarled at her. The murderer. The one that kidnapped Susie.

The one who was dead.

She squeaked in shock as the truck jumped forward, nearly running her down. Zoe shouted for help when she realized she was witnessing a car theft. Her nerves ratcheted to high, as she watched the truck careen down the parking lot lane. Suddenly, the truck skidded to a halt at the far end.

Three figures stumbled into the road toward the truck. The passenger door shot open as they neared. Zoe watched the figures shuffle inside, but she couldn't believe what she was seeing.

She blinked her eyes quickly to clear her head and gawked at the sight again.

Skeletons piled into the stolen truck.

The truck sped around the corner, picking up speed.

Zoe started running after them, all the time yelling for help at the top of her lungs. Still, no one came to her aid. She darted in between cars, in an effort to get in front of the truck. She had to slow him down somehow, because she knew what she saw.

"Zoe!"

She turned her head mid-pursuit and spotted Agent Allen running toward her. The serious look on his face startled her, but she kept chasing after the truck.

"What are you doing?" His harsh cry vibrated, whip-like, through the air.

Zoe pointed to the truck and called between gasps of air, "That truck! Stop it!"

As soon as she said the words, the truck veered to change course and drove straight toward her. Mid-sprint, her foot caught against a parking lot curb, and she didn't have time to correct her footing.

She attempted to regain her balance, but her speed was too great. The freefall terrified her, but she had no way to stop her tumble. Her head cracked against the cement curb a second before the rest of her body hit the ground.

Pain scattered her thoughts, then everything went black.

***

Erik saw Zoe tumble in the path of the oncoming truck. Her head bounced off the curb, and he knew an instant of fear. He wouldn't get to her in time before the vehicle struck her. Erik didn't think about his decision. The one thought on his mind was to make sure Zoe was unhurt. Later, he would look back and realize he made the wrong decision. He should have gone after the man. His training told him to go after the man.

But in the heat of the moment, he chose Zoe. He lifted his arm toward the truck and growled, *"Im hayats'k'its' stats'ir."* The spell in his Armenian birth tongue burst from his lips. Power shifted inside him, moving through his limbs and pushing into his fingertips. Wind roared before him, and he sprinted toward Zoe.

The gust of wind hit the truck, causing the driver to twist the wheel to keep control. The truck bounced around Zoe's still form, but continued on, not slowing down. For a moment, Erik watched the truck skid around the corner and disappear from view.

Wasting no more time, Erik bent, pulled Zoe into his arms, and made a run for his car. There was a chance the truck would double back to finish what it started, and he couldn't allow that. Zoe didn't move in his arms, as he sprinted to safety. Settling her in the back of his rental, he jumped in the driver's seat without checking her vitals. He pulled out of the hospital's parking lot, turned toward his hotel, and prayed she survived her fall.

In the rearview mirror, he caught sight of her head lolling to the side, like a doll. He wrestled with the idea of taking her back to the hospital. They were better equipped to handle head trauma, but there would be uncomfortable questions on how she came to her current condition. He wasn't ready to deal with the paperwork of a walking corpse yet.

He'd came face-to-face with the necromancer turned revenant.

And he'd simply walked, no; he simply ran the other way.

Chapter 12

"**I** need a doctor."

Zoe woke to that perplexing statement and an excruciating pain in her head. The agony was unlike anything she'd experienced before. Her brain felt as if it had been pulsed in a blender, chopped up in small, painful bits, and shoved back inside. Slowly opening her eyes, she glanced around and, once again, found herself in the middle of an unknown bed.

No. The bed wasn't unknown. Her surroundings became familiar. This room belonged to Agent Allen. *Oh, Lord*, she thought. *What did I do this time?* Did she somehow get drunk and pass out? Oh, please, no.

Then, she remembered everything.

She'd gone to the hospital to meet with Susie. Then, she spied the murderer from the cemetery stealing a truck in the parking lot.

The *dead* murderer.

Anxiety made her heartbeat faster. How had a dead man escaped from the morgue, and why would he steal a truck? She was sure that was not a logical reaction, from a man declared dead only hours ago.

Zoe must have made some sort of noise – hopefully not some helpless gasp or whimper – because Agent Allen walked through the door toward the bed. Dark hair spilled almost boyishly over his midnight eyebrows. A nicely fitted button-up shirt hinted at his well-toned physique. He'd changed out of his mud-splattered apparel. She wouldn't even get into how well his slacks fit. The way they hugged his hips was enough to send her into heart palpitations, or give her a brain aneurysm.

"I've sent my location," he spoke into the phone, but his eyes locked onto hers. Zoe's pallor worried him, and he hoped the doctor would arrive quickly.

The searching gaze sent heat into Zoe's cheeks. Her head pounded, reminding her of her fall and subsequent skull beating. What happened after she lost consciousness? She couldn't remember anything, other than falling after she tripped on the parking curb. Obviously, the agent managed to get her to safety.

Unless you are in a coma, and he is in your dream state, her brain suggested. She ignored her brain and asked, "What happened? I remember falling, but how did I get back to your hotel room?"

Erik sat down on the bed next to Zoe. He reached to put a comforting hand on her leg, but thought better of it. Instead, he laid his hand on the small pillow nestled against her thigh. She'd managed to distract him enough, without any real physical contact. If he touched her, who knew what decisions he would make that would turn out for the worse. "You fell and hit your head."

"Yeah, I remember that part, but I saw the man from the cemetery. What happened?" Pain washed over her again, engulfing her in a wave of dizzying nausea. Her injured brain lodged some sort of war on an invisible foe in her head. She turned a slow glance toward the agent, waiting for him to fill in the details.

She knew what she saw. Susie's kidnapper broke out of the morgue, stole a truck, and drove off to who-knew-where.

"The truck almost hit you, but you got lucky." He didn't tell her magic was the only thing that saved her life, and he didn't get into details on Dale's revival from the dead.

"Did he get away?"

Erik rubbed the back of his neck. Another lock of dark hair fell over a brow. "I chose to help you over apprehending him."

Shock stole her words. She gently touched her head as she thought about what might have happened, had Agent Allen not been there. "Thank you" was all she could say.

Ritual Of Blood

"I made an icepack for you," he declared, as he rose and disappeared into the main room. A moment later, he returned carrying a plastic bag with ice.

He handed it to her, and she swore his eyes shifted uncomfortably. She suspected he didn't want her asking questions about the murdered man. She sat silent for a moment and gently held the icepack against the side of her head. She winced as she touched a particularly sore spot.

Guilt traveled through Erik, but he pushed it away. This was part of the job. Sometimes the innocent got involved, and it didn't always turn out the best for them. He expected the revenant to rise, but he had not expected him to use the air vents to get out of the morgue. The time it took Erik to figure out Dale Hicks had escaped almost got Zoe killed. "How bad is your pain?" he asked, avoiding the more serious conversation.

Now it was Zoe's turn to grimace as the ice shifted in the plastic bag. "Hurts like I smacked my head on cement."

He nodded and tried to resist smiling at her wry words. "Seems acceptable since that is the truth."

The humor in his words caused her heart to skip a beat. He couldn't be flirting with her, but she still relished the sentiment, even in the midst of the worst headache she'd ever experienced.

"I called for a doctor to check on you." His eyes searched her face, as if looking for signs of distress.

She wanted to tell him she didn't need a doctor, but the pain in her head scared her. It would do no good to foolishly decline medical help, especially if she was seriously hurt. She wisely kept quiet. Her stitches hadn't even been removed yet, and she'd managed to hurt herself again – both times near the same man. Was she cursed? Because if not, the world had some explaining to do. At the moment, she didn't think the world would actually take the time to explain the injustices to her, so she settled on Agent Allen doing the talking.

Apparently, Agent Allen had other ideas. He didn't want to talk.

Zoe gritted her teeth at his reticence. Detective Williams had shown Zoe a picture of the body. Susie declared her kidnapper dead. She wasn't imagining things. "The man driving the truck was the same one from the cemetery."

Erik glanced a moment at Zoe, flexing his fingers. He suspected she recognized Dale Hicks; from the way she was running after the truck at the hospital lot. She didn't need to stick her nose in his business, so he had to get her off the trail as quickly as possible. She was in over her head, and she didn't even know it.

Hell, the police would be in over their heads soon enough. The Lakewood police force wasn't equipped to fight the undead. The revenant Hicks had to be located, and Erik needed to find out who had the demon's book. It would end badly if they had no idea what they had in their possession, and if they did it would end even worse. Once the book took a hold of the person's spirit, they would be hard to track.

Until the killings started again.

But Zoe was a different matter altogether. He couldn't perform magic with an uninvited guest nearby. He needed to get her out of his hotel room as quickly as possible, once he was sure she was well enough to travel.

Only, he did invite her into his hotel. Hell, he invited her right into his bed. His body stirred at the image, but her questions about Dale Hicks derailed his lusty thoughts.

Fighting the urge to close her eyes against the pain in her head, Zoe softly persisted, "Can you tell me how a man who is supposed to be dead, steals a truck in broad daylight? "She refused to give up on the dead man-walking subject. She lightly covered her aching eyes.

Erik watched her battle her pain and realized he didn't have a logical rebuttal to her question. At least not one she was prepared to comprehend. Before he could begin an explanation, his phone rang. Zoe's doctor had arrived. "I will be right back," he told her as he rose from his seated position next to her and left the room.

Zoe cracked open one eye and watched him leave the bedroom. She wanted to trust him, but she had more questions than answers. His refusal to address her question concerned her.

Ritual Of Blood

There was still the possibility he was a terrorist, and planned to blow something up with the mysterious chemicals in the bottles.

Voices mingled in the main room before an older woman with blond hair, pulled back in a severe ponytail, walked into the bedroom. She moved to the side of the bed and looked down at Zoe.

Trying not to squirm under the direct examination, Zoe stared back with limited success. The doctor's image shimmered and divided in two. Her eyelids slid closed, and she struggled to keep them open. No matter how hard she tried, they slid back down, blocking her view. The pull of sleep danced on the edge of Zoe's consciousness, and she found herself drifting off.

A bright light shining into her eyes startled Zoe awake.

The doctor leaned over her and yanked up an eyelid, moving a small light back and forth across her face. "Hello, Zoe. I'm Dr. Blackwell. I heard you took a hard spill. Your pupils look good. Are you experiencing any dizziness?"

Zoe didn't shake her head, but she answered, "A little. I'm seeing double, and my head hurts a lot."

Dr. Blackwell sent her an easy smile. "I would imagine so."

The doctor smelled of mint and something else. A faint whiff of bourbon. What? Did Agent Allen bring a drunken doctor to examine her? Ire rose in her blood, but her body responded by a dizzying set down, in the form of nausea and lightheadedness.

Turning, the doctor spoke to the agent, "From my brief exam I believe she has a slight concussion. If you notice pronounced slurred speech, trouble walking or seizures, take her to the hospital immediately. She should stay in bed for the rest of the day and avoid driving for the next twenty-four hours, at least. She can have over-the-counter pain relief, if it's needed." Then, turning to Zoe, she stated, "That's a pretty big bandage on your cheek."

"Yes. I ran into something a few days ago." She slid a quick glance to Agent Allen.

"Did you have stitches?"

Zoe gave a tiny nod. The pounding in her head took on an extra beat.

"May I have a look to make sure everything is healing properly?"

"Yes."

Dr. Blackwell gently peeled off the bandage and touched the scar. "Would you like me to remove your stitches? Your scar has healed nicely."

She lightly felt her cheekbone. The offer would save her a trip to the doctor's office. "That would be helpful." Frankly, Zoe would agree to anything if people would be quiet and let her sleep.

"Yes, it seems to be very superficial. It will be a moment."

The doctor pulled a pair of scissors from an unseen pocket and proceeded to trim the ends. With a smooth pull, the stitches came out easily. Zoe felt her cheek again, but only slightly raised skin met her fingertips.

"Try not to bother the area. You don't need to apply anything special to the site. Two to three days from now, you can moisturize it, if you choose." She rose, patted Zoe's leg, and nodded to the agent.

"Thank you," Zoe called out softly.

"I'm glad I could help. I hope that we won't meet again in this same capacity. Take care, Miss Hunt."

Zoe closed her eyes before the doctor left the room, and she felt sleep rush over her senses. An instant later, her head rolled to the side on the pillow.

Panic surged through Erik. He took a step toward Zoe, but the doctor touched his arm – an effort to stop him. "Let her sleep. She is fine." Blackwell stared at the wizard in front of her. She'd worked with him before and liked him. This human side of him was something new.

"Thank you for coming so quickly," Erik told the doctor quietly, as he walked with her to the front door. "I didn't want to take her to the hospital if I could avoid it. There would be too many questions, especially given her name being on the police radar."

"Are things getting out of hand?"

Erik shook his head. "No, a few miscalculations."

Dr. Blackwell narrowed her eyes. "You usually don't have

miscalculations."

"I am only human, shocking as it is. I cannot live forever without a few mistakes. I have a grasp of what's going on now, and I'm getting close to finding the book. When I do that, one less book will be out in the world calling to its next servants."

"Then you would be out of a job," she said in a teasing tone.

Erik shook his head, his eyes bleak. "No. There is always something out there waiting to step in the line. I don't think I'll ever be out of a job."

The doctor opened the hotel door. "Well, be careful. And take care of the girl. She seems to be taking this all-in stride, considering she has no idea what you're up against."

"Provided she didn't get brain damage from hitting her head on concrete," Erik remarked dryly.

"She will be fine if you follow my recommendations. Call me if there are any changes or if some new symptom arises. Now that I know you are in town; I'll make sure to be available if needed again."

Erik thanked the doctor and closed the door. He needed to think of a plan on how to proceed finding the new necromancer, as well as tracking down the newest revenant. And the helpers. There was veritable army on the ground nearby, provided the necromancer was a local. Oh, and he had to keep Zoe safe. That wasn't part of his job description, but somehow, she had managed to land smack dab in the middle of this mess.

He toyed with the idea of the revenant seeking out Zoe due to the fact of the missing book. He didn't know if the revenant would actually pursue her again. He did know where she lived, but he wasn't sure what motivated the new revenant at this point. The police had collected no ancient spell book in their sweeping of evidence at Dale Hicks's house. No book meant one unhappy revenant. The book was possibly in the hands of a new necromancer, but Erik needed to be sure it wasn't in the stack of books he shielded from view back at Dale Hicks's hideout. By tomorrow, all manuscripts and books gathered from Dale's would be taken to a storage unit and processed by a team under the employ of the Vatican.

Penny Pearson

As for Zoe, Erik would keep her near, for her own safety, until he could figure out who had the demon's book.

Chapter 13

Erik's plan was exactly opposite of what Zoe had in mind. She wouldn't stay a moment longer in Agent Allen's hotel room. Not again. If she could get her body to cooperate, she would thank the agent for helping her, and then leave for the comfort of her own apartment. She attempted to sit up, but her stomach roiled, threatening action if she proceeded to try any funny business, such as walking.

Well, she would have to wait a little longer, until her brain didn't feel as if it were going to fall out of her head, then she would leave. She still had no idea if he was a good guy or not. On one hand, an Interpol agent seemed like a good thing, but on the other, his appearance was too mysterious.

Sure, he saved her from a crazed – possibly walking dead – lunatic who tried to run her over with a stolen truck, but that didn't mean he didn't have evil plans of his own. Unless he told her exactly what was in those duffle bags he hid in his room, she would leave as soon as her body quit holding her hostage.

The door opened, and Agent Allen peeked into the room. The doctor must have left, Zoe surmised, for he entered alone. The serious look on his face worried her slightly. There was still the elephant in the room that needed to be addressed, namely the supposedly dead man who could drive. "Okay," Zoe began as she watched him approach. She would not let him continue to ignore her questions. "I think it's time for some answers."

Erik shook his head, his face not giving anything away. "I cannot talk about police business."

"Police business would have taken me to the hospital to have me examined for extensive injuries, not brought some fly-by- night physician to the hotel room."

At Zoe's words, a tick developed in his jaw. "Dr. Blackwell isn't fly-by- night."

"She's not a doctor in a hospital!" Zoe heatedly exclaimed, but instantly regretted it. Her head yelled at her for getting so sassy. She touched shaky fingertips to her temples and closed her eyes to sooth the pain.

Erik leaned toward her. "You must rest." When she opened her mouth to argue, he offered, "When you wake *after a few hours of rest*, we will talk more about what happened. I realize you have questions, and I can give you some answers." *Not all,* he added silently, *but some.*

She didn't want to be satisfied with his response, but his words slightly mollified her. Settling a little deeper against the soft pillow under her head, she asked suspiciously, "Did your doctor say it was safe to sleep?" The icepack slid to the side of her head, but she left it alone.

"Yes," Erik told her. He gently moved the icepack to shift it to a more comfortable resting spot. "Get some sleep. It will help your head. When you wake up, if you feel up to it, we'll get you something to eat."

Zoe smiled at that. The offer of food sounded wonderful, even with the intense headache. She didn't like missing meals and looked forward to seeing what he would produce. Squeezing her eyes closed to ease the pounding pain in her head, she murmured, "I would like that, but then we talk." Sleep fortunately overtook her a minute later.

Erik stayed next to Zoe and watched her sleep. He needed to move away and work on his plans for his next step, but couldn't make himself leave her side. The delicate skin of her eyelids entranced him, and he watched her take a deep breath before settling into a deeper slumber. A minute longer, he finally roused himself to leave

Ritual Of Blood

her and get some work done.

Back in his own bedroom suite, he dialed Jenny on his cell phone.

She didn't answer normally, but went right into egging him. "Dude, you've lost a body already! The police are freaking out."

"I know that," Erik growled, instantly in a bad mood. "What details do you have?"

"Dale Hicks is now listed as MIA, along with some accomplices of the skeletal variety. Their belief is someone from a religious cult, probably satanic in nature, came and stole the bodies. They are thinking multiple suspects are at large. Logical guess, considering the alternative."

The alternative being a dead man walking out of the morgue under his own volition with skeletons, barely held together by ligaments and tissue, following close behind. But reality was always stranger than fiction in his line of work. For the last seven-hundred years, he'd trained and studied, hunted and detained various demons, devils, and poor unfortunate souls. He'd never known anything differently. Today was not atypical.

Except for the woman sleeping in the next room.

"Erik."

Jenny's voice captured his attention. "I heard you."

"Did you? I asked if you needed help. Last time we talked, there was only one dead body. Now there are two. Or is it three now? Don't think I don't know you called Blackwell. Who got hurt?"

Holding the cell phone with one hand, Erik pressed his fingers against the bridge of his nose. "The woman was injured."

"The witness?"

"Yes." He waited for Jenny to break into a jaunty song that likened him and Zoe to some sort of lovebirds kissing in a tree. But it didn't happen. She wisely stayed quiet. He continued, "She will be fine. She tripped and hit her head."

"What do you need from me?"

Erik needed Jenny to remove Zoe from his presence, but he couldn't say that because it actually could be done. The woman had done nothing wrong. As long as she stayed out of his way during the investigation of finding the location of the new necromancer, she wouldn't need to be placed elsewhere. In answer to Jenny's question, he told her, "I need to have a pickup and delivery of Zoe's car. It is at the hospital, and I don't want to raise alarm bells with her car being in the middle of a crime scene."

"I'm on it," Jenny told him. There was a flurry of taps on the phone, as she typed in her computer. "Oh, a storage unit has been located and ready for Dale Hicks's items, when you give us the word."

"Good," Erik said. "Have Zoe Hunt's car brought to my hotel. I'm working on locating the necromancer, obtaining the book, and ending this. I will let you know when to send the team in to recover Hicks's items."

"Sounds relatively easy." Jenny ending the sentence on a strange note. As if she didn't really believe her words.

"I will check back with you tomorrow, unless you find out something before then."

"Will do. Laters."

Erik frowned as he slipped his phone into his pants pocket. After working for the Vatican's secret department for five years, Jenny still had no respect for her elders. He eyed at his closet, before walking over to pull out the biggest duffle bag.

Evidence of Zoe's earlier meddling from the previous day showed in the form of a missing plastic tie on his bag. As a security precaution, he had set a spell to alert him if the duffle had been opened. He didn't know what prompted Zoe's curiosity, but he would ask her once she felt better. He glanced in the direction where Zoe was sleeping. His eye narrowed, and then Erik pulled out a large book.

Unlike the necromancer's book, his book held the workings of white magic spells. Setting the book down on the table, he searched for his needed ingredients. He was going to attempt a location spell that would search for any dark magic. Usually such spells were unsuccessful without a personal item from the object in question. This had the potential of a needle in the haystack outcome, but he would attempt it, until he could leave the hotel in search of the revenant's belongings.

He pulled a pinch of salt from a drawn leather bag and quickly created a circle around him. It served to capture in the elements of his spell and formed an isolated barrier. With a quick glance down at the book, he recited the words to summon any sort of reaction. Nothing happened. He reached deeper inside him, pulling at his power, but still nothing happened. He wasn't disappointed. He didn't expect the spell to yield much of anything, but it was worth a try.

Erik knew the revenant had to be on the move, but he didn't know where he was moving. There were a few different possibilities. He needed to get some sort of personal item from Dale Hicks's cabin. When he did that, his location spell would work. He called the magic back, cleaned up his materials, and placed everything back where they belonged.

A sound from Zoe's bedroom captured his attention, and he moved to see if she needed help. She stood, staring warily at him, in the doorway. Her pale face and bloodshot eyes told Erik she still felt awful. "Zoe, what are you doing? You haven't slept nearly long enough to help your body recover."

"I'm having trouble sleeping. I keep seeing the man. What's his name? The police didn't tell me."

Without thought, Erik answered, "Dale Hicks." His jaw tightened in effort not to say more. She didn't need to be involved. It was too dangerous.

"Can we sit down?" Zoe hated the breathy sound of her voice. But if she talked any louder, her head would explode into a million pieces. Or her brain would slide out of her skull and plop onto the floor.

"Would you like a Tylenol? Dr. Blackwell said it would be fine."

"Oh, did she?" Zoe stopped her wise-ass comment that fought to come out. "Yes, please." The amused look he cast her made her wonder, if he could see her grit her teeth.

He came back with a glass of water and two white pills. She

quickly took the medicine and leaned back in the chair, hoping the pain relief would kick in soon. Her stomach flipped sourly, and she licked her dry lips. The need for answers outweighed her need for comfort, so she got right to the point, "I thought the killer was dead."

"The police declared him dead when that was not the case."

Zoe stared at him. He knew more than he was saying. "Why would he steal a car?"

"I don't have the answer you are looking for."

"Tell me the truth," Zoe pleaded. Her head hurt unbearably, but she sat in front of him expecting him to tell what was going on. There was more to this whole affair than anyone was willing to let on. "Am I safe? Is Susie safe?"

"It's possible Dale Hicks – the murderer and kidnapper – will think you have something that belongs to him. There is a chance he will attempt to reach out to you."

His words puzzled her. "I don't have anything of his. How could I? I saw him for a split second in the cemetery. That's it. I've never seen him before. Is this because I took a picture of him?" It unsettled her to think she endangered her friends and herself because of a thoughtless action. If she never would have taken the picture, it was possible she wouldn't have been in this position.

"The picture had nothing to do with it. Today was a bad case of being in the wrong place at the wrong time. I am pretty sure the picture you snapped of him, is the least of his worries right now."

"But now he's free again. A man presumed dead, who's now driving around!" Zoe's face grew flushed at her words, and she fought a wave of dizziness. "So, what happens next? When can I go home?" The words sounded brave to her, but a small part was terrified the killer was waiting in the parking lot for her.

The haunted look in her eyes told Erik she feared the return of the necromancer, and he agreed with her reluctance. He didn't know what Dale Hicks was thinking. He didn't know if he still thought Zoe was some part of his plan.

He stared so intently at her; she became warm under his gaze. She fought not to squirm, determined to match his stare.

Ritual Of Blood

"I want you to avoid your apartment for the time being. I don't know where Dale Hicks is going."

"What about Susie? Isn't she in danger?"

"I don't know." That was the truth. The necromancer had Zoe's blood for future use, he didn't know if Susie was in the same boat. Dale could track Zoe down. He didn't know if the necromancer had time to do any spell work on Susie.

"Did you call the police department to let them know Dale Hicks is still alive?" she questioned.

"Are you asking me if I did my job correctly?"

"N-no," she stuttered. "I thought it would be a good idea to get more people involved."

"I know what I'm doing. You didn't get enough rest. Go back to your room. I told you we would talk after you slept enough." He stared at her. "You didn't sleep long enough."

He raised his eyebrow in the most infuriating manner, and Zoe saw red. "You can't treat me like an unruly child and send me to my room."

"I am not treating you like a child. I am treating you like a person that nearly had their head cracked open." His voice rose a moment before he drew a deep breath. "It is my job to keep you safe. I know what I'm doing. Don't worry. I'll be working while you sleep," he told her in no-nonsense voice.

The urge to argue battled within Zoe, but she managed to tamp it down as she quietly walked back to her bed. She gingerly rested her head against the soft pillow and let her eyes drift closed.

Chapter 14

Zoe woke with her head blissfully quiet. The room was dark. She could see into Agent Allen's bedroom and spied him carrying an armful of laundry, before he tossed it on his bed. He grabbed a large wooden stick and moved it to a nearby corner. Tilting her head to the side, Zoe wondered why a grown man carried a large stick around. He turned to face her, and he immediately moved the stick out of sight. She threw her legs over the edge of the bed and slowly rose.

She really wanted to ask about the stick.

She did not ask about the stick. Instead as she walked toward him, she inquired as politely as she could stomach, "Have I slept long enough?" Her attitude was pretty crappy, but she had a good excuse. She'd been terrorized not once, but twice, by a murderer who was dead, but still walking.

He glanced at his watch. "Three hours. I'd say that is enough. For now." Her face was pale, but her eyes were clearer than before, and she didn't appear to be on the verge of a collapse. However, to be safe, he waved to the couch. "Sit down. We need to get you some food. Would you eat pizza if I ordered one?"

Her stomach agreed with his suggestion, even though she and Susie had ordered a pizza yesterday. Erik called the order in and brought her a Coke from the nearby vending machine in the hallway. He opened the can and poured the drink over some ice. His fingers touched hers as he handed her the small plastic cup.

"How do you know Dale Hicks's isn't waiting outside to attack?" she asked.

"I would know," he told her cryptically.

"No, really." She pointed to the staid, dark blue chair across from her. "Sit. You owe me some answers, then I have more questions, and then you owe me more answers."

He smiled at her. "I'm not sure that is how this works."

His smile caused her stomach to flutter. "Yes," she retorted, trying to stay on track. "It works this way. *You* tell me what is going on. *I* have a better chance at survival. It's quite simple."

Then, he laughed. "You bring dramatic up to the next level." His eyes searched her face, still smiling.

Zoe grew more serious. "Really. I'm asking you to tell me what is going on. You've fed me lines to placate me, but I don't think you are being completely truthful."

Erik was reluctant to get into a head-to-head conversation with her. The need to tell her about him rose every moment he was with her. He'd never told anyone, outside the Vatican, who or what he was. Zoe could never understand, and he'd never take the chance. His secrets kept people safe.

When it became evident Agent Allen wasn't going to talk, Zoe narrowed her eyes. "Okay, let's try this." Her dry tone bordered on hostile. "On Friday, I stumble across the murderer, Dale Hicks." She counts on her finger. "Saturday, an *Interpol* agent comes to Boston Township to investigate a murder." Another finger count. "Sunday, my friend gets kidnapped by Dale Hicks – still the murderer from the first night." Third finger comes up. "Monday, nothing exciting happens, other than almost getting run over by a dead man who stole a car." She stopped talking and looked at him expectantly.

"That sums it up."

Annoyance at his simplistic response rippled inside her, and Zoe huffed out a breath. Before she could question her good sense, she blurted, "Tell me what's in your bags."

The agent's eyes grew round before narrowing. He straightened in the chair and leaned forward. "The bags that belong to me? The ones you rifled through. The bags that were *hidden* away in the back of the closet? Are those the bags you are talking about?"

Under his direct stare, Zoe felt her courage leak away. Oh, why would she ask him such a question? What if he was planning something illegal? She just let him know she was on to his game, while she sat across from him at his mercy. She would never be able to make a run for it, not with her near concussion.

"Never mind," she said weakly. Her eyes darted away from his steely stare. God, it was getting hot in the room. Her brain supplied, *it's not getting hot, you idiot. You have been found guilty in the court of Agent Interpol.*

"No," the agent said in a deceptively pleasant voice. "What did you see in my bags?"

"I'm sorry. I shouldn't have said anything."

"What did you see?" Agent Allen continued to stare at her, offering no respite from his chilly tone. He would not let her off easy.

Deciding she had no better option, she went for the truth. "I saw old knives and bottles of liquid. Not your normal police paraphernalia, I'm positive. Everything about this case – the murder, Interpol – seems off. The news reported the murder initially thought to be ritualistic in nature. Then, I find the really old knives in your bag, and I thought..." she trailed off.

"You thought what?"

She grimaced a second, almost hating him for his smugness. "I thought you were a terrorist."

He blinked. She thought he was a terrorist, and she dared to beard him in his own den? Her troubled gaze lit a fire in his belly, and he burst out laughing.

Zoe worried at his laughter. She didn't like that he found her funny. There was nothing humorous about this! "It's not funny! Anyone would have assumed the same thing!"

Still laughing, Erik wiped the corner of his eye and said, "You are not anyone normal. Because any normal person would never have dared go through an international agent's items, *in his hotel room.* I am not a terrorist." He could tell Zoe that much. Hopefully, it would mollify her into complacence.

"Then why do you have all that stuff?"

"It's part of my job. It's forensic in nature."

Zoe stopped her line of questioning. His reasoning sounded reasonable, but she still thought there was more to the story, however she chose to be quiet. Her gaze shifted to her bare feet, and she muttered, "Sorry for assuming the worst."

"Kind of the downside of snooping," he quipped. "One tends to assume incorrectly."

"Why isn't someone from the local police force here, asking us questions?" Zoe leaned back against the couch and rested her head, as she awaited his answer.

"They are conducting their own investigation."

"Why is this place not crawling with officers?" Zoe persisted. She watched enough news to know the police wouldn't sit idly by, after a body goes missing from the morgue. "How did Dale Hicks walk out of the morgue?"

"I don't have the details," Erik said elusively.

"Tell me what is going on!" Frustration sent her temper soaring.

Erik shot her a determined look – as in, determined not to say anything.

She slowly stood as she threatened, "If you don't tell me what is going on, I will go to the news. I will tell them such a fantastical story, that they can't help but investigate!"

"They will think you're crazy," he shot back, not rising to her bait.

Narrowing her eyes, she hissed, "The news loves crazy people, haven't you heard? It sells numbers and ratings, and I'm pretty sure a dead man walking will turn a lot of heads."

"You'd be willing to put innocents in danger?"

"No," she snapped, "but I want answers. I don't buy the story you are feeding me." The look she sent him conveyed desperation, but she didn't care at this point. "I want the truth."

Erik's resolve melted, but there would not be an easy way to tell her the truth. The world she lived in was different than the reality he knew. Demons weren't something she dealt with on a daily basis. "Would you believe me, if I told you that you were better off not knowing?"

Zoe shook her head. "No. Please, tell me what is really going on."

He stared at her for a moment. So long, in fact, Zoe thought he chose to ignore her request. Then, he stood up, pulled his wallet out of his pocket. One second later, someone knocked on the door. Jaw dropping open, she watched him open the door and greet the pizza delivery girl.

"Thank you," he said as he took the pizza and handed the cash over. He kicked the door closed behind him and grinned at Zoe. "Hungry?"

She silently nodded to him.

"Stay where you are. I'll bring it to you."

Zoe's mind whirled. "How did you know the pizza was here before she knocked?" Did he have some observation camera set up in the hallway? "How…"

"…Did I know to open the door? I felt her coming," he told her simply.

"You felt her coming?" she parroted. "Like a dog feels a thunderstorm?"

Erik wanted to deny her referring to him as a dog, but realized her assumption was somewhat correct. He imagined a dog would feel the pressure of an approaching storm, similar to the same manner he felt pressure build when the protection spell around the parameter of his hotel room was disrupted. With a wry smile, he handed her a slice of pizza on a paper plate and said, "You are correct."

Gratefully she took the pizza and tried her hardest not to devour it in less than thirty seconds. Her stomach grumbled for more. The agent offered her a second piece. "This isn't going to distract me," she promised. She glanced at him as he sat down in the chair and balanced the pizza slice. "You can tell me in between bites."

"You are merciless." His eyes held hers. He would do it. His profession wasn't common knowledge, but not unheard of in certain circles. Heck, for the first three-hundred years as a fledgling wizard, everyone knew what he was. They sought him out because of it. He wouldn't even get into the mystical societies in the late 1800's.

But in recent times, he withheld his wizard status. He knew how demon and witch hunters would handle his confession. Now, he was about to find out how a perfectly non-magical woman would take his admission.

Chapter 15

"**I** hunt demons."

Agent Allen's words caught her by surprise, and Zoe nearly choked to death on pepperoni pizza. She coughed and gasped, trying to dislodge a hunk of meat from her windpipe. Eyes tearing, she accepted the plastic cup the agent offered and swallowed desperately. Eventually, she stopped hacking, and her breathing returned to normal. With a raw throat, she croaked, "What did you say?"

If Zoe was shocked at his words, Erik was floored. He didn't know what came over him. He did not intend to tell Zoe about himself. His outwardly façade had been carefully constructed, and with one statement, he'd sucker punched it into near ruination.

Zoe gripped her pounding head and grumbled, "Near concussions and choking fits are not good for a body. I think I must have misheard you." Suddenly, out of nowhere as if to accompany his completely asinine statement, a vision tore through her mind of skeletons jumping into the stolen truck at the hospital. She forgot about seeing the walking skeletons getting into the stolen truck.

How could she have forgotten that?

The agent's talk of demons must have jogged her memory. With wide eyes she studied him before saying, "I saw skeletons." *And you hunt demons.*

"What?" Erik stared at Zoe for a moment, caught off guard by her words.

"I saw skeletons get in the truck."

"Really?" Zoe must have seen the necromancer's helpers following Dale out of the morgue.

"I'm not crazy," she pronounced. Her eyes lifted to his. "But yet, I heard you say you hunt demons. You don't seem surprised to find out skeletons are jumping into cars. In fact, you don't seem worked up over a walking dead man. *Who are you?*"

Erik frowned, and pinched the bridge of his nose. Explanations ran rampant through his head. The most favored being, he would tell her he said, *I want lemons*, not I hunt demons. He told her that. "I think you misheard me." His tone was firm, yet not condescending.

"No," she drawled the negative sentiment out. "I know what I heard. And I know what I saw. I think they go hand-in-hand somehow." Leaning forward, she pointed her pizza at him. "Spill it! There is some crazy shit going on, and you need to tell me about it!" A loose piece of cheese sailed through the air and landed on the floor between them, as she forcefully punctuated her sentence.

Erik laughed at her expression when she noticed the cheese. He hadn't laughed in so long; he'd forgotten how good it felt. Reluctantly, she joined him in his mirth. Soon, they were wiping tears from the corners of their eyes.

"I'm sorry," she giggled, "this isn't a laughing matter." Her heart stilled when she noted his boyish expression. Butterflies knocked at her stomach, but she pushed them away. She refused to have a crush on him. She knew nothing about him, other than he just declared to hunt demons and tried to backtrack with some hogwash about wanting lemons. Jeez! Did he think her an imbecile? "Really, Agent Allen," she began, but stopped short. "Is that really your name?"

She knew instantly she'd struck a chord as soon as she asked the question. "Come on!" she held her hands up. "Please, I'm tired of all this subterfuge."

He leaned back against the chair. "My name is Erik Vardan."

"Not Jordan Allen?"

"Correct," he confirmed.

"Why?" she asked simply.

Ritual Of Blood

"It's not wise to use real names around certain kinds of criminals." He took a drink from his cup and set it quietly on the table beside him. His empty plate perched on one leg, wobbling slightly.

"Criminals such as demons and skeletons?"

"I cannot confirm or deny." He refused to rise to her bait.

Eyes widening, she cried, "You already confirmed! There is none of this elusive lingo any longer."

Rubbing tired eyes, Erik realized his lack of sleep over the last two days had caught up with him. He didn't require a lot of time to recuperate, but he did need at least a couple of hours to restore his energy level. Sleep pulled at his eyelids and his arms screamed at him to find a bed soon. No, beds weren't even necessary. He'd take a spot on the floor. Anything to get some sleep. "I realize you have a lot of questions, but I need time to rest before I start tracking down Dale tomorrow. I suggest you do the same. In the morning, we'll figure out what our next steps are."

Zoe didn't argue. He did look worn out. Nodding carefully, she said, "Thank you for dinner. We'll talk in the morning."

Smiling, he rose and escorted her into the spare bedroom. "Yes, we will."

Zoe tripped, stepping around a low table. Erik reflexively placed his hand on her waist, steadying her. The warm contact stirred him, and he instantly dropped his hand. Her eyes sought his, but she said nothing.

Zoe told Agent Allen – no, Erik Vardan, good night and softly closed the door. Erik Vardan. She liked that name, for some reason she thought it suited him. He was like an onion peel, with layers encasing more layers. Granted, he was the best smelling onion, but still an onion. Squeezing toothpaste on her toothbrush, she stared at her reflection in the brightly lit bathroom.

The lights cast an almost-sickly tint to her skin, but she'd never been at a hotel with bathroom lights that didn't make her look ill. She peered at her scar, but it was barely visible. It healed quickly. If only the matter of the murderer could be put to rest as easily. While she took a shower, she mulled over the facts she knew:

Penny Pearson

Dead murderer no longer dead, skeletons walking around, a *maybe* demon hunter posing as Interpol agent.

Did that about cover it? Yes. Those were the facts. She should throw her overactive olfactory senses in the mix, but didn't know where they fit. Maybe a sinus infection could cause her sensitivity to certain smells. Shrugging the silly idea away as she stepped into the shower, she thought about Erik. She vowed that tomorrow she would learn the truth about him and his fabled demons. She didn't think she believed in such things, but she did see skeletons clamor into a truck driven by a previously dead murderer earlier in the day.

She was on her way to crazy town. It was possible men in lab coats would come to take her away. And no one would believe her story. It made no sense to a logical person.

A half hour later tucked in bed; Zoe drifted off to sleep.

The dead invaded her dreams. She thrashed and twisted to escape Dale Hicks, as he plunged his knife at her. The knife sank into her arm from elbow to wrist. Screaming, she tried to pull herself free from the weapon. He sneered at her and twisted the knife. Zoe cried out again.

Erik burst through Zoe's door, not knowing what to expect. He didn't detect intruders. He caught sight of her flailing in the bed, battling an unseen foe. His hands found her writhing body and instantly knew Dale reached out to Zoe ,in her dreams. The new revenant used Zoe's blood to track her in dream state. He didn't know for what purpose, but it definitely wasn't a friendly visit.

"Zoe," he called to her. The bed protested when he moved onto it and took her in his arms. Closing his eyes, he whispered a charm, shutting off outside forces, and Zoe's body went still. She opened red-rimmed eyes to peer at him. Fear slid slowly from her gaze. Shaking fingers gripped his shirt, and she breathed harshly in the darkness.

"What's happening?" she whispered as reality slowly drained in. "I've never had a dream like that."

Erik reached over to click on the bedtable light. Zoe slept in a worn bright blue t-shirt and long flannel pants. He saw a thin red line rapidly disappearing on her right arm.

She followed his gaze and gasped, staring at the vanishing mark. The dream had felt real. From the looks of it, it might have been real.

"Don't move," he told her and strode from the room.

At a loss, Zoe stared after him. She reached for the covers to pull them over her quaking body. The warmth from the heavy blanket provided a little comfort. When he returned, he gripped something within his palm. "What's that?" she asked with some reluctance.

He held up a necklace and said nothing as he circled the braided rope around her neck and tied it quickly in place. A small stone dropped against her collarbone with a solid thump. Picking it up, she peered through the dim light at the object. To her surprise, the bright red stone began to grow hot within her grasp. "What in the world?"

She let go of the necklace and as it fell, she caught a whiff of something dark and musky. She must be sleep deprived. It was the only explanation for why she smelled things while sitting in her bed.

"This protects against dark magic. It's not great in the day, but at night, I recommend you wear this. The stone warps magic in close proximity to the wearer. It also helps to protect against incoming spells."

"Magic?" Her thoughts interrupted her power of speech. A moment later, she nearly lost her mind. "Do not tell me Dale Hicks is Freddy Krueger."

Erik look at Zoe in confusion. Eyes widening, she stuck her chin out and proceeded, "You know, the guy from *Nightmare on Elm Street?* The one that kills people through their dreams? I *do not* want to end up like Johnny Depp." This last was delivered with verve.

"The revenant doesn't have the power to kill you through your dreams, not directly," Erik said reassuringly.

Her arm told another story. "But he cut my arm."

Gently taking a hold of her elbow, he tilted her appendage toward the light. "It's only a scratch on your skin. It is not a cut."

"But there was a knife!"

"Only in the dream."

Zoe resisted the urge to pull at her hair. "But my arm had a mark on it."

"Yes."

Now, she resisted the urge to pull out *his* hair. "Doesn't that constitute hurting me while I sleep?" Her voice ratcheted up a level, but she paid it no mind. She was mad. How had she gone from normal to paranormally haunted in a span of a few days?

He shook his head as he glanced down at his watch. "He can't kill you or cause any real physical injury. He can, however, prevent you from sleeping. Keep the necklace on and that won't be an issue. Try to get a few more hours of rest. It is only four."

Zoe knew she would be getting no rest, not when Freddy Krueger was out there. She didn't tell that to Erik. It was unsettling how quickly she got past the fake name. Agent Allen was a thing of the past. So, she didn't tell Erik Vardan she would go back to sleep. She simply covered herself up with the oversized comforter, and mumbled, "Good night."

Chapter 16

Early the next morning, Zoe pulled on her jacket and slung her purse over her neck and shoulder. The soreness from her fall had disappeared mysteriously after the dream. She walked next to Erik expectantly.

"What are you doing?"

Wide eyed, she told him, "Coming with you." Zoe realized as she came out of her bedroom, that Erik was preparing to leave. She had no idea where he was going, but she wasn't going to stay at the hotel by herself. She'd had enough of the wait-and-see expectations. It was time to take charge.

Erik shook his head, and then scowled when Zoe nodded, seemingly at odds with his statement. "You are staying here. I will not be long."

"Oh no," she disagreed as she stepped forward. "I'm not staying here by myself. There are skeletons out there!"

"Which is why you are staying here."

"No," she said obstinately. "I'm going with you." She held out the necklace he'd attached around her neck the night before. "Remember spooky things can come after me, even when I'm sleeping? You can fill me in on all the details about Mr. Hicks on the way to wherever it is we're going. Besides, what if the skeletons know how to pick locks? Or open vents and crawl through? You don't mean to leave me here defenseless, do you?"

Realizing he was wasting precious time he couldn't afford;

107

Erik surrendered the potential fight. "Don't slow me down," he warned, before he opened the door and waved her through.

As Zoe and Erik walked to his car, she watched him out of the corner of her eye. She was going to ask him to do something that he wouldn't like. Taking a deep breath, she dove in. "Can we stop by Susie's?" She watched for signs of an eruption, and she quickly backed up her request, "I want to make sure she's okay. She's been through so much. I want to make sure she doesn't need anything."

Erik stopped and shot her an exasperated look. "You promised to keep up with me. Now you are asking for a side trip to a friend's house?"

"Yes," she shot back. She pulled her hood over her head to block out the biting wind. Hair waved in front of her eyes, and she pushed the stray locks further into her hood. "Yes, I'm asking to stop by a friend's house. A *friend,* who was kidnapped by a murderer and a dead guy. The same dead guy you are looking for! How do you know Dale Hicks isn't trying to kidnap her again, to finish what he started?"

It was highly improbable Dale would go back for Susie. She wasn't his original target, but it wouldn't hurt to stop and see the woman, in case Dale or his minions were in the vicinity. It would also give him time to question Susie on her experience with the necromancer.

Zoe took his silence as a refusal. "Please," she said softly. "It won't take long." She'd gotten worried when her several phone calls to Susie this morning went straight to voicemail. Susie always answered her phone. Zoe teased her about how eager she sounded when answering. This wasn't like her not to take calls.

Erik peered at her wide eyed, truly understanding her concern for her friend. "We can stop and see her briefly."

"Oh, good!" she cried, almost hopping in excitement. "I promise to keep it quick." Then she spotted her car. "My Focus! How did my car get here?"

Erik spoke with a twinkle in his eye. "Interpol? Remember?"

"Really, you're still claiming to be from Interpol? I'm pretty sure Interpol doesn't hunt demons."

"I actually work for the Vatican, but my Interpol credentials are quite real." he said evenly. He'd already told her what he did, where he worked shouldn't come as too much of a shock.

Zoe mulled over his declaration and wondered if she was getting in the car of a superhero, or a crazy person.

***

They drove to Susie's without many words between them. Erik was trying out different theories, and Zoe was trying to imagine, scientifically speaking, how skeletons could actually walk.

Erik found a parking spot almost directly in front of Susie's house. Zoe quickly got out of the car, and Erik followed her to the front porch. Susie lived a few blocks from Zoe's apartment, and not much farther from the hotel.

Her friend had been through a terrible ordeal, and on top of taking care of her ailing mother. It made sense to stop by and see if she needed anything. Zoe would quickly check up on her friend and then leave.

Susie's house was a cute, two-bedroom brick cottage, with character oozing from its scalloped eaves. She loved Susie's house. Zoe had told her friend many times, if she ever wanted to move, she called first dibs. Knocking quickly on the door, Zoe stepped back and listened for movement inside the house.

The floorboards creaked, heralding Susie's arrival. She opened the door with a scowl on her face and stared at the two of them.

"Hi, Susie," Zoe began awkwardly. "I wanted to see how you were doing. Do you need anything?"

Susie shot a distrustful glance at the tall man standing behind her.

Zoe quickly introduced the agent, keeping his story intact. "This is Agent Allen. Do you remember seeing his business card on Sunday? He's from Interpol, and he's assisting with the murder case." Perhaps if she thought about it later, she would wonder why she didn't introduce him as Erik Vardan. It *was* his real name. At least, she thought it was his real name. But it was easier to introduce him as a character already in play.

"Oh, yeah," Susie said with a short nod and a sidelong look at the agent. "I remember seeing his business card on your counter." Then, she looked up, almost as if hearing something in the other room. Turning her attention back to her guests, Susie told Zoe, "You didn't have to check up on me. I'm fine." She eyed Erik with distaste and stepped back reluctantly, to allow them entrance in her house.

Slightly taken aback by the anger in Susie's tone, Zoe cocked her head and regarded her friend. "I wanted to make sure you were okay. You *were* kidnapped," she reminded Susie. "In my parking lot! Be grateful that you have such a thoughtful friend," she added teasingly. The need to lighten the mood intensified.

A scent of rot crept through the air, and inwardly Zoe stiffened. It was the same smell as before – the cemetery, the hospital, and the parking lot. All the same foul, deathly smell. Goosebumps rose on her arms, and she breathed in through her mouth. Glancing around, she didn't see any dirty dishes that would account for such a rotten smell. She shot a look at Erik to see if he reacted to the stench, but he didn't seem affected.

"Everything turned out fine."

Susie's words snapped Zoe out of her thoughts. She must be imaging things; otherwise, someone else would have mentioned the scent. "I'm happy you are safe. Is there anything you want to talk about? You've been through a lot. I'm sure it's healthy to talk about what happened to you." Zoe tried to capture Susie's gaze, but Susie continued to stare coldly down at the floor. It was as if a pouting child stood in the place of her friend.

"What's to talk about? The man tripped, hit his head on a rock, and he died. He got what he deserved, in my opinion." Susie stepped in front of Zoe, to stop her advance into the living room. "Look. I need some time alone." Her eyes shifted to stare behind Zoe, and they widened ever so slightly. Then her eyes shifted back to Zoe.

"But do you need any help with your mom? I can stay if you

would like me to."

Erik watched the interaction between Zoe and Susie, and knew Zoe wasn't going to be happy with the outcome. It was obvious that Susie needed some alone time, and she wasn't going to accept anything else. Her dislike of police was unfortunately common, especially in those who are reminded of a traumatic event.

"Thank you for stopping by. I'll call you tomorrow." Susie walked to the door and opened it in a blatant signal of *get out*.

End of discussion.

Flabbergasted, Zoe stared at Susie. She glanced over her shoulder to see what caught Susie's attention earlier, but the room was empty.

Before turning to walk to the front door, Erik spoke for the first time. "Ms. Monroe, how did the man capture you?"

Through narrowing eyes, she said in disdain, "He blew some sort of dust in my face. I don't remember anything after that."

Maybe that is the smell, Zoe thought. All the fine particles must be impossible to clean, thus the lingering smell.

"Did the kidnapper say anything to you?"

"No," Susie said shortly. Her impatience was palpable.

"I hope you get some rest," Erik told her, seeing her tolerance of visitors was at an end. He lifted his hand to guide Zoe out the door, but instantly lowered it. That sort of familiarity would get them nowhere.

As Zoe stepped outside, the tree branches moved slightly, and a flash of white caused her to start. It was only falling leaves, she told herself. No monsters lurked in the shadows. Nothing was there. She remembered how jumpy she was in the days after the murder. Potential danger lurked around every corner. She expected the killer, or at least his skeletons, to jump out of every shady spot. No doubt, Susie was feeling the same and needed some time alone.

"So where to now?" Zoe asked after buckling herself in the seat. She wouldn't be upset over Susie's refusal to open up to her. When her friend was ready, she would say something.

"How about lunch before we go out to Mr. Hicks's house?"

Her stomach agreed instantly with his suggestion, so she

nodded. "Sure."

Turning into a local mom-and-pop diner, Erik escorted Zoe inside. The menu consisted of sandwiches, salads, soups, and more. Zoe ordered a grilled cheese, much to Erik's entertainment. Wisely, he kept quiet.

When the server left to turn in their order, Zoe couldn't hold her questions any longer. "How long have you worked for the Vatican? How did you train for your job? What exactly *is*, your job?"

Grinning, he took a quick drink of his Coke and said, "Longer than I should admit. Very carefully. Senior Researcher."

"How long?" Zoe latched on to his first answer.

"I can't answer that."

"Can't or won't?"

"Both," Erik parried.

"What's your scariest case?"

That caught him off guard. He imagined when people learned where he worked; they would bombard him with questions about the Vatican and the Pope. Zoe was interested in what he did. An uncomfortable feeling settled at the bottom of his stomach, and anxiety had him questioning his decision to tell her what he did for a living. "I can't talk about it," he told her again.

She huffed and folded up a paper napkin into a triangle, before pushing it off to the side. She tucked it next to the ketchup and regarded him.

Erik Vardan (probably). *Demon Hunter* (supposedly). *Master of the cheekbone* (surely). *Lord of the lovely chest and shoulders and –* (definitely, and she should stop thinking about that). Not that she was paying attention to those things. No! She was sitting across the table from a normal man, eating a normal lunch. There was nothing special about him. She tried to tell herself that from the moment she met him. She needed to get back on track, so she stated, "Then, we'll talk about something else. Is it normal for a kidnap victim to want to be alone?"

Erik could delve into this subject without giving away any company secrets. "Everyone reacts differently to trauma. Some want to surround themselves with compassionate souls to comfort them. Others want solitude in order to process what happened to them. Your friend seems to be the latter."

She mulled his words. She understood people reacted differently, but Susie had always been one to rely on her friends. Her reactions puzzled Zoe, but if Susie didn't want the help that was offered, there was nothing she could do. "I guess so."

"She will be fine. In a few days she will be more her normal self," Erik told her.

The server brought their food, and they ate quickly. Erik was fully absorbed eating his hamburger, and Zoe forced herself to think of something other than his elegant fingers cradling his luscious-looking bun. Her grilled cheese sandwich did taste wonderful. As she chewed, Zoe tried to imagine what the murderer's house looked like. Would it be creepy with blood and spiders everywhere? Probably not, she thought. The police would clean up the crime scene. There wouldn't be any blood, but spiders were probably a different story. She shivered at the thought.

Determined to curtail her creepy imaginings, Zoe pulled her cell phone out of her small purse. Erik stood at the counter to pay their bill. The urge to call and check on Susie again tugged at her, but she knew when to take a hint. Susie needed space. Instead, she called Tiffany, to see if Susie had reached out to her. Tiffany was shocked to hear about Susie's abduction and subsequent escape.

"I'll drop by tomorrow evening," Tiffany stated. "I'll let you know how she's doing."

"Okay and thanks. She didn't act like she wanted me around, and I don't want to upset her."

"Not a problem. I'll talk to you tomorrow."

Zoe tapped the end call button and turned to catch up with Erik.

Chapter 17

Dale Hicks's house wasn't what Zoe expected. In her mind, she imagined a rundown fixer-upper, but her imagination fell short. Reality shattered that illusion. The house wasn't creepy; it was horrifying. The outside walls vibrated with malevolence, and the shuttered windows seemed to seal in the evil.

When Erik drove her into the woods, Zoe expected him to drive back out and continue down a habitable road. No. He drove further into the veritable wilderness and parked in front of the newest horror movie house. Zoe gulped, as she leaned forward in the passenger seat, to peer up at the monstrosity. The sun, streaming through various trees, illuminated the age-worn wooden siding and hollowed out the front door space, creating an evil ambience that didn't sit well with her.

"Not very inviting, is it?" she spoke softly.

"It's not supposed to be."

Glancing at him, she made a face. "I was going for chit chat. You don't have to be such a downer."

"You sound like Jenny," Erik muttered.

"Who's Jenny?" Zoe crossed her fingers and toes, and maybe even her eyes, in hopes that Jenny wasn't his girlfriend.

"She's my research analyst back in New York."

Her heartbeat slowed. Okay, she could deal with a research analyst. Way better than a girlfriend. "She's probably very wise."

Erik couldn't resist a snort. "No. She's too young to be wise."

Zoe leaned against the car door in a questioning gesture. "Yeah, like you are so old. What are you? Thirty-five? Thirty-six. So old." The sarcasm nearly dripped from her words onto the floorboards.

"Not quite," he told her elusively.

"Oh, let me guess," she said with some heat. "You can't discuss that, either."

"As a matter of fact, yes, you are correct. I am not able to talk about my age."

"Why?"

"Not practical."

"Not practical?" Zoe parroted. "What about aging isn't practical? It's life. I'm twenty-eight. I'm not too proud, to tell you my age."

"Being proud has nothing to do with divulging my age."

"Sure it does," she shot back.

"No, it doesn't." He could feel a heat rise within him at her teasing.

"Maybe you don't know your age. Are you an orphan with no record of a birth date? That would explain a lot."

"I am not adopted." That was a lie, but he wasn't going to tell her. He also wasn't going to tell her he didn't know his birth date. Those records weren't kept when he was born.

She narrowed her eyes. "Maybe my question scattered your wits, and now you can't remember your story and have to backpedal on your facts."

"Fine. I'm over seven-hundred years old," he said curtly.

That had her backpedaling. Over seven-hundred years old? Then she glared at him. "Is this some joke? First, you tell me you hunt demons, and now you say you are hundreds of years old? You must think I'm the biggest idiot in the world. Well I'm not, and it isn't funny."

"I am usually not funny," he told her seriously. That was true. There was nothing in his life that he did for fun. His calling was to hunt demons and protect the innocents. Fun rarely entered into the picture.

Ritual Of Blood

She reached over and smacked him on the arm. "Quit messing around! I want answers."

"I've told you the truth," Erik said. He looked at Zoe and had an urge to lean forward and take her in his arms. Her lips glistened, and her mouth formed the most delicious moue. "I've told you against my better judgment. I do not mess around, and I treat this very seriously. I realize it might seem extraordinary, but it's the truth."

Her eyes widened, at his somber expression. Questions bombarded her. Too many to voice. "What –" She didn't know where to start. She could get around hunting demons as a career choice, if one believed in skeletons, walking dead, and, well, demons. But seven-hundred years old…

No, there was no getting around that one. She would have to barrel straight through it.

Before he could stop himself, Erik reached over to touch her cheek.

Zoe's body melted at the light stroke. His warm hand caused her breath to hitch.

"I will explain what I can later. First, we need to get in that house, so I can investigate before the next round of forensic agents come back on shift."

She nodded silently, still feeling the imprint of his fingers after he'd pulled away. Handing her a flashlight, they both exited his car and walked toward the house. "Why do I need a flashlight?" Zoe questioned.

"There is no electricity in the house. Believe me, you'll want the flashlight."

The look he sent her didn't make her feel better. Her stomach knotted tighter with each stride, as she grew closer to the house. Steps creaked, as they walked up the porch stairs, and Erik motioned for her to stop. She waited, as he cautiously opened the door. And she waited and waited.

Moments passed, and still, he didn't move.

"What are you waiting for?" she whispered to him.

Erik closed his eyes against her interruption and cast out

another spell, to detect any undead within. The house stood empty. With a sigh, he turned to her. "Could you please refrain from talking?"

Her mouth popped open in offense. Inwardly, Zoe seethed. How dare he treat her like that? She wasn't his, research analyst! "I can talk if I want to," she gritted out.

Drawing to full height, he turned back to send her a telling look. She didn't shrink away, he noted. "Please. Listen to me. If you cannot, I will take you back to the hotel." He didn't wait for her to reply. He opened the door wider and walked through.

Duly chastened, Zoe walked close on his heels. Her eyes took in the dark kitchen. Even with the late afternoon sunlight filtering in, nothing good could be said of the where, once upon a time, someone ate a meal. "This is disgusting," she breathed. Dirty dishes decorated with old food, and fuzzy science projects piled high in the metal sink. Her nose wrinkled involuntarily.

"Did I ask you to come with me?" Erik spoke over his shoulder. He didn't keep the hint of impatience out of his tone.

She bit her lip. Damn. He had a point, but she couldn't help but look around and cringe. "Are you sure it's safe to be here?"

"You are in the house of a ritual murderer, who arose from the dead, along with the skeletons you saw. There are things at work here, that you can't even fathom. You do realize it was safer at the hotel, right?" Erik wanted to scare her. She would be more cautious if fear dogged her steps. Hopefully.

She shook her head. "No, I'm pretty sure I'm safer with you. There are skeletons out there."

Involuntarily, his eyebrow lifted at her words, and he said sarcastically, "There could be skeletons in here."

Her gaze took in the rooms. "No, they are not. We would know if a walking skeleton was here. You would know, right? Since, you hunt demons? Kind of like spider sense. Or pizza sense." This last she said under her breath.

"Do you think I have spider sense?" This time he couldn't help but laugh. He wondered briefly if she'd confused him with a superhero.

Ritual Of Blood

"It's not nice to laugh at someone," Zoe told him dryly.

"Apologies," he muttered, while the image of spiders danced in his head. "Come, we are heading to the basement first."

Wisely, Zoe kept quiet; all the while, her brain wished she stayed at the hotel.

Chapter 18

The house was eerily quiet as Zoe and Erik made their way toward the basement. The familiar rotten smell invaded her senses the further down the stairs they walked. "What is that smell?" she asked as she covered her mouth. Her stomach revolted, and she desperately hoped she wasn't going to be sick.

Not here, and not in front of the seven-hundred-year-old man!

He's probably seen a few people throw up in his lifetime, her snarky brain told her.

Too busy trying to not cast up her stomach contents, she ignored her stupid, unhelpful brain.

"I don't smell much," Erik said.

Harrumphing, she plugged her nose and said nasally, "Be glad you don't. This is horrible." Zoe stepped down lightly onto the basement floor. She shined her flashlight in a circle around her, peering at her surroundings. "What exactly are we looking for, again?"

"I'm looking for a particular book."

"What's the name of it?" She narrowed her eyes at a dark shape, in the far corner of the room. Did it move? She stepped closer, and breathed a sigh of relief, when her light revealed a five-gallon bucket full of fire kindling.

"It doesn't have a name."

Very helpful man, she thought spitefully. "What does it look like?"

"Old."

Zoe gave up. Let the jerk find his old book, without her help. Bending down, she picked up a screwdriver from the floor.

Erik sighed, and said, "Don't pick anything up. Technically, you are not supposed to be here. The forensics team hasn't finished cataloging everything."

"Then why are you allowed to sift through books?" she snapped.

"I work for Interpol, remember?" He flicked his flashlight in her direction, illuminating her form.

"I thought that was a ruse."

"No, I am an agent for Interpol. Truly, Agent Allen, at your service."

Her hands went automatically to her hips. "If you were truly at my service, you would answer my questions with more information."

Erik smiled. Her patience was wearing thin; he could see she was on the edge of erupting, and for some reason, he liked to get a rise out of her. "You could help me with something," he told her.

Turning to look eagerly at him, Zoe nodded.

"You can go upstairs and be on the lookout."

"Lookout? You mean, be on the lookout for skeletons?" Excitement and trepidation bubbled up within her chest at the idea.

He shot down her excitement. "No. Be on the lookout for the police. Let me know if you see any cars headed to the house."

She didn't want to be the lookout for the police. She wanted to stay down here, to unearth something helpful for the investigation, but there was no way to deny his request. Skeletons weren't really going to knock on the door and make themselves at home. It would be fine. "Fine," she said, as she sulked away.

At least she would get away from the horrible smell. Upstairs, it was quiet. Too quiet by her estimation. Watching for the police in the kitchen was not an option, so she headed to the other rooms on the first floor. Limited sunshine gleamed through the dirty glass windows. Curtains hung in tatters, and bits of cobwebs floated in

Ritual Of Blood

the breeze of some nearby draft. A thick layer of dust covered the old wooden floor, and Zoe carefully stopped into the room.

An old couch, so abused it was impossible to tell its original color, sat along the far wall. Defiantly it seemed to issue a challenge, daring anyone to attempt to sit down on it. Zoe had no desire to test fate by getting near the monstrosity. Hell, for all she knew, the skeletons could have spawned from the thing. With a shiver, she turned and spied a dark stairway.

Maybe Erik was looking in the wrong place! Hope burst through her, at the thought that she would find his elusively described book. Then she could cram it up his …

A flash of white streaked by the closest window. She froze mid step. *What was that?* Running to the window, she tried to peer out, but it was too cloudy with grime to get a good visual. Without thought, she raced to the front door and threw it open.

Her eyes scanned the woods surrounding her and tried to see what had run past. Nothing was there. She rubbed her eyes and glanced again, but still nothing. A full minute went by, but she never caught another glimpse of anything white, or any other color, for that matter. The air was unusually quiet. Even the wind died down, so the branches didn't rub together. The trees didn't creak under their own pressure. It seemed all surrounding the house held its breath, waiting for something.

That thought caused a shiver to run through her, and she turned back, after one last glimpse. Suddenly, she didn't feel like being the lookout for police.

Chapter 19

Erik invoked his earlier concealment spell, and the giant stack of books appeared before him. The flashlight he'd placed on a shelf over his head illuminated the work area. He truthfully didn't hold out much hope that the book would be located this easily. He bent down to study a title. The demon's book might not be here, but he couldn't disregard the chance to see what the necromancer was working with.

A wizard, or necromancer, couldn't remember every spell needed, thus he had to have books nearby, that contained everything at his fingertips. The books would provide insight on what magic the user was utilizing.

He frowned at the sound of Zoe's footsteps on the boards above him. Cursing his inability to say no to her, he shut out the racket she created and concentrated on the work in front of him. Picking the book on the top of the stack, he opened it carefully and instantly knew it wasn't what he was looking for. Book after book yielded similar results. As the pile grew smaller, he knew his search had been fruitless. It wasn't here.

"Erik," Zoe called down. "I'm coming down."

He scowled. "Your job is to watch for anyone coming to the house."

"Yeah, well, I've changed my mind," she hollered. Then she began clopping her way down the stairs. As she neared the bottom, her foot caught on something, and she lunged forward.

If Erik detected any ghosts, he would have sworn one planted a fist to the backside of Zoe and sent her flying. As she stepped forward, her foot came down with a hollow echo. It brought to mind clacking coconuts. He quickly caught her, before she tumbled to the floor. His hands slid around her waist, and the heat of her body set his on fire.

Not able to resist, he asked, "Do you have coconuts hidden on your person?"

Zoe stared up at Erik, entranced. His arms held her firmly in place, and she could feel his fingers pressing into her sides, holding her steady. The scent of him filled her, causing her to breathe in a sigh. Her fingers involuntarily gripped his arms, and the strength of them captured her imagination.

Then, his words hit like a splash of cold water. Coconuts? She glanced down quickly at her shirt. What in the world was he talking about? Then she remembered the hollow sound, as she tripped on the bottom step. She turned to study the floor, but it looked like the rest of the floor. The all-dirt floor. But she had heard the sound, and so did Erik. Something must be there.

She shimmied out of his hold and gingerly stepped over the area. When her foot came down with a hollow clopping sound, Zoe turned, surprised eyes to his. Erik scowled at her. Without waiting for permission, she bent and started scrubbing at the floor with her fingers. Instantly she found the edge of something metal. "Look!" she gasped. "I found something! What if it's a secret compartment?"

The excitement in her voice seeped into Erik. She did manage to find something. What it could be was anyone's guess, but he was anxious to find out. He knelt beside her and aided in the recovery efforts. They unearthed a lid that was about two feet wide.

"It is! It's a secret compartment!" Her eyes sparkled, even in the dim light.

Wordlessly Erik motioned for Zoe to move back. He searched through his wards, for any sign of the necromancer's magic attached to the buried item. He felt no push against his magic, so he opened the lid. Instantly, blackness covered his vision and slithered into his mouth, choking him. His body bowed under the onslaught, and he scrambled to recover his senses. The dark magic swirled within him, to block his own powers.

Zoe cried out in surprise when Erik fell back, appearing to battle some unseen foe. "Erik!" Leaping forward, she settled by his side and took his hand. "Erik," she repeated again. A nauseating smell rose up, nearly suffocating her. Fingers locked around his, she held tightly. "What's going on? What's wrong?"

Unable to answer, he continued to push at the magic. Darkness covered him completely, hatred smiling and taunting him. Reaching out for a center, he called on his faith. Little by little, he began to feel the evil lessen. Soon, he found his voice and commanded Zoe, "Take the box."

Zoe peered past Erik, into the hole created when he had opened the compartment's lid. A box not eighteen inches long, sat nestled safely inside. With an unsure glance at him, Zoe bit her lip. He knelt on the ground, breathing harshly. His jaw clenched in pain. Would the same thing happen to her, if she touched the box? She had to take the chance. Erik wouldn't put her in danger if he expected the same thing to happen to her. Why she thought that, she didn't know. Why she *knew* that, she didn't know for sure. It was only a feeling.

She quickly reached in and grabbed the metal box. Nothing happened at the contact, so she pulled it out and cradled it to her. It was weighty for such a small object. "I have it," Zoe declared, all earlier levity gone. Anxiously, she watched Erik as he sat up. Pain filled his gaze, and he shook his head, as if to clear it.

"Hold on to it. We're taking it with us." Fire lit his entire body when he moved his legs to stand. Ignoring the pain, as best he could, he pulled himself upright.

"Let me help you," she told him. When he held his hand out, blocking her, she realized he didn't want to get near the box. Nodding, she waited for him to stand on his own. "Will you be okay in the car with this?" she asked as she glanced at her new possession.

A box that waylaid a man, suddenly, and with no warning.

What the hell was going on? She wondered wildly. It felt like a normal metal box. She didn't feel anything strange. It wasn't hot, it didn't talk to her, or do anything strange – it was …a very smelly box.

Still stunned by what had happened, Zoe watched wordlessly, as Erik closed the lid on the now empty hole. He pulled the dirt with his hands atop the area and rose to stomp on it, making it look like a normal dirt floor again. He motioned for Zoe to start moving. She walked up the stairs and listened to Erik's increasingly firm footsteps behind her. He must be feeling better, she mused. At the top of the stairs, he closed the door and hesitated a moment. His mouth moved, as he waved his hand.

Seeing her confused look, he explained, "I don't want the police aware of my return to the site. It will only raise questions. It was a simple concealment spell. Let's get to the car." The necromancer's black magic would wear off slowly, but he needed to get Zoe back to the hotel. He didn't know if Dale's security force was nearby, but he didn't want to take the chance. A wave of nausea hit him, and he took in a deep breath. His ribs and chest felt as if a vice was closing in. The necromancer managed to score a point. It troubled him that he hadn't detected any magic, before he opened the compartment.

Even if the magic had been stronger, it wouldn't have killed him. Probably. But it showed Dale Hicks took precautions, that his predecessors didn't. When Zoe called, "I'm driving back to the hotel," he didn't argue.

Erik's silence spoke volumes. Zoe shot him a worried glance. "Are you sure you're okay? You look terrible." His skin was pale, and his jaw set in a hard line, and his eyes told his pain. Her gaze tangled with his, and for a moment, her heart stopped.

His step stumbled, and he concentrated on walking, not staring at her like a moonstruck fool. When they reached the car, he handed her the keys. "You can put the box in the back."

"Will it be safe?" Then she rethought her question. "Will *you*, be safe?" She had no idea what happened back there, but she understood something was at work that she couldn't see. Whatever was in the box was dangerous.

"Yes, the worst is over. I need a little time to recover."

Nodding, she put the metal box in the back of the car. After sitting in the driver's seat, Zoe started the car and adjusted all the mirrors. To her amusement, her leg length was the same as Erik's; she didn't need to move the seat at all. The maps app on her phone guided her safely to the hotel. No skeletons jumped out. No one chased them. It was peaceful. So peaceful, in fact, that Zoe thought Erik had gone to sleep. The drive helped her focus on what she knew. She knew a dead bad man was walking around. She knew skeletons weren't far behind. She knew Erik wasn't what he seemed.

So, where did that leave her?

Right in the middle of something she didn't understand. Why was the murderer not dead? What could he possibly be after? She didn't have the answer to those questions.

Erik opened his door after she parked, and went to the back of the car to get the box. The spell had dissipated, leaving only the metal box. Dale Hicks warded the opening, but not the contents. Apparently, he thought the initial spell would have been enough to incapacitate most individuals.

"Do you want me to carry that?" Zoe pointed to the box he held.

"No. There's nothing harmful left. The spell was on the act of opening. The necromancer wanted to discourage anyone from getting in. It would have been enough, in most cases, but I'm not the average person." The word "necromancer" sent a shiver down Zoe's spine.

They walked inside and empty hallways greeted them. He waited for Zoe to catch up and said quietly, "All of this you've seen, and I've told you, must be kept to yourself."

Shooting him a "no duh" look, she told him, "As if anyone in their right mind would believe me. I still don't believe! But your secret is safe with me, old man from the Vatican."

The teasing light in her eyes, ensnared him. He liked her.

Damn.

His still-recovering body wanted to do more than like her. It wanted to pin her to the nearest wall and take what he wanted.

No. He couldn't do that. However, much he might want her. He had work to do and making love to her, wasn't in his plans. His depleted energy level made him vulnerable. Once he rested, he would have more control. Erik wondered if he shouldn't call Jenny and have her set Zoe up in a safe location – away from him. His thinking would definitely be clearer, but the idea of her not being around didn't sit well with him.

Zoe followed Erik into his hotel. "I think you should get some rest. You really don't look well."

"I don't feel well," Erik mumbled, as he sat heavily down on the couch. He set the metal box beside him.

"Get some rest." He eyed the box, and Zoe groaned. "I promise to leave it alone until you wake up. Not thirty minutes ago, that thing nearly knocked you out. I'm not an expert on the Vatican and its apparent top-secret departments," she said as she made air quotes, "but it doesn't take a genius to figure out you need to take a time out."

Exhaustion pulled at him again, making it impossible to argue. He patted the box. "I agree. I'm going to take this to my room."

"Is it a good idea? I mean, are you safe sleeping in the same room with it?"

Smiling slightly at her concern, he explained again, "Its harmless now. I, basically, tripped an alarm when I first opened the compartment. Now, it's just a box."

"I wonder what's in it," Zoe whispered.

"After I've recovered, we'll find out. Oh, and the Church doesn't have secret departments, it has secret orders."

Zoe liked the sound of that. He almost considered her part of the team. Too bad she didn't know who the other players were.

Chapter 20

Dale shook his head in disgust. The damn wizard was going to be a problem. A skeleton came back with reports, that the wizard and the girl from the cemetery were going through his house. They would have to be dealt with. He needed to stop any further snooping from the duo. He couldn't afford for them to track down his new master.

He didn't expect revenant life to be this difficult: a delicate line of keeping the white wizards from finding the necromancer's whereabouts, and at the same time mentoring his putative master on what's expected in their role.

Mammon made it clear, he would not take failure lightly.

Plans ran through his head. Dale shot down some, but others had potential. Organizing his thoughts, he began to pull together his strategy to bring down the wizard. Dale wasn't planning to visit the demon anytime soon, not after the last visit. Once his plan worked, the wizard would be taken out of the equation.

Suddenly he felt scorching liquid roil through his limbs. Gasping in pain, he didn't think he should be able to feel as the walking dead, Dale helplessly waited for the pain to fade.

The girl with the wizard, Mammon spoke in his mind. *Add her to the equation. She was your intended target before you foolishly managed to die. I want her.*

The pain left as suddenly as the voice in Dale's mind, and he turned to his skeletons. "It looks like we have a new addition on our to-do list, boys."

Zoe waited for Erik to wake. The hotel room was too quiet, so she turned on the TV. The stillness drove her crazy. Her body didn't want to be still. The urge to sneak into Erik's room and take the box overwhelmed her, becoming almost too much to resist. She wanted to know what was in the box. It had to be something important. No one would dig a hole in his or her basement, to hid minor treasure.

No. There was something big in there. Sounds from Erik's room set her pulse racing with excitement. She eagerly waited for him to exit his room with the box.

And she waited.

Frowning, she wondered if maybe Erik hadn't woken up. It was possible she was mistaken. Again, she heard more noise. He was definitely awake. Zoe rose from the couch and made her way to Erik's door. "Erik," she called. "You're not opening that box without me, are you?"

Movement behind the door stopped. Zoe stood, barely breathing, and strained to hear any sound from him. "Erik, I'm not kidding! I found the box; therefore, I should be able to see what you find in it." She hated to sound like a third-grader fighting for her right to play with a toy, but at this point, she didn't care. There was treasure in that-there box!

The door opened suddenly, and Erik paused in the doorway, staring down at her. She couldn't tell if he was amused or not. Then she looked at him. He was fresh out of the shower. His dark hair glistened with droplets of water, and the scent of him nearly knocked her senseless. She shook her head. "I swear you need to stop wearing that cologne."

There would come a point, when she might have to beg him to cease with the scent. It was too much for her. If he wouldn't desist, she would have to leave. Because she would make a fool out of herself, by throwing herself at him.

And that was what would happen, if he didn't stop wearing the soul-melting scent.

Ritual Of Blood

Erik looked puzzled. "I'm not wearing cologne."

Zoe wanted to cry. And she wanted to lick him. All over. *No, no, no!* There would be no licking. There would be only box opening and crime solving.

No licking.

"Oh," she simply said. Desperately she searched for something else to say. "Are you feeling better after being... zapped?"

He smiled at her phrase and nodded. His brain was slow to respond, after her first question. She thought he smelled good. From the way she refused to look him in the eyes, the answer was yes. He decided to let her off the hook. "Yes, I feel much better. It was an unfortunate surprise. Makes me realize I must be more vigilant in the future."

"Did it hurt a lot?"

"Yes," he confessed. "Like the devil."

She made a face and stepped back from him, realizing she was inches from his chest. "Do you want me to get you something to drink? I can run to the pop machine."

Erik smiled at her use of the word *pop*. He'd travelled extensively and found only a few regions in America used that word, to describe carbonated beverages. He liked the word. He liked it even better when she said it. Shaking his head at himself, he turned his attention to more serious matters. He knew she was anxious to see what was inside the box they recovered in Dale Hicks's basement.

But the box would not yield the treasures Zoe expected. There would be nothing pleasant inside.

When Erik shook his head at her offer of getting a drink, she widened her eyes at him. "Let's see what's in the box." Excitement laced her voice, as she urged him to get on with it.

"You do know there will be nothing pleasant in here, right?" Fair warning would be delivered, he decided. She was unused to the gruesome artifacts in his world.

Zoe stared at him and let the words sink in. "What's in there?"

Erik turned the dirty metal box in his hands. Objects inside shifted and slid around. "I am assuming this belongs to Dale.

Therefore, its items collected for Mammon."

"Mammon?" Zoe echoed softly.

"A demon. Come, let's sit down at the table." He led her to the nearby small dining table. He sat down in the padded seat and waited for Zoe to do the same. Erik stared directly at her and asked, "Are you sure you want to do this?"

Nodding, Zoe tried to send him a reassuring smile. He began to worry her. "Yes, it will be fine."

Still giving her a skeptical look, he flipped open the fastener that held the box shut.

"Wait!" Something urgent lit her eyes. "How do you know you're not going to get hurt again?"

Pleasure spread through him at her remark, but he concentrated on the object in front of him. "It will be okay." He didn't tell her he had conducted a counter spell, while he rested in his room, in case Dale Hicks got even more creative with his magic. Without further words, he carefully opened the lid.

Zoe leaned forward.

Her mind processed the various items in the box. Some sort of leathery piece of something, a tarnished necklace with a golden fish encased in clear glass, hair collected into a ponytail, a roundish meaty substance, and a stench of dark magic.

Her stomach revolted at the remains of human flesh and organs, before her brain could fully comprehend what it was seeing. Bile rose in her throat. Twisting away from the box and Erik, Zoe stood to distance herself from the items. Tears stung her eyes, and her throat closed up, as she gasped for breath. Erik touched her shoulder gently. She wanted to turn to him, use him to forget the human artifacts in the box, that they stole from a dead murderer's house. Her skin grew clammy from the threat of vomiting. "I'm sorry," she managed.

He said nothing, only continued to touch her. Before long, her body settled down. She lifted her gaze to his and expected to find him with a superior look on his face. But he didn't gloat. He didn't even look sympathetic. There was only concern.

Erik asked, "Are you okay?"

Ritual Of Blood

Her gaze met his, but she couldn't speak. Her eyes travelled to the box of morbid curiosities. She walked to the table and stared in the box. With a shaking hand she pushed the hair around. Horror spread, as she realized the hair had skin attached at the end. Someone had been scalped. Her vision grew blurry. The room spun.

"Zoe, look at me."

Erik's voice cut through her burgeoning panic. She forced her eyes to meet his. Her lips trembled, and she damned herself for being weak. He warned her nothing good would be in the box. In her mind, she playfully made up items that could be inside, but she never thought it would be honest-to-God body parts. "What kind of man does this?"

"Sit down." He pulled her away from the table and led her to the couch. After Zoe's color returned to her cheeks, Erik continued. "Dale Hicks is a practitioner of black magic."

Her mind railed against his explanation. "But why keep body parts in a box?"

"It is for ritual magic. Embedded in each article is some or all of the victim's life force. Dale can utilize the energies to power his rituals, bargain with evil spirits, or create mystical devices."

"But why?"

Erik grimaced. "I can't say for sure. I can only try to guess his reasoning. Every person choosing to do magic – white or black – has different reasons. My guess, is once upon a time, Dale stumbled across a ritual that helped him. Maybe it was money, fame, or health." He sighed. "I don't know, but something swayed him to walk the dark path. There are always demons looking for people to do their bidding. The person has to be receptive enough to pick up on the otherworldly chatter."

Zoe glanced at the box again. "Can this demon," she paused, sorting through her memory for a name. "Mammon, get through now?"

"No." He shook his head and put his hand on her knee. "Dale was feeding power to the demon, but Mammon has no desire to come to earth, where he would be vulnerable. Whatever the demon is using the power for by definition, cannot be good. I came here to track down the spell book, that collects power from his helpers. No book means no energy for Mammon."

"And you haven't found the book yet."

"Correct. I had hoped it was in the pile of manuscripts, in Dale's basement, but that wasn't the case. It is a good thing we found this box, though. I can deactivate any magic feeding the demon." He rose and walked back to the table.

Zoe walked behind him, to peer over his shoulder. "Okay," she said breathlessly. "I have to know. Is that a heart?"

Chapter 21

Zoe had to ask. Because it looked like a heart.

"Yes," Erik told her evenly. She wanted to be involved, so he told her the truth. "It is a human heart."

"Is it from that boy, from the cemetery?" She shivered at the thought of the murderer cutting out the organ, and the fact that she'd stumbled across him doing it. Bile threatened to rise again, but she ruthlessly tamped it down. She wouldn't get sick, she told herself. She was made of sterner stuff.

"It is possible," he conceded. "The ME's report did conclude the heart was missing. It's logical to think, that is his heart."

Both stared down at the body part in question. She bit her lip, not sure if it was an effort to stop from laughing, or from crying. So many emotions ran through her, she wouldn't bet one way or another.

"Are you going to give them to the police?" she asked, referring to all the items within the small compartment.

"Yes. After I'm done with them."

"What are you going to do? You said they might be magically feeding the demon."

Erik nodded. "I will do an abjuration spell, to neutralize any remnants of the necromancers work."

That sounded exciting. "Can I watch?"

Smiling, Erik said as if reading her mind, "It's not very exciting. I say some words. There will be no fireworks or flashes of light. Only energy leaking away into the universe."

The idea of watching Erik make the bad magic go away, kept Zoe's thoughts of sliced out hearts and scalped heads at bay. She would concentrate on the good they were doing, and not the evil that had taken place.

Erik touched her arm, and Zoe's heart beat faster. She was slightly disappointed when he told her, "I will be right back. Don't move or handle anything."

Lusty thoughts wilted, replaced by anger. "What? I'm an adult you know. You don't have to treat me like a child."

"I didn't mean it that way," Erik replied tersely. "I realize you are not a child." God, he knew she wasn't a child. He needed to end this infatuation, so he stepped closer to her.

Zoe's breathing stopped, as soon as his body neared hers. Dark eyes met hers, and she read serious intentions in his gaze. Was he going to kiss her? *Yes!* Her brain happily chorused. Finally, those fine lips were going to lock with hers! She glanced up at him and tried to react normally when he bent to kiss her.

But he didn't kiss her.

Erik froze a fraction, before his lips touched Zoe's. There was nothing else he wanted more than to take her lips and show her exactly what he thought of her. Every cell in his body needed him to do it. He couldn't think straight until he tasted her. For three days, his body ached in ways he thought he'd lost.

All because of Zoe.

But he couldn't. He had the strength not to kiss her, but he didn't have the strength to pull away.

Zoe opened her eyes, when she didn't feel his lips. His dark gaze bore into hers. "Are you going to kiss me?" she whispered. Lust whipped through her body, making her clench her teeth in need. It was strange that he stopped. She searched his face for some clue on why. When he gave nothing away, she told him, "I wouldn't mind if you did."

Her words nearly undid all of Erik's resolve. He forced himself to step away from her and noticed her look of disappointment, before she could stop herself. She couldn't have felt it as keenly as him, he thought with a groan.

The denial hit Zoe square in the chest. He didn't want to kiss her. She should have been too old to have hurt feelings, but there it was. His rejection stung. An apology sat on the tip of her tongue, but she refused to speak. She had nothing to apologize for. Nothing happened.

Which was good.

She would keep telling herself that. She glanced down at the carpeted floor, as he retreated to the table once again. Kissing him would have been a huge mistake. One, it was highly inappropriate. He was a man of the law, or the cloth. Two, she didn't know him enough to kiss him. She didn't even know if he snored. Three, if she kissed him, she might not stop.

Therefore, she did the only thing she could think of. She pretended nothing happened. Almost kiss? What almost kiss? "What's next for the box," Zoe asked him, all business-like and not kiss-like.

Erik should have been pleased at Zoe's reaction, but he experienced an opposite emotion. *Hypocrite!* His mind shouted. He would continue to treat her coldly; therefore, no lapses in judgment would occur. He took the bone she'd thrown him. "I'll be right back."

Zoe silently watched Erik walk to his room and disappear, only to return minutes later with two smaller boxes in hand.

"Once I complete my circle, you cannot cross the barrier," Erik explained, as he sat down, and opened one box and scooped out a handful of white powder. A small stream slithered from his grasp.

"You're spilling it!"

He flicked a glance at her. "It's only salt, and I'm doing it on purpose to create a protective barrier for the magic. The circle will ensure the energies dissipate safely. I will use clover for the actual incantation."

"That sounds ominous," she remarked. The salt falling to the floor mesmerized her mind.

"It can be."

She peered at the remaining box. "So, clover will help?" She wasn't sure how a flower, could help send bad demon magic to where it belonged, but he was the ancient expert. "Can I be here when you do your thing, or do I need to leave?"

At this point, she almost wished he told her to leave and go back to her apartment. She could nurse her pride in the comfort of her own home. But what about Dale and his skeleton minions? Would they come after her?

"No. You can stay. Try to stay quiet to minimize distractions, though."

Zoe sank down on the couch and watched Erik finish pouring the salt in a circle around the table, that held the box of gruesome discoveries. Sitting down, he mouthed a few words she didn't understand and pulled out the clump of long hair.

The scent of rot wafted over her, causing her stomach to revolt at the stench. She covered her nose and said without thought, "That smell is nauseating." Deep breaths calmed her stomach and nerves, and she told herself she could handle whatever he was doing. He would make it better, and she was going to help catch a murderer.

Erik glanced at Zoe out of the corner of his eye. It was very dangerous to lose concentration in the middle of performing a spell, but he wondered at her comment. There wasn't any smell he could detect. After completing the abjuration spell, he would question her.

A half hour later, Zoe realized Erik was correct. Nothing exciting happened, during the "magic releasing" spell. Her mind did make those exact air quotes. There were no tortured sighs of murdered victims, no squeals of anger from evil spirits, not even a little smoke. Only the horrible smell, that seemed to creep up on her ever since the murder.

Erik gently closed the box and turned toward her. "You didn't believe me when I said nothing would happen."

She wrinkled her nose and admitted reluctantly, "No. You were right. I have to admit I did expect, *something*."

Ritual Of Blood

His eyes lit with humor. "I told you that you wouldn't see anything."

"Well, I should have," she told him crankily. "It certainly smelled bad enough." She wrinkled her nose at the memory of the caustic scents.

"I think you may have experienced more than you let on." His eyes captured hers, as he walked over and sat down beside her.

Zoe felt his nearness, and her heart sped up. With a quiet, tortured sigh, she decided she really needed to find a man, an eligible man. These feelings prowling around her, were a huge inconvenience. Then his statement pulled her attention away from his physical form. "What?" she asked, in confusion.

"What did you smell when I was at the table?"

Wrinkling her nose, she shivered at the memory of the stench, but shrugged off her unusual reaction. "I'm sure it's nothing. Sometimes I smell something really awful for no reason. It's like when you open a trashcan, and the horrible stench hits you in the face."

"How long have you experienced this?"

Zoe fell silent as she thought back to its origination. "The murder. It's stupid," she said quickly. "Don't mind me. I'm overwhelmed with all of this. It's probably some sort of psychological reaction."

It didn't sound stupid to Erik. He got up and walked to his room once more. He picked three items from one of his bags and came back to her.

As he sat, she smelled the heavy scent of leather. Intrigued, she said, "Whew. What is in the box?"

Erik eyed her. "It's salt and clover." He held up each box to show her.

"Really? Gosh, it smells like a horse saddle."

He laughed. "I've never heard salt and clover described as smelling like saddle leather. You have a curious sense of smell."

So, she thought irritably, *I am unkissable, and have a screwed-up sense of smell. Wonderful.*

An idea began to form in Erik's mind. This new sensory

experience began when she stumbled across a ritual murder. During a full moon. The experience was enough to put her senses on high alert. She might not practice magic, but her body was perceptive enough to it, to respond. She was a sensitive.

And this made her even more valuable to him.

"When did you smell the rotten smell last?"

She thought for a moment before saying, "At Susie's." Erik's brow furrowed, but Zoe hypothesized, "I think her belongings triggered it. The lingering smell. I experienced the same smell when I came across the murderer, Dale, stealing the truck. Right before the skeletons jumped in the car. Oh, and at his house, too."

"And the good smell. How often do you experience it?"

Zoe felt heat rise in her cheeks. How could she answer that truthfully, without coming across like a complete nut job or psycho stalker? *Every time I see you,* would be the proverbial nail in the coffin. Instead, she said, "When I went through your bags."

Erik knew then, she had a small bit of magical elements in her. Her senses had been alerting her the entire time that she experienced white and black magic. "Being in the cemetery, during a full moon, at midnight, during a ritual murder opened up your senses."

She laughed when he told her that. "That's crazy! Why would my sense of smell suddenly become wise to magic? I don't even believe in it."

"You don't have to believe in it. Your body doesn't operate on beliefs. It exists; therefore, it's reacting to your nearness to different magic."

Scowling, Zoe commented crankily, "Great. Now, *follow your nose,* has a new meaning for me."

"It's actually a good thing."

The picture of her walking around, sniffing the air for bad magic wasn't appealing to her. "No, it's not a good thing." She disagreed with him. She didn't want to smell things like some sort of human bloodhound.

Erik chose to let it lie, for now. She needed time to realize how helpful it could be. He stacked the boxes of herbs on top of each other and returned to his room. As he zipped his bags closed, his cell phone rang, and he answered it.

"Agent Allen, we have a murder scene we'd like you to have a look at."

Chapter 22

Zoe stared at the door, after Erik closed it behind him. There had been another murder. He hadn't told her much; only that the police wanted his assistance on a new murder case. She shivered and turned to stare around the room.

But her eyes kept straying to the box of people parts. Hearts, hair, and skin. She was officially creeped out. At the moment, her mind was telling her to get her stuff and get out. Put as much distance between that box and her as possible. She felt torn apart by the indecision of what she should do. The logical side of her said to stay. Erik was the expert who could keep her safe. The illogical, and the most persuasive, side of her said, to get the hell away from there. She didn't ask to be in the middle of some supernatural crime spree.

Zoe nodded to herself and set off to gather her things. She couldn't stay with the box of dead things, that sat so casually on the table. Those parts once belonged to living people. She strode into the bedroom and grabbed her bathroom supplies, stuffing them in her suitcase. She knew Erik would be livid once he found out she'd left, but she couldn't think of a better solution. Her apartment was her safe haven.

She would be fine.

***

Erik walked up to the intersection of two busy roads. An ambulance and five marked police cars sat on the berm. At least a dozen officers were present. Sergeant Vega spotted his approach and motioned him over. Watching his step, he made his way over to the man.

"Agent Allen, you took your time getting here," the sergeant said, in a bothered tone.

Erik shrugged off the words. "I got here as soon as I could."

Vega pointed to the ambulance. "Vic is inside. DOA. We have a few witnesses. Whoever did this wasn't shy about getting caught."

"I appreciate the call, but what makes you think this has anything to do with the Hicks case?"

"Well, it seems our dead man grew legs and walked."

Centuries of practice made it easy to shoot a surprised look at Vega. "What? Is that a charming American idiom, I'm not familiar with?"

"Damnedest thing. The body and the skeletons are missing. We assumed accomplices came in. Something happened to the video feeds. We got no visual. I don't know how it's possible, but that's the situation at the morgue.

Then, we got a call that whackos wearing clown clothes were accosting a driver at this intersection. When we arrived, only the victim was here. His car had been stolen."

Erik watched as the medical examiner walked onto the scene. He didn't look at Vega when he asked, "What made it strange enough, to call me?" His presence in their investigation didn't sit well with the locals. They had to have something very disturbing to call him.

"The vic was stabbed repeatedly. Excessively. We're not used to this here. The fact that the murder weapon was a knife … Well, I'm sure I don't have to tell you the murder weapon of choice around here, are guns."

Erik nodded. The coincidence of another homicide by knife within a week of the initial, didn't escape him. "Well, show me what you got, and maybe we can find the murderers and our missing dead fellow."

Ritual Of Blood

***

Zoe parked her car and sat for a moment, staring at the building. She wasn't afraid to go to her apartment. She was just questioning her rash decision. A neighbor waved to her, and she felt her tension ease. All she wanted to do was get back to normal, to do that, all she had to do was pretend everything was okay.

Picking up her bag, she quickly strode across the parking lot toward the main entrance. The hall was empty, and she let herself into her apartment with no interruptions. Her apartment was exactly as she left it. It was a secure building. It would be very difficult for a dead man and his skeleton minions, to sashay into her building.

Once again, she told herself, that she was safe.

Her stomach also rumbled, telling her she was hungry. A quick glance in her fridge determined, it would be grilled cheese night. Thirty minutes later, she happily munched on her sandwich and barbeque chips, while watching a home improvement show. Sleep pulled at her, so she decided to call it a night.

You need to call Erik and let him know you left his hotel.

That thought popped up as she washed her face. But she shook her head and said out loud, "I don't owe him anything."

Only, she did. He saved her life in the hospital parking lot. He helped find Susie. He trusted her with a secret so outlandish, no one in their right mind would believe her. Her actions certainly didn't speak of someone grateful for his help.

No. She wasn't in some horror movie in which a killer stalks her. She was in her apartment, and she was going to bed. She would deal with her actions tomorrow. Right now, she would go to sleep and dream good thoughts.

Zoe woke in the night, to the sound of faint scratching. Her eyes searched the pitch-black room for movement. Carefully getting out of bed, she listened for the sound, but it stopped when she stepped forward. She noticed her alarm clock read 3:56 a.m.

The sound never repeated itself, so she crawled back in bed, to fall back into a fitful sleep.

The next time she woke, the sun was high in the sky. She cursed to herself for oversleeping. She had to get some work done today, or it was possible she'd be fired from her relatively enjoyable job. She walked to her bathroom and stretched her arms above her head with a loud yawn.

A quick shower energized her, and she finally began to feel normal after the last few days. As she dried herself off, she spotted one of her favorite shirts hanging on her towel rack. "There you are!" she cried happily. Scooping up the shirt, she went to her bedroom to dress.

Her favorite jeans probably could use a wash, but she pushed it off to another day. Comfort was key. She pulled on her newly found shirt and headed back to the bathroom to blow-dry her hair.

She leaned over to aim her dryer at the under part of her hair. Shaking her head and working her fingers through her blunt bangs, she hummed a tune before she smelled something. A wave of rot caused her stomach to drop. Instantly, she straightened and came face-to-face with a skeleton.

It stared at her through black eye holes. Its round skull shone duly in the bathroom's light.

Zoe couldn't move, frozen for an endless second, to voice any sort of horror at her surprise visitor. But once that moment broke, she screeched in terror and push frantically at the creature.

In her mind, her shove should have dislodged the bones from its frame, causing it to collapse in a heap. No such thing happened. The skeleton advanced on her, silently yet effectively blocking her exit out the bathroom door. She tossed her hair dryer at it, but the damn thing fell harmlessly to the ground, as it reached the end of its cord.

Next, she threw toothpaste, a toothbrush, a hairbrush, a bottle of face wash, and a basket of old cosmetics. The skeleton showed no signs of discomfort. She tried again to shove it away, but it seemed held together by an unseen force. Frantically, she searched around for a better weapon.

Her eyes focused on the shower rod. She jumped up in the shower and tore at the wooden pole. It gave way instantly, and she waved it at her attacker like some flag-bearing lunatic. "Get back!"

she hissed through gritted teeth.

The figure's bones moved, eerily gesturing to her. Still, it never spoke, but Zoe wasn't about to make friends with some demon spawn. She thrust the curtain rod at the skeleton, but it grabbed the end and almost ripped it out of her hands.

She pulled it back to break contact and swung again. The rod went underneath one of its ribs, and she jerked her weapon up. The skeleton slid down the pole, almost falling on top of her. She yelped and accidently let go of the curtain rod. The skeleton tried to right itself, but had trouble getting un-skewered.

Zoe took the opening.

Rushing past the unearthly minion, she barreled out of her bathroom and slammed the door closed behind her. Breathing heavily, she twirled around to stare at the object that separated her and a walking skeleton. Her heart pounded loudly in her ears.

Oh, why did I leave Erik's hotel?

She had no time to answer her question, for she watched in fear as the bathroom handle turned slowly. She leapt forward and yanked the door closed, stopping the skeleton from opening the door. It pounded menacingly. The most frightening thing was that the creature made no sound in its anger. Bones scratched frantically at the wood, and it pulled on the door handle harder and harder.

Zoe sank on her bottom and pulled back to keep the door closed. She spotted her phone. It sat thirty feet across the room, charging on the table next to the couch. Damn! Running the odds of letting go of the door, getting to her phone, and calling for help, all the while fending off a skeleton attacker, didn't seem in her favor.

So, she did the only thing possible. She held on for dear life.

Chapter 23

Erik cursed for the fifth time in the last forty-five minutes. He hung up the phone. Where the hell was Zoe? He intended to let her know not to expect him at the hotel for at least another hour. It had been a long night, and the officers working the case were in the process of preparing to hand off their work to the next arriving shift.

He didn't need the sleep, but it would seem suspicious if he continued to work the case tirelessly for so many hours without any semblance of rest. Sergeant Vega looked as if he was sleep walking, and the other officers fared little better. He closed his eyes as he rubbed his forehead to portray exhaustion, rather than the loss of patience with a certain woman who failed to answer her cell phone.

"We've been over this a thousand times," Vega was saying to his team. Bleary eyed, he pointed to an officer. "Lean on forensics to produce some fingerprints, so we can start doing legwork. I want these maniacs caught ASAP! We can't have the media catch wind of this, either. They'll make it look like a slasher flick in no time."

Erik agreed with Vega. The media tended to dramatically enhance the news. And as sensational as the crimes in Lakewood had been lately, they'd have a field day. He wondered if the murder was the handy work of the new necromancer. It was always a toss-up on how soon the newest inductee would start sending ritual offerings to the demon.

Glancing at his watch, he worried about Zoe. It was past ten in the morning. She should be up. He stepped away from the group of officers and dialed Jenny.

"Yo, what's up?" she answered impertinently.

"I need to see if you can get a ping off of Zoe Hunt's cell phone."

Jenny sighed into the phone. "Tell me you didn't lose her."

"No," Erik growled. "I didn't lose her; I want to make sure I know where she is." *Which should be at the hotel*, he thought to himself. "Just do it, please."

"Since you asked so nicely, give me a second to locate her."

While Erik waited for Jenny, he waved to Vega, as he exited the room with two other officers.

"Get some sleep," the sergeant ordered Erik. "We'll meet back at 4 p.m."

Erik nodded in agreement, but turned his attention to Jenny when she came back on the line. "If you were hoping she was at your hotel, I'm sorry to report Zoe is not there. From the GPS on her phone, she is back at her apartment."

"Damn it," he swore. "Thanks, Jenny. I'll get with you in a bit, once I find out why she left the hotel."

"Okie-dokie. Try not to storm in there like some medieval knight." She snorted.

His eyes narrowed at her words, and he shook his head. "Someone should put you on warning for your customer service."

Jenny barked in laughter. "I deliver perfect customer service to you and all the others. I'm sorry you can't handle my coolness."

She hung up on him.

He didn't notice, as he was too busy storming out of the station. The cold air hit him straight in the face. Grimacing, he got in his car and drove toward Zoe's apartment. She had a lot of explaining to do.

***

The skeleton stopped pulling at the door. That terrified Zoe. What if it found a way out? What if it was creeping up behind her? She cast a nervous glance over her shoulder. An hour had passed since she trapped it inside her bathroom. She sat, still holding onto the handle, while listening for any movement. Nothing. She wrestled with the idea of opening the door to see if it was still inside. Or should she try to run for her phone and call Erik?

Releasing the doorknob, she straightened and paused. Her hand hovered nervously, as she decided to peek inside the bathroom. She carefully turned the handle and pushed the door open a crack. The towel rack limited her view, but she saw no sign of the skeleton. Zoe opened the door wider.

A bony hand reached out and pulled the door out of her grip. She screamed as she scrambled to pull the door away from it. Without a sound it reached a worn grey skeletal hand toward her. She batted it away and pulled harder on the knob. The door slowly edged toward her, yet the skeleton continued its efforts at escape. Using every bit of her strength, Zoe jerked the door.

It was enough to dislodge the skeleton, and the door slammed shut. The creature once again resumed its scratching and clawing on the other side. Zoe sank down and held the door closed and wondered how long she could hold on.

A sound at the door sent her heart racing up to her throat. Someone knocked, but Zoe knew she couldn't get up to answer it. She couldn't scream for help, either. The idea of some innocent soul coming to the rescue wouldn't end well. She didn't want to open that can of worms. No, she would stay right where she was at and hold onto the door, until her shoulders fell off.

Bright light flashed around the edges of her front door. Zoe didn't know if she should let go of the handle and make a run for it, or take her chances with whatever was on the other side of the door. An instant later, Erik burst through the opening, sending the door crashing to the wall.

Zoe's heart skipped a beat at the sight of him. He looked like an avenging god. A very angry avenging god, but still an avenging god.

Erik stopped in his tracks as soon as he spotted Zoe sitting on the floor, pulling against a door handle. "Umm, what are you doing?" he asked suspiciously. He noted her hair was wet.

"I caught a skeleton!" she cried with a mix of unholy glee and frustration.

"What?" His voice snapped with tension. How the hell did a skeleton get into her apartment?

"A skeleton," she declared, still hanging on to the door handle. "It's trapped in my bathroom. I trapped it!"

Erik stepped forward and concentrated beyond the door. Sure enough, he sensed the foul blackness of an undying soul. The skeleton had to have been sent on this specific mission, for they did not think on their own at this stage of decomposition. Looking back at Zoe, he asked, "Are you okay? Did you get hurt?"

She shook her head. "No. I managed to keep out of reach."

The skeleton clawed wildly at the door again, startling a squeak out of Zoe. Erik motioned for Zoe to rise, as he considered his options.

The first being to destroy the creature. Fewer of the necromancer's minions walking around would be better. The second being let the creature loose and follow it back to its home base. He might get lucky enough to bag both the new necromancer and the newly undying Dale Hicks.

"I think we should let it go and see what it does." She eyed him quickly and added, "As long as you think it's safe. Plus, I don't know how we would explain skeleton bones in my trash can."

And that was the riskier choice. Erik didn't like taking risks, but it would be helpful to find out where the skeleton would go if it were turned loose.

Erik thought furiously. He wanted to use the skeleton, and if he magically cut the ties the skeleton had to the necromancer and demon, he would lose any foothold he had to ending the case. "I will set it loose. If we can keep it moving, it might be very helpful."

"Hold on, then. You have the door, right?" She gazed up at him with eyes sparking with excitement. "I have to get my shoes and coat on. He might move fast, and I don't want to slow you down."

"You're not coming." His voice held a hint of steel.

Ritual Of Blood

"Oh, yes, I am! I'm not staying here. That *thing* got in here somehow. Where there is one, there could be another. It's very strong, and I don't want to take any chances. I don't want to die by the hands of a skeleton."

She smiled at him, and Erik felt his body tighten.

"I should say, *bones*. I don't want to die by the bones, of a skeleton. You know, because he doesn't have hands. Just long white bones?" Her voice trailed off when Zoe realized he was looking at her as if she were crazy. She turned in search for her shoes, coat, and purse.

So what if he didn't find her funny? She needed him to get that walking skeleton out of her bathroom.

Realizing he had no choice but to bring her, Erik waited and planned how the release of the skeleton was going to happen. He could conduct an invisibility spell for anyone they might encounter while setting the skeleton loose. This would only help with sight, though. He had to keep the skeleton on a straight path out of the building, as he couldn't mask physical contact.

Zoe stood beside him with a determined look on her face. "I'm ready."

Chapter 24

"**O**kay, I want you to go out of the building in front of me. You leaving the premises should be enough to motivate him."

Zoe was fine with that idea. She had no intention of walking beside her skeletal attacker and holding his hand as they walked out of her apartment building. "What if he makes a run for it?"

Erik shrugged. "I'll try to contain it as much as I can." He reached inside his coat pocket, and then held his car keys out to her. "Head directly to my car. I parked in front of your car. When you get in, lock the doors."

His words sent shivers down her arms. She was putting herself directly in the path of danger, and she was doing it willingly. What was it about this man? She had taken care of herself so long, and the fact that she was willing to let him keep her safe, was hard to understand. She took the offered keys, and his touch set her on fire.

Erik's fingers tightened around hers, and he didn't let go. He stared down at her hands, resisting the urge to do more. He forced himself to loosen his grip, before he did something they both would regret. It was a constant fight between his brain and his body, whenever he was around Zoe. Once again, his brain whispered for him to get her out of the picture. She could be relocated, until the danger had passed. It would take a phone call.

One phone call and all his troubles would be removed.

Only, he didn't want to remove his troubles. He wanted her

by his side, trouble and all. He liked her. So, he relinquished the keys and turned his back to her. "Go. I need to do a tracking spell, before I turn him loose."

"Can I watch?" She wanted to see more magic. He used some sort of magic to get in. Zoe glanced at the door in concern. Her door better not be broken. The Vatican would be buying her a new one, if that were the case. She glanced back at him and wished for the millionth time, she could haul off and kiss him. Her body could only handle so many touches and glances, before it went up in flames.

"No, you can't."

Her stomach dropped when she thought she said her kiss comment out loud, and he was answering her back. Then he continued.

"I need you out of the apartment, in case things go wrong."

Zoe didn't like the sound of that. "Will you be in danger?"

Erik turned to look at her. Her concern washed over him. Resisting the urge to haul her in his arms, he shook his head. "I will be fine."

"Should I learn some magic?"

He laughed at that. "No. Horrible idea. Training takes decades to master."

"Oh, that's right," she said sarcastically. For a moment, she forgot there was a skeleton that attempted to attack her behind door number one. "Oh, you are right, O' fabled magician from the past."

"I'm not a magician, and I'm not some time traveler."

"You said you were born hundreds of years ago. So, that makes you from the past."

He shook his head and stepped toward her. "You were born twenty-eight years ago. That makes you from the past, as well."

"Yeah, well. You do magic. Therefore, you are a magician."

Erik spoke through gritted teeth. "I. Am. Not. A. Magician."

Zoe threw him a sassy smile. "Ah-ha! Struck a nerve, did I? Geez. You would think, throughout all your years, you'd have been called a magician. A lot."

Ritual Of Blood

"I'm a wizard," he corrected her. He took another step in her direction.

They were almost touching; he was so close. She couldn't resist. "Like Harry Potter." It wasn't a question. It was a statement.

It was a statement that brought about his downfall. He slid his hands in her silky hair and pulled her into his body. "Not Harry Potter," he growled an instant before he kissed her. He caught her gasp with his mouth, while his hands tightened around her waist.

Zoe closed her eyes and sank into his wild kiss. Every part of her lit up like a torch. His hands burned her skin, and she wanted more. She gasped against his mouth, as his tongue stroked her lips.

Wild scratching raked the air around them, and both pulled apart. Erik instantly muttered a curse, and Zoe jumped away from the skeleton's waving bony arm. Erik forced the skeleton's arm back and slammed the door shut. His eyes locked on hers and he said, "You should go. Now."

Biting her lip, Zoe nodded. Her brain was still fuzzy from his kiss, so she silently grabbed her purse and headed to the door. With a quick look at him, she bade, "Be careful."

Be Careful. Erik frowned after she shut the door. That was not the first time she told him to be careful. He'd lived too long, and rarely did people think of his safety. Certainly, no one at the Vatican, dared utter such a sentiment to him. Her worry for him should have irked, but it only emboldened his need for her.

Zoe pushed the button for the elevator while her thoughts whirled, still discombobulated from Erik's kiss. Her lips continued to tingle and deep down, she knew she wanted more. What in the world was wrong with her? From the moment she stumbled across the murder at the cemetery, she fumbled from one crazy decision to another. How else could she explain helping a *wizard* fight off skeletons, as if she was Sinbad fighting off the Evil Magician's skeletons?

The elevator dinged, and the door opened. She stepped inside and was down on the main floor in a matter of seconds. The entrance was empty. Relief shot through her. She imagined it would be tricky to get a walking skeleton out of the building, without someone losing their mind and screaming in terror. She spotted Erik's car and walked swiftly toward it.

She had no idea how much time she had before Erik would set the skeleton free. For the first time since the attack, she wondered how the skeleton got inside her apartment. She would check for holes or removed air vents. It might be as simple as that. Maybe the skeleton knew how to use a screwdriver.

Five minutes later, Erik walked out of the building. Zoe didn't see the skeleton. She rolled down the window and shouted, "Where is it?"

Erik scowled darkly and motioned for her to be quiet. She bristled as his reaction. No skeleton could be seen. Did it get loose and run away? As Erik grew closer, she asked again, but less loud. "Where is the skeleton? Why are you walking so calmly?" Her gaze scanned the area, for any sign of the missing creature.

"It's right in front of the car. In fact, he seems to be looking at you."

A chill moved over her. "What are you talking about?"

A small cloud of gray dust appeared in front of the car, startling Zoe.

Erik cursed.

"What was that?"

Erik ran his fingers through his hair and said sourly, "That was the skeleton being destroyed."

"What do you mean destroyed? Why did you destroy it?" she asked in exasperation.

He glared at her through the window. "I didn't destroy it. Either the skeleton had orders upon capture, or someone else caused it."

"Darn. That would have been really helpful."

Erik glanced at her and noted she seemed genuinely disappointed at this turn of events. "Let's get back inside. I need to get some things in order, and then we'll head back to the hotel."

"I can't stay with you!"

"Do you want to stay at your place and take your chances with any returning skeletons?"

Ritual Of Blood

Zoe slammed his car door harder than needed. She shot him a sheepish look before taking up the fight again. "There's no guarantee more will come back."

"There is no guarantee they won't."

She huffed her unhappiness and watched the cloud from her breath dissolve in the air. "I won't be any safer at your hotel."

Erik cast her a sidelong look. "You will be."

"Typical male statement," she retorted.

"It has nothing to do with being male. I have spells to keep you safe. I have already warded my hotel, so you are safer there."

"But they could be watching us now and follow you back to the hotel."

"I have precautions."

Zoe couldn't argue against something she didn't understand. "You need to teach me magic," she stated.

Chapter 25

"**I**'m not teaching you magic."

She rolled her eyes and asked him caustically, "Not a good teacher, huh?"

Erik loved the angry spark in her eyes. It was better than the opposite, which would be uncontrolled panic. "I'm a great teacher," he told her calmly. He should stop with the teasing, but it was too enjoyable. Very rarely had he experienced such emotions when he was with someone.

They walked into the elevator, and the door closed. For a split second, Zoe wished he would take her in his arms again. However, that didn't happen. He seemed determined not to repeat his actions. He must be very sensitive about Harry Potter. At that thought, she snorted a quick laugh.

"What's funny?" he asked. Her swift change in emotion, caught him off-guard.

"I was thinking that you must dislike Harry Potter."

He drew to full height. "I'd rather not be compared to some adolescent fictional character."

She couldn't help but ask, "Does the Vatican keep copies of all his books? Maybe some of the officials of the church are part of a Harry Potter book club?"

Erik tried to keep a straight face, but it was impossible with her impertinent questions. "No," he began. "There is no Harry Potter book club, at the Vatican."

"Have _you_, read Harry Potter?"

"No."

Zoe narrowed her eyes at him. He was lying. "You have!"

Erik shook his head. "No, I haven't."

"No!" she cried. "You have! Your face dropped a little. You're lying. I bet you are a closet Potter fan. You probably have a sorting hat you wear when you're reading."

It was too much. Erik burst out laughing. "Truce. I plead the fifth. I chose to not incriminate myself further."

She smiled up at him. "Truce." A warm feeling settled in her stomach.

The elevator door opened, and they walked to her door. She let them in and took off her coat. "I guess I will pack again. Do you know how long, I will be away?"

Erik glanced into her bathroom and took stock at the destruction inside. "Probably a week, maybe more." He picked up her toothpaste and handed it to her. "Smart thinking about the shower curtain. Bet that surprised him."

"Yeah, but it didn't take him long to get loose."

"Bought you enough time, I would say."

She stood beside him and spotted her toothbrush. It was wedged in the far corner. She mentally added new toothbrush to her shopping list. "I will stay a week, but no longer. I won't be away from my apartment any longer. Besides, what exactly am I hiding from?"

"Skeletons?"

"But why? Why would a skeleton be after me?"

Erik sat on the tall chair by the breakfast bar. "I'm trying to figure that out."

"Can you tell me what's really going on? I've seen a murder, a dead man walking, and an attacking skeleton. You are an ancient wizard." She thought for a moment. "Why the hell am I not more freaked out?"

Warmth lit his eyes as he looked at her. "I can't answer the freaked-out question. But I must confess, I am pleased you are not freaking out. You are making a decent witness."

Ritual Of Blood

Zoe narrowed her eyes again. "See? There you go, saying good things, then following up with insults." She pushed against his shoulder.

His hard, muscled shoulder.

All this extra time with him, was a drug to her libido. She couldn't pull away. She wasn't one to make the first move, but for him, she would be willing.

Erik closed his eyes against the sensation of her fingers on his shoulder. He fought against the wave of lust. "Don't do this," he warned.

For a moment, Zoe froze. Insecurity reared its ugly head. She pulled her hand away and glanced down. "I'm sorry," she told him softly. *This was why you never made the first move*, her brain taunted.

Erik watched her turn away and cursed himself. A part of him applauded his efforts. It was better this way. She would be nothing but trouble, and if he became attached to her, they both could be in danger.

He knew he did the right thing.

But his body moved on its own volition.

Tears welled in her eyes. She was too old for this! Tears? Over a man who'd rather not kiss her again? Fingers wrapped gently around her arm, and she met his hungry stare in surprise. His dark eyes called to her, and her entire body froze, as he cupped her jaw.

His grip on her tightened perceptively, and he bent to take her lips. Zoe ran her hands up his chest to hold onto his shoulders. Her hips aligned with his, and she rubbed against him. Her hands travelled further, and she sank her hands into his hair. She pulled on his hair, and his tongue touched hers, as if in reward.

Erik kissed Zoe's lips until he couldn't think rationally. He had to stop before things went too far. His job dictated his time, but his cock had other ideas. He pulled back a fraction, and for a moment, Zoe followed his mouth. He licked her lips, and her eyes opened in surprise.

He grinned down at her. "That got your attention."

"I'd say."

"We need to go. I have to get you back to the hotel, before

Penny Pearson

leaving for the station."

In a daze, Zoe nodded. Her limbs felt wobbly, and her head light. He had kissed her senseless, yet she wanted more. This would never work, she thought. But her body didn't want to listen to her brain. To keep things light, she said, as she went into her bedroom to collect her things, "You will have to tell me sometime what house you were sorted into. I'm guessing Ravenclaw."

Erik didn't answer.

Minutes later, she towed a suitcase and lugged a large bag over her shoulder. A quick glance around her apartment, assured her she didn't forget anything. "I'm ready," she declared. "I'll meet you at the hotel?"

"Yes. I want to make sure you don't encounter any trouble on your way." He didn't like that the necromancer's skeletons were actively seeking her out. The safest place for her would be with him, but he couldn't bring her to the police station. At the hotel, he'd set up new, stronger wards. They would keep anyone wielding magic at bay.

Zoe nodded at his words. She wanted to stay safe and not have a repeat skeleton attack. "It's like you are my bodyguard."

His eyes met hers. He scowled, but said nothing.

Apparently, he didn't like being called a bodyguard, either. So, she egged him on, "Bodyguard by day, wizard by night. Or would that be reversed? Probably wizard by day, bodyguard by night. When we have time, will you tell me about being a wizard?"

"There's not much to tell," he said, as he held the door open for her and her many bags.

"How old are you?" she asked cynically. "Six hundred and something?"

"Seven-hundred."

"Oh yes. Nothing to tell about. What you experienced the last *seven-hundred* years of your life, is so inconsequential. Tell me one thing about yourself before we reach our cars."

Erik thought for a moment. "I was born in 1302."

Zoe sucked in a breath. "That was a long time ago," she said quietly.

Ritual Of Blood

Desolation crept into his gaze, and she wondered about his family – gone so long ago. "Are there many like you? Hundreds of years old?"

"Quite a few. Some of us work together, while others work alone. The Vatican assesses our abilities and assigns accordingly."

A million questions formed in her brain, but she stood in front of him wordlessly. Erik pulled the handle of her suitcase out of her grip and nodded to the back of her car. She unlocked it quickly for him. "Thank you," she told him as he straightened.

His eyes bored into hers. Her breath caught at his look, and she couldn't help but ask, "We're making things worse, aren't we?"

Erik thought for a moment. "More than you can imagine."

Chapter 26

On the way to the hotel, Zoe's thoughts wavered back and forth between Erik's last words to her and attacking skeletons. By all rights, her entire brainpower should have been focused on fending off walking bones out to assault her. They were unusual and dangerous.

But Erik could be dangerous too, her brain offered. *Dangerous to our heart.*

Zoe wouldn't lie to herself. She found him unusually attractive, also she found herself liking *him.* She liked the way he tried to act serious and keep things in order. She liked the way he took the time to make sure she was safe. She wouldn't even get started on the way he smelled. So what if the entire olfactory experience was due to stumbling across a ritual murder, during a full moon at midnight?

The fact that he was a self-proclaimed wizard, should send her running while screaming, in the opposite direction. If she really thought about it, things were spiraling out of control. Maybe she was delusional and making everything up in her head. That made more sense. But with every passing street sign, she knew she wasn't delusional or dreaming. This was real.

She thought about her skeleton attacker, and to keep things light-hearted, she named him Skelly. What would Skelly have done, if he had managed to capture her? Was not his job to take her or kill her? Zoe was glad she didn't have to find out. The idea that demon-driven creatures were after her, was frightening. Even if magic existed, she didn't have any skills. Erik would have to teach her, she decided.

Being a Wednesday afternoon, the hotel parking lot was almost completely empty. Erik parked his car next to hers. "I have to go as soon as I get you settled," he told her.

"I can get into the hotel room. You already said you warded, or whatever," she said as she waved her hands, as if holding a wand, "the hotel room. Go to the station."

Shaking his head, Erik continued walking beside her. "I want to check on some things before I leave." The list of spells available to protect a residence ran through his mind, but he would need to find the right book to conduct the spell. It would take no more than fifteen minutes, and then he could head back to meet with Sergeant Vega. If he stayed a team player, he might be able to view the body of the man murdered yesterday.

Zoe wheeled her suitcase across the floor and into what she called, *her* room. Erik's eyes followed her, even though he knew he should leave her alone. A girl from Ohio shouldn't be able to enthrall him so completely. He never should have kissed her. Now, he only wanted to do it again. Turning away, he walked to his room to locate the book he needed.

"I wasn't kidding around, when I said you should teach me some magic," Zoe insisted when he came back into the main room. She was seated at the table, but pushed the container of Dale's relics slightly away from her.

From the way she frowned, he could tell she was still disturbed by the macabre relics. "I'll take the box with me when I leave." He would drop if off by the storage unit, before going to the station. He knew items were being categorized and sorted. The box would be a welcome addition.

Relief slipped through her and settled her stomach. She dreaded sharing the hotel with a box that contained a heart, hair, and skin of various pieces of dead people. It was beyond creepy. "Thank you for taking the box. But you didn't answer me."

She was like a dog with a bone, Erik thought sourly. "I cannot teach you magic."

Ritual Of Blood

"Yes, you can."

"I can't."

"Yes, you can!" she burst out. "I'm a quick learner, and you already said I have some magical abilities, hence my smart nose."

He stood before her. "Have you accepted Jesus Christ as your lord and savior?"

That question caught her off-guard. "What?"

"Is Jesus Christ your lord and savior?"

"I heard you the first time," Zoe shot back. "I was questioning what religion, has to do with magic."

"It has everything to do with magic. You have to be a believer."

"That doesn't make any sense!" Anger made Zoe dizzy. "You're making that up."

Erik stared at her. "No. I am not. I am from the Vatican. *The Vatican*." He let that sink in. "My magic works, because of my beliefs."

"Okay, not magic, then."

"Buy a gun," he suggested. Her glare should have melted his flesh. Not a good suggestion, he learned.

"I'm not going to buy a gun." Her words dripped like acid. "I'll stick with shower rods."

Erik nodded, glad to have the "teach-me-magic" conversation over. Flipping through his spell book, he found what he was looking for. He scanned the incantation, and the familiarity of it fell into place. "Stay here," he commanded, as he rose and strode out the door.

Zoe scowled after him, but turned her attention to the discarded book that sat on the table. The book was wider than a sheet of paper and thick. Its pages were yellowed, and she turned to the first page to see if there was a publish date listed. No brick and mortar publisher printed this book. It was handwritten, and from what she could tell, many hands went into the making of the book. Page after page, she scoured through the text.

The words made no sense to her; they were Latin. "This is crazy," she whispered. "Why would I possibly think, I could learn magic?" Noise in the hallway alerted her to Erik's eminent arrival, so she quickly shut the book and slid it to its original spot.

"You will be safer here, now with the added protections. I have to go, but later tonight I will be back."

"Okay. Hope your day is productive."

Erik thought she looked guilty of something because she wouldn't meet his eyes. He took his spell book off the table and returned it to his room. On his way out, he said his goodbyes and left with a sense that she was going to get in trouble again.

Chapter 27

Zoe's stomach growled in hunger. She should have thought about food before Erik left three hours ago. The idea of running into Dale Hicks or one of his helpers didn't sit well with her. She thought about calling Tiffany, to see if she wanted to meet for supper.

When she talked to Tiffany earlier in the week, she'd said she'd be happy to check on Susie. Maybe Zoe should invite her over, and she could bring some dinner for them. She decided to call Susie, too.

Tiffany didn't answer her phone, so she left a message, and then called Susie. Susie didn't answer her phone, either. She left a message for Susie, as well. As she searched for nearby delivery places, the front door opened quickly. Zoe's heart jumped in her chest, but she didn't have time to do more than jump to her feet. Erik walked in, carrying paper bags. When he spied her, he grinned. "I thought you might be hungry."

She nodded wordlessly and followed the smell of chicken to the table. "Oh, yum," she breathed. Her mouth watered as she pulled fried chicken, mashed potatoes, coleslaw, and biscuits out of the bags. "Did you read my mind?"

"I hope not. That would be an invasion of privacy," he retorted, as he removed his coat and flung it over the back of the couch.

"However it happened, thank you for bringing food. I tried

calling Tiffany and Susie to see if they'd be willing to bring over food, in exchange for my great company. I had no takers."

"So, you are saying I saved your day," Erik teased. She must be starving, he surmised, because she was nearly licking her lips in anticipation of her dinner. He opened the bag and tossed her a biscuit.

Zoe caught the flying object and scowled at him. "Hey," she warned. "These biscuits deserve better treatment!" To show how much better treatment, she took a large bite and chewed with relish. She closed her eyes at the taste of the buttery goodness.

Her look of ecstasy nearly undid Erik. Turning away from her display of biscuit love, he pulled out the plates provided and dug around for the plastic silverware. He placed them on the table and motioned for her to join him.

"I'm surprised you are back so early," she told him. Her eyes widened as she glanced at the food before her. She pointed her finger at a container. "Can you pass the coleslaw? This is the best stuff ever."

Smiling, he handed the carton to her. "Better than biscuits?"

"Oh, yes."

God help him. He concentrated on her earlier question. "I assumed you were hungry and wanted to bring you something, before you decided to venture off on your own."

She grimaced and rolled her eyes. "You aren't going to let me live it down, are you?" When he shot her a questioning look, she reminded him, "The skeleton in my bathroom. I'm not your prisoner. I can come and go as I please."

"Can you?" Erik asked her, as he lifted his eyes from the piece of chicken he was cutting with a ridiculously small knife. "I can't guarantee I will be nearby to save you, if you continually wander away from the safe zones."

Zoe nearly choked on her coleslaw at his words. "Okay," she said when she could talk. "I think you need to fill me in on what exactly is going on. A week ago, I had a normal life, now my life may be in danger from a dead man and his skeletons. Skeletons and walking dead!" She shook her head, but took another bite of coleslaw. "I need you to tell me how long I'm going to be here. This isn't logical for me to stay at your hotel. I have a life, or I used to. I need to get back to it."

"I don't know how long."

"Fill in the details, then. I'm trying to understand how we got to this point. Right here, right now, but I feel like I'm in a foggy haze. My facts don't line up. For all I know, a demon is going to knock on that door."

"No demons are going to be knocking on any doors."

"Oh, excuse my misconception," she told him. "You said you were after a demon's book."

"The demon won't come here. He recruits individuals to do his work. The more recruits he gets; the more power he's given."

"What does he need power for?"

Erik shrugged. "Every demon is different. Some want it to buy the equivalent of a pack of cigarettes in prison. Others want enough power to enable them to take over more territory."

"What about the demon Dale Hicks's is involved with?" The biscuit tasted like straw in Zoe's mouth when she talked about Dale. She didn't want to think about all the people he killed.

"Mammon is a greed demon. He tempts and ensnares with wealth and fame. He grants treasures to earthbound individuals, in exchange for magical power. He's demanding more and more recently. He needs it for something big. Throughout the years, the M.O. of the recruits follow the same path. The ritual spells start out small, as they are learning the different spells and enchantments. Then, as time goes by, the rituals get bigger. For instance, one of the recruits started with birds, and then moved to rabbits – things he could trap easily. With each killing, he began to get more confident. As each killing grew in size, finally getting to humans, the necromancer was able to buy time from the demon."

Zoe stared at Erik. "Necromancer?" She'd heard of the word, but didn't know what it meant.

"A necromancer is someone who technically brings someone back from the dead. In this case, the necromancer transfers the ritual sacrifice's soul into the demon's possession. That soul feeds the demon's power, and the demon grants extra time on earth to the recruit. In my time, I've discovered that the necromancer earns extra lives for each killing, but in small portions."

"Why does this sound like some crazy Dungeons & Dragons?"

Erik smiled faintly. "Where do you think some of the D & D material comes from? Life is stranger than fiction."

By now, Zoe didn't think she wanted to eat anymore – not with all the talk of murder. She pushed her plate away from her, but kept her eyes trained on Erik's face. "So, you're saying Dale graduated from woodland animals to people?"

"Yes. But since he's died, he's no longer the necromancer."

Zoe furrowed her brows. "He's not?" This was getting confusing, she thought.

"No. A necromancer has to be alive. Now he's transitioned to a revenant."

"Oh my gosh, all these names." She put her fingers to her temple. "How long have you been searching for the necromancer?"

Erik rose and gathered all the trash. Zoe piled her napkins on her plate and handed them to him. When their hands brushed, her body reacted instantly. Tamping down her lust, she waited for his response.

"I've only searched for Dale for about six months. There are several copies of this one particular demon's book circulating. It has a life of its own, and it speaks to people willing to listen. It offers riches or fame. And like the circle of life, this book and the demon exact its own circle. The person offering allegiance to the demon goes from necromancer to revenant to zombie."

"But what are the skeletons? They aren't the zombies, are they?" Zoe was beginning to wish she hadn't gorged herself on KFC biscuits. Her stomach roiled at the zombie prospect.

"No. The skeletons are the final phase. They have a finite amount of time, before they turn into dust."

"Like the skeleton that attacked me in my apartment. He exploded into nothing."

Erik nodded. "Correct."

"How are we not overrun by all the demon's evil doers? With

various books out there, why aren't we tripping over necromancers and zombies?"

"A new book takes a long time to create. The zombies are the scribes of the books. They can no longer go out for fear of discovery. Their motor skills have declined rapidly. They write until their skin rots away. At this point, they no longer have the conscious thought they need to transcribe the manuscript. They will move to the final skeletal phase. They are only soldiers following orders."

"Luckily zombies are not the fastest writers."

"Yes. It takes multiple rounds of necromancers going through the various phases to finish a book. Then, there is the fact the book might get lost. The book cannot move on its own, so it only has the ability to put an S.O.S. out and wait for someone to answer."

Zoe looked up at him. "Now you are trying to find the book that Dale had before it falls into someone else's hands."

It seemed an impossible task.

Chapter 28

"**D**o you have any idea where Dale's book is?" Zoe settled down on the couch. She kicked off her shoes and propped her feet on the coffee table. She figured that if she were going to be stuck in the hotel with him for the unforeseeable future, she'd might as well make herself at home.

"I was hoping to find it at the cabin. It would have been there since Dale had taken Susie to that location."

"Since you haven't located the book, does that mean someone has already taken it?"

Erik quirked his mouth. "I think something happened to it. I believe Dale had it with him when Susie was taken." It was incredibly easy bouncing ideas off her. Almost too easy. He wasn't one to work with a partner. By his estimation, he should dislike her line of questions.

"Were there lots of people at the house when Susie was found?"

"Yes, and even more that I probably didn't see."

"Can you catch Dale and ask him?" Zoe yawned and waited for him to answer. She wondered how hard it would be to catch a … What was he called now? Oh, yes, a revenant. She would definitely have to take notes so she could remember all he told her. Erik remained silent, and an idea popped into her head. "What if I'm the bait?"

"What?"

His sharp voice took her aback. Her eyes grew round as she explained, "Why can't you use me for bait to draw him out? That way you can find out where the book is and maybe where the new necromancer is located."

Erik didn't like her idea. In fact, he hated it. "No."

"I think it's a brilliant idea. I can help you. Plus, if this helps you catch everyone faster, I can get back to my life again. I really don't like the fact that skeletons are attempting to catch me for some nefarious purpose."

"No. End of discussion."

"There has been no discussion!" Zoe cried. "I'm willing to help! How often do you have someone willing to be a victim?"

"Are you listening to yourself?" Erik shot back. "You will get yourself killed."

"I won't," she promised.

"This isn't a game. You are mortal."

And he wasn't. He didn't have to say it, but she felt it. She was a lowly human in his world of magic, demons, and wizards.

Erik rose from the couch and stood over her. "There will be no more talk of this. I am going to bed now, so I can get to the station early tomorrow. I will be further along in the investigation, and we can get you back to your normal life."

Without me, Erik almost said, but the words wouldn't come out. He refused to make a fool of himself, so he turned and walked away.

Zoe stared after him in disbelief. Why wouldn't he take the help she offered? The idea of offering herself up as a sacrifice didn't exactly sit well with her, but she had confidence in Erik to keep her safe. It was a shame he didn't have the same belief. She headed to her room.

Sleep didn't come easy, but around midnight she drifted off to sleep, clutching the red stone necklace he'd given her for protection. From the moment Erik placed the pendant around her neck, Dale never attempted another dream invasion. She didn't know if it was pure coincidence, or if the necklace really had magical powers. From what she was learning, she was leaning toward the latter.

Ritual Of Blood

When she woke, gray light peeked out from between the heavy red window curtains. Stretching, she glanced at her watch and gasped at the time. It was almost nine!

She had to sign into work and get a few things done, before she ventured out of her room. There was no sign of Erik, but a note on the round table filled her in on his absence. He'd gone to the station and didn't know when he'd be back. Her ire rose at the thought that he'd assumed she'd willingly wait for him.

She would find a way to help him out. He might not like the idea of her offering herself as bait, but he wasn't there to stop her.

***

Erik arrived at the station the same time as Sergeant Vega. The victim of the suspicious murder was officially identified to the media yesterday afternoon. Four reporters asked for comments, but he silently walked by.

Detective Williams nodded to him as she entered the briefing room. Erik sat in the first row and waited for Vega to give updates identified throughout the night.

Williams leaned over from her seat behind him. "Have you seen Zoe Hunt?"

He lifted an eyebrow in question.

She gave him a knowing smile. "I was wondering if you'd seen her since she'd visited Miss Monroe at the hospital."

"Not that I recall."

The intrepid officer shot him an incredulous look. "Really? Hospital video showed you exiting the same door as her on Monday."

Erik nodded. "I was searching all exits."

"The murder suspect's body hadn't been reported as missing yet." Mistrust kept into her gaze.

"Correct," Erik said calmly. "I was clearing exits, in case the accomplices decided to make a visit."

Detective Williams sat back in her chair. Her body language read she was unhappy with his answers, but couldn't actually find anything in his explanation that led her to believe otherwise. He twisted around to look at her and said cryptically, "She is safe and sound."

***

Zoe set her jaw and marched toward her car. She was going to see Susie, then tempt the fates by parading around town in an effort to draw out a revenant and some skeletons. The weather warmed a little, and instead of producing snow, droplets of rain fell.

Once again, she was leaving the safety of Erik's hotel; but she refused to sit idly by, while she could be doing something. Her 'doing something' might possibly get her killed, just like he'd told her, but she'd be doing it on *her* terms. What she would do when she spotted the bad guys was still a currently unformed plan, in her mind.

As she'd told him, she wasn't one to own a gun. She refused to; ergo, there was no need to discuss it. Erik's book of magic might have been helpful, but she was deluding herself if she thought she could really learn magic. As long as she wasn't caught unaware and alone, everything would be fine. Her plan would be to identify the culprits and track down where they were heading. Then, she would call Erik, he could come and do his magic spiel, and things would be better.

He would leave.

She would go back to her quaint, lonely apartment.

He would embark on the next dangerous mission for the Vatican.

She didn't need a man like him. To be clear, she said aloud, "I don't need a man like that. I was perfectly fine before he came here." Besides, she reasoned, what would a wizard want from her? Shouldn't he fall for some sort of sorceress or witch or mermaid? Refusing to be brought down by melancholy, she started her car and set off for Susie's house. There would be no more thoughts of Erik in any sort of romantic capacity, she told herself.

At a stop sign near Susie's, Zoe spotted a lost car flyer, with a

182

picture of a white cat lounging beside its smiling owner. She hoped the little cat would be found soon. It wasn't good for an indoor cat to be outside in the cold winter. A police car stopped at the opposite side, and Zoe held her breath for some reason.

She hadn't broken any laws when she left Erik's room. There was no reason to be nervous around the police. They were the good guys. The police certainly had no idea what Erik did, when he wasn't Agent Allen. They probably didn't know half the story. She moved through the stop sign and continued without any incidents.

When she parked, Zoe noticed Susie's car wasn't in its usual spot. It was possible she was at work. She decided to knock on the door anyway. The front door was answered almost immediately. A nurse in bright colored scrubs smiled at her and asked how she could help.

"Is Susie home?" she asked.

"No, I'm afraid she's not. She stepped out for a moment." The short woman smiled at her.

"Rita, who is it?" came a voice from the other room.

The nurse lowered her voice and asked, "What's your name, dear?"

"Zoe Hunt."

Nurse Rita said in a lilting voice, "It's Zoe Hunt."

A moment later, a scraping sound neared, and Martha Monroe, Susie's mother, appeared. A huge smile pasted on her pale face. "Zoe! I haven't seen you in a while! Come in." She slowly moved back to allow Rita room to open the door.

"Are you sure, Ms. Monroe? I don't want to tire you out."

Martha slashed her hand in the air. "Bah. I relish the company. I hardly see anyone other than Susie or Rita. Come sit down and chat with me."

Smiling, Zoe sat obediently on the couch. Martha sat on a chaise recliner. "I'm really glad you are feeling better."

Bright eyes lit up, and Martha spoke, "I tell you, I thought the Lord was coming for me, but now I see he was only fooling."

Zoe was so happy for the Monroe family. It had to be hard on Susie to watch her mother be so sick. "Susie talked about getting you on a new treatment. It must be working."

"Yes," she agreed. "I have more energy in the last day or two. It's been almost a month since I've felt well enough to get out of bed. That's why Susie isn't here right now. She went to the store to buy me some rocky road ice cream."

Zoe laughed and looked up when Rita walked into the room.

"Ms. Monroe, let's take a short rest. I know you are feeling much better, but we don't want to press our luck." The shorter woman turned with a look at Zoe that read, *help me make this easier on her.*

Zoe understood and rose. "That sounds like a great idea. You don't want to push yourself. Will you tell Susie I stopped by to see her?" She didn't want to raise any concern in case her mom didn't know what happened. She'd been through enough, and Zoe wasn't going to put more pressure on Susie's terminally ill mother.

"I will, Zoe. It was so nice to see you. I'll tell Susie, and if I don't, Rita will help me remember."

Rita smiled at Zoe, as she put a protective hand around Martha, then she walked through the room.

"Keep getting better, Ms. Monroe," Zoe bade, as she stepped to let herself out the front door. "Bye."

As she stepped outside, the rain splattered on her face. The wind picked up, driving the little droplets. She had to look down to shield her eyes, to ease the stinging. A bright flash of light illuminated her vision, and suddenly a car hurtled down the driveway toward her.

Chapter 29

Zoe jumped out of the way and breathed a sigh of relief, there was no repeat of the hospital parking lot.

When Susie got out of her car, she said in a rush, "I'm so sorry, Zoe! I nearly didn't see you."

"It's okay. Lucky for me I'm quick on my feet." She hunched into her coat to try to block the rain. "I visited with your mom. She looks amazing. Her new medicine must really be working."

Susie's eyes lit when she looked toward the house. "I think we've finally found something that works. She's had more energy than usual."

"It looks like you've recovered from your ordeal, too. I wanted to tell you again that I'm really sorry."

"It wasn't your fault." Susie opened the back-seat door and pulled out two bags of groceries.

Nodding, Zoe cleared her throat before saying, "Has anything weird happened to you since you've left the hospital?"

"Weird? No. Same old stuff. Other than Mom feeling better. Why? What's going on?"

Staring at her friend, Zoe realized she couldn't say anything. Susie's mom was sick. She couldn't unload all her nonsense on her. It wouldn't be fair. Not to mention, Susie would never believe her story of skeletons, dead necromancers, and demon books.

No. She would deal with it on her own. Besides, if she involved Susie, she might be putting her friend in danger. They were after her, not Susie.

Zoe smiled and hoped it didn't look unnatural. "No, nothing is going on. I think I'm just weirded out by the murder. Then when you were kidnapped, it got my mind working."

"Okay, if you're sure." She shot Zoe a concerned smile, before she said, "I need to get inside."

"Oh, right. Yes. Let me know if you need anything, okay? I'll call tomorrow."

Susie waved as she walked to her front porch. "I will. Thanks for stopping by."

When Zoe got to her car, the wet began to seep through her jacket onto her shoulders. The car's heater warmed things up quickly, and Zoe thought about what she needed to do next.

Oh, that's right, she thought sarcastically. *I need to try to get myself captured by the undead!*

She started her car and drove away from Susie's house; only for the fact that it would be construed as strange, if she continued to stay parked in the same spot while she wrestled with her options.

There was only one option that she should choose: go back to the hotel. That was the smartest, safest, and sanest choice she could make. She didn't know the first thing about self-defense, and that was what she would need if she tried to track down Dale Hicks and his minions. Then, if she did manage to find them, what then? Tie them up with bungee cords? Because that was all she had in her car: Bungee cords.

It was a horrible idea, and she realized it now. She needed to get back to the hotel, and hope Erik never found out about her lapse in judgment. Her stomach growled as she drove through town, and she spotted her favorite sandwich shop.

She'd run in, pick up a turkey with provolone cheese sub, and go back to the hotel.

Five minutes later, she stood in line and ordered her food. She handed the cashier her credit card. Something flashed by the corner of her eye. Turning, she tried to figure out what she had seen, but only an empty, wet street stood before her. She shrugged it off as an overactive imagination and turned to the woman who handed her credit card back.

On her way to the car, she caught another flash of white. Narrowing her eyes and peering down the street, Zoe willed the figure to move again. The street ran between the backsides of stores, effectively blocking out sufficient sunlight. Again, she spotted the flash of white. With a quick look over her shoulder, she jogged down the darkening street in pursuit. Her sandwich bag bounced against her leg, and she tightened her grip on her lunch.

Halfway down the street, she stopped and searched the area around her. Several cars were parked along the side of the road, but the street was empty.

Her cell phone rang, nearly causing a heart attack. She fished it out of her purse and recognized Erik's name. Uh oh. "Hi there," she answered with a light tone.

"I find myself asking you the same question over and over again."

Confusion caused her stumble over her words. "W-what question?"

"What are you doing?"

Color drained as she realized she'd been discovered. How did he know she wasn't in the hotel? He had to have been tracking her. "Are you spying on me?" Anger pulsed through her, causing an ache in her temple. She continued to watch the street for any signs of trouble.

"You do know my line of work, right?" he questioned, sarcasm lacing his tone. "At what point will you listen to me?"

"Probably never," Zoe shot back. Her eyes flicked up and saw a white figure twenty feet in front of her. Comprised of bones and nothing else, it walked toward her. "Oh no," she breathed. "I have another skeleton."

She heard Erik swear, but kept the phone pressed against her ear. "Should I run?" she whispered. Her eyes never left the skeleton as it advanced steadily. It's hollowed out eye sockets appeared to see her movements. She backpedaled to keep distance between them.

"Don't run."

The voice came from directly behind her. She shrieked and

swung around in terror, her sandwich bag falling to the ground. Erik stood... with his big stick. He had the most amazing ability to be at the right place at the right time.

His eyes latched on to the skeleton, but he told her, "Move behind me."

Shooting a quick glance over her shoulder at Dale's helper, she did as he ordered.

Glad to see that Zoe listened to him for once, Erik stepped forward and cracked his staff against the ground. At his arrival, the skeleton stopped his movement. He could feel the skeleton attempting to communicate with someone. He whispered a spell, and power ran through his arms and into his staff. The smooth red oak warmed as the incantation gained more energy. *"K'un hima."*

The skeleton instantly fell to the ground.

Behind him, Zoe gasped and cried, "Is he dead?" She realized those were the most ridiculous words she uttered today. Of course, he was dead! He was a skeleton.

Erik didn't say anything, only turned to her with a frown.

He was mad as hell, Zoe could see. He had rescued her again from a stalker skeleton. She glanced at the pile of bones, but nothing stirred. He moved toward the creature, and she jumped up next to him. "What are you doing?"

Rain fell harder now, and she pulled her hood up over her head.

"I need to act fast if I want to try a tracer spell." He shook his head. "Why, Zoe, did you leave? I wasn't expecting to do this, in the middle of town. I haven't even had a chance to make sure this particular spell works. Your rashness might have ruined the best chance we had to put a stop to this."

Erik knew he spoke harshly, but he was short on patience. He would first have to perform a concealing enchantment to make them invisible, and then conduct the tracking spell. He'd been working on a new one, but hadn't gotten to see if it worked. He couldn't use a spell he'd previously worked. The skeleton would react immediately to the familiar magic. It had to be unused.

Erik admitted to himself that having a skeleton nearly hand

delivered to him was a plus. He just didn't want to admit it to her. She was dangerous enough at this point. To tell her she helped things progress faster could be fatal.

She stared at the unmoving skeleton and watched rain pelt off its dingy bones. Erik's words hurt, but she knew where they came from. She might have ruined things for him. This wasn't some movie or book where she could go off on her own and save the day. She tried to explain, "I thought if I found Dale or the skeletons it would help you out. You were working on another case."

He scowled at her and shot back, "A related case. Two murders now. Are you planning to offer yourself up as the third victim? Because I refuse to watch you tie yourself to the nearest pole and wait for them to slice your throat."

His brutal words tore at her, and she felt helpless tears well in her eyes. With trembling lips, she declared, "I was trying to help." Her eyes met his.

"I don't want your death on my conscience, because I failed to keep you safe. I'm not a bodyguard. I'm only a wizard, trying to keep this demon from causing more death."

She was another number in his quest at getting his bad guy. The irrational part of her was sad, because she wasn't special to him. She was one in the crowd of people he encountered while tracking the demon, Mammon. She wanted Erik to like her, to –

Zoe stopped that thought. He'd never want her in that way. He was t passing through, and once he found the book that would be it. He would be gone. "I'm sorry," she told him, but she wasn't exactly sure what she was sorry for.

Chapter 30

Erik nodded at Zoe's apology and stared at her. Her trembling lip called to him, and a primal need shot through his blood, raging through his body. The irrational hunger took him by surprise, and his thoughts narrowed to the simple act of touching her. He cursed himself a fool for the thousandth time since he met her. He didn't have much time to set his spell on the skeleton.

Never had he let his emotions take over. The street around them grew darker as the clouds unleashed another torrent of rain. Her bright eyes met his, and he knew he would do anything for a taste of her. "I am going to kiss you." Erik growled, resisting the urge to take her lip between his teeth.

Zoe's heart knocked against her chest in anticipation. Her entire body lit on fire, and she would have done anything for his kiss. She asked in a whispered voice, "Is this the fabled old-world charm you're showing?"

"Where and when I grew up, men didn't ask for a kiss. They took it," he warned. "I'm trying to be gentlemanly in warning you." His hands slid around her waist, and he heard the swift intake of her breath. When her lips parted and her eyes took on a bright look, he knew she wanted him as much as he wanted her.

Erik leaned down a fraction and took her lips. Her soft mouth parted under his, and he deepened the kiss. Her hands instantly clutched his jacket and pulled him closer. She tasted of mint, and he wanted more. He slid his hands over her waist and anchored her to him, his wooden staff creating erotic sensations against her back, as he clutched her.

Thoughts beat at him, but he refused to give into reason. The sensation of her body against his, caused him to groan. The sound brought clarity and consequences, and he pulled away. He shouldn't have kissed her just now. Hell, he shouldn't have kissed her the previous times. He should have let her get her fool-head kidnapped by Dale, or his skeletons, or the new necromancer, or the demon. Then, he wouldn't be standing in freezing drizzle, with a rock-hard erection.

"Is this what you do when you are angry at someone? Kiss them?"

Zoe's inane comment bought him out of his inflections. He stared at her humor-filled eyes and wondered if she had really suffered a concussion, when she fell and hit her head on the hospital parking lot. Perhaps Dr. Blackwell had misdiagnosed Zoe's injuries. How could she be joking at a time like this? After he'd kissed her? After what she'd seen? "I did ask nicely," he retorted, at a loss for further words.

Zoe caught the incredulity in his expression. She'd taken him by surprise with her remark. She'd been known to deflect uncomfortable or super private moments with humor. Well, she had to admit, it was probably more humor on her side than the other party's, but humor nonetheless.

"You're very frustrating," he admitted with hint of disapproval lacing his voice.

His breathy words against her lips sent shivers through her. She couldn't stop herself. "What happens when you're happy?"

"You're not going to find out," he growled. They stared down at the fallen skeleton. "I'm going to do the tracking spell on him, but then I have to go back to the hotel to get my things. He's going to lead us to Dale."

Worry squeezed Zoe's heart. Was he ready to go after Dale? She should have thought about the next step in her decision to go looking for skeletons. It was possible she rushed Erik, and he was going into some magical battle unprepared, because of her rash actions. "Don't you need help? Isn't there anyone from the Vatican that can assist?"

He calmly regarded her. "I don't need help." No trace of ego or pompousness laced his words.

She stayed quiet as he leaned over the skeleton and uttered foreign words. A second later, Erik took her hand and pulled her down the alley. "Wait! I'm parked in the other direction!" She pointed to the brick building. He continued to silently pull her the opposite direction. "I can't leave my car here! What about the skeleton? Aren't we going to follow it?"

"I'm taking you to your car, and you are going to drive straight to the hotel." He wrapped his fingers around her wrist and set off walking. "We need to be out of sight before the skeleton is released from my holding spell. If we are around, he will go up in dust like the first one."

Zoe nodded and kept pace with him. "I'm parked over in front of that sandwich shop." She hesitated a moment, then asked, "Do I have time to go inside and get another sandwich? I dropped mine out there."

The look he shot her told her without question, that his answer was a firm no.

"Okay, I'll wait," she finished lamely. "I wasn't very hungry anyway."

She was a liar, but Erik couldn't take the chance the skeleton would move faster than he expected. Zoe would have to go hungry, for a while longer. He waited for her to start her car and drive, before he jogged to his own to follow her to the hotel.

Back in her car, Zoe took a trembling breath to calm her nerves. Skeletons and kisses were too much for her. She honestly didn't know which one terrified her more. It didn't take long to find a parking spot and meet Erik at the hotel's entrance. She glanced at him, trying to detect any leftover emotion from him, but he was fully focused on the task in front of him.

Erik wasn't focused as much as he wanted to be. As he gathered his supplies for confronting Dale, his mind kept thinking about Zoe. His body wanted more of her. She was important to him, and he was confused about how such a thing happened. He'd worked other cases where women were involved, and none of those women ever tempted him half so much. Something was different about Zoe.

It could be her constant need to be in trouble. Or her relentless need to talk back to him. Or her ceaseless need to kiss him, with such passion. Her eyes called to him. She didn't have to tell him she had growing feelings, as well. Her eyes told on her. But if he didn't track Dale and the new necromancer done, their budding passion would go nowhere. He had to stay on the top of his game, only for the fact that Zoe was in danger. Dale continued to send his helpers after her therefore, she must be important.

"Can I help?"

Zoe's voice pulled him back. He watched her bite her lip as she waited for his response. Was she worried for him? Some part of him liked the idea that someone cared what happened. He knew everyone at the Vatican wanted him unhurt, but that was for the job. There were not many centuries-old wizards alive today. He was a rare commodity in the eyes of the church – only for his talents.

Zoe seemed to want him for more than his demon hunting talents. "No, I'm almost ready."

Out of nowhere she asked, "Do you like doing this?"

Zipping up a bag, he thought about it before answering, "Yes. Even though every case involves the same elemental sameness – i.e. a demon, each case is different. It keeps me on my toes."

"Have you ever been hurt chasing after demons and ghouls?"

He smiled. "A lot, but I'm hard to kill."

Zoe didn't want him to get hurt. She rubbed the stone on the necklace he'd given to her. "How are you going to capture Dale?"

"When the skeleton leads me to him, I will banish him."

"That will take care of him?"

"Yes."

"Good. Then it will be over?"

Erik shook his head. His jaw tightened. "No."

"No? But you got Dale. He's the murderer!"

"But the moment Dale died, the book called to a new necromancer. It won't be over until I get the book."

Ritual Of Blood

"But won't there always be copies of the book? This case will never end." Despair shifted inside her. How could he keep doing this year after year? Decade after decade?

"The police do the same thing. It's about law and order. In the Vatican, we have the same. We do what we can. It will never be over. The question is can we stay on top of it, before all hell breaks loose?" Shoving a few more things in his bag, he peered at Zoe. "I am going." He paused and delivered a stare worthy of any general. "You have to stay put. Do not leave this hotel."

Zoe rolled her eyes at him. "Don't you want to see if my third time is a charm?"

He stepped up until his body nearly touched hers. She had to lean her head back to peer up at him. His eyes strayed to her lips, but he finally met her gaze. "Let's see: first time, attacked by skeleton. Second time attacked by skeleton. I don't think you should press your luck."

As he turned to leave, Zoe reached for his hand. He looked at her in surprise. Her mind turned to mush at her actions. "Please be careful. I know I always say that, and I haven't really earned the right, but –"

She didn't have the words to tell him how she felt, so she showed him instead.

Zoe leaned up, closed her eyes, and set her lips tentatively against his. At first, his lips didn't move. Her mind warned that he wasn't attracted to her. Horror colored her face, as she thought about how to untangle herself from him, and manage to save face. But a second before she pulled away, he responded.

His lips opened, and he took control of the kiss. She sank into him with a sigh when his hands travelled up her waist to the small of her back. He bent her over to kiss her harder and pulled her hips into his. She gasped at the contact and grew dizzy. When his hand rose to cup her jaw, she nearly lost her mind.

Erik was unsure how long they kissed. Too long and not long enough. He pulled away and captured her gaze. "I will be careful. Please, stay put." Then he turned, grabbed his things, and closed the door shut behind him.

Chapter 31

Erik pushed all thoughts out of his mind, as he concentrated on pulling the tracer spell on the skeleton. If things worked out the way they were supposed to, the skeleton would return to Dale, or the new necromancer. From there, he would stop Mammon's helpers. The capture wouldn't fix everything, but it would result in a few less individuals running around, doing the demon's bidding.

Once he located his tracer, he would be able to track the skeleton's movements. By putting the skeleton under, it had no idea a tracer spell had been conducted. When it woke up alone, Erik assumed it would go back to its home base, and he would follow it. Unlike the tracking spell he performed to locate Susie, he didn't need a personal object from the subject. It would have been obvious that the skeleton had been compromised.

Instead, he would utilize his abilities to find his own magic. Since he had been the spell caster, he alone could trace where it went. The map on the console between his two front seats, and with a few whispered words of recall, a pinprick lit the paper, illuminating his destination.

The skeleton's location on the map read it was relatively nearby. Unsurprising, considering the skeleton had a limited shelf life and wear and tear ate away at that life. He worked on his plan as he drove. His phone rang. "Hello Jenny." He prayed she hadn't called him to say Zoe was on the move again.

"Are you in route to an interception?" she asked.

"Yes."

"I thought I'd give you some forensic info the police received from the dead motorist. Details arrived from the lab about ten minutes ago."

Sgt. Vega expected something soon. He wouldn't be disappointed it appeared. "Anything unexpected?"

"No fingerprints," Jenny related.

"Not surprising since skeletons have no fingerprints. It proves my theory that this was done by the new necromancer. It reeks of immaturity."

"Why would you say that?"

Erik stopped at a red light. "Witnesses described the attackers wearing garish clothing. Someone's making a statement. The new necromancer is declaring his territory."

"Makes sense. The lab also reported they discovered the vic's tongue was missing."

Erik grimaced, hoping the man was dead when that deed was done. "So it begins. He's not wasting any time before giving ritual offerings to the demon."

Jenny sighed. "No, he's not. On a brighter note, how is Zoe Hunt?"

"She's fine," Erik said, offering nothing more.

"Okay, I can tell you don't want to share intimate details. How long has it been since you had a girlfriend? Have you ever had a girlfriend?"

Now it was Erik's turn to sigh. "That is none of your business."

"Ughh," she moaned. "You wizards are so tight-lipped! Marc won't say anything about Lena, even though I ask him. You know she makes cow eyes at him every time they are together. And don't even get me started on Dominick."

"We are all too busy hunting the bad things," Erik said between clenched teeth.

"Well, once in a while, you need to stop and smell the roses. Or girls… If you know what I mean."

Erik could almost see Jenny giving him an exaggerated wink. He didn't need her telling him to stop and smell Zoe. He knew her scent, but he ruthlessly put it from his mind. "Is that all you have to report on the victim?" He needed to keep Jenny on track to deliver the facts, not play wizard matchmaker.

"Yes." Her tone belied her frustration.

"To keep you up to date, I am tracing a skeleton back to its lair."

"Oh!" Jenny's voice rose a pitch. "That is excellent news! Do you have everything you need?"

"Yes," he responded. Jenny always ensured he had every magical item available. At the moment, his arsenal was fully stocked. "Goodbye." With a tap, his line with Jenny ended. He glanced down at the map and noted he was minutes away.

The location was on the outside of town, and the residential areas had been left behind. Streetlights lit the road and illuminated the warehousing district. Metal buildings sat in the distance, dark and the perfect location for nefarious beings doing nefarious things. He pulled over and turned off his lights. He would walk the rest of the way. Taking out his staff, he filled his pockets with paraphernalia that might come in handy if things grew difficult with the revenant. The number of skeletons, and even other revenants, were unknown, and he didn't want to go in without everything he needed. He slid a bottle of holy water into his inside pocket of his coat, as well as several herbs such as wolf's bane and verbena.

Before venturing off to destroy a revenant, Erik pulled his Armenian cross from the inside of his shirt. The ancient relic had been with him since he was thirteen years old, when a Knight Templar saved him from a life of thievery. The pendant assisted with everlasting life and was a symbol of the Armenia people. His abilities were even more powerful when he drew in the use of the solar cross. He started his quiet trek between the abandoned warehouses and pulled up his shields in order to not giveaway his presence.

Silence surrounded him, other than the soft swish of his footsteps. Small gravel under his feet made little noise. With a quick glance at his map, it read the skeleton was directly in front of him. Erik tilted his head back to take in the giant warehouse.

Penny Pearson

In the darkness, the building looked to be a light tan with a darker brown entrance door, probably made for arriving customers. Three large garage doors for semi-trucks were set off further down the building. The windows were pitch black, giving no hint to the evil forces inside.

He was in the right place; he could feel the dark magic emanating from inside. It wasn't a strong feeling, more like a gentle knocking against his limbs. But it was enough to alert him. Making his way around the building, he searched for a way inside.

As luck would have it, a broken window at the back volunteered to aid in his breaking and entering. His jacket was thick enough to protect him from the shards of glass as he crawled through. When his feet hit the ground, he pushed himself against the wall. He checked his invisibility spell, and everything seemed to be working. It took a few seconds for his eyes to adjust to the almost pitch-black visibility within the warehouse. Faint outlines took shape in front of him, and he proceeded carefully, not wanting to give himself away with a misplaced footstep.

Erik stayed close to the wall and slid into the next room. There were no signs of Dale or any of his helpers. He continued until he heard faint voices in the distance. Adrenaline tried to hurry him forward, but he kept his cautious pace. It would do no good to give up the element of surprise. Moving forward, he listened until he came upon a room lit by gas lanterns.

"If you were followed," Dale was threatening in a gravelly voice.

Erik leaned forward slightly to glance around the corner. He spied Dale standing beside a table. The skeleton wavered slightly next to him. Deciding to end the game, he stepped out in full view.

Dale instantly sensed his movement. He whipped his head around and shot the skeleton a furious look. "You were followed!"

"Your training should have taught you not to be so bold. It wouldn't have been so easy, if you hadn't sent so many helpers out to find Zoe Hunt."

"I was following orders," Dale said unhappily. "My actions are not solely controlled by me. The demon is impatient."

Ritual Of Blood

"Why?"

Dale shrugged as he leaned against the table. "Surely you don't expect me to know. He's a demon. I'm a human."

"How did you find the book?"

Dale eyed the wizard. He wouldn't give information unless he got something in return. "If you let me go, I will tell you."

Erik smiled in the flickering light. "That doesn't work." He pointed his staff and said, "*Stipel khosel.*" The compulsion spell loosened the revenant's lips.

"It spoke to me as I drove past a house. No one lived there, but I found the book under some floorboards in a bathroom. I took it home and learned what I needed to do." Dale shot angry looks at Erik, but couldn't stop talking.

The spell was compelling, too powerful for a revenant. "How long have you had it?"

"A year and a half."

"Was the kid in the cemetery your first human sacrifice?"

"Yes."

Erik stared at the man. "What spell were you using?"

Dale tried to stay silent. He wasn't going to talk because he feared what the demon would do more than he feared the white wizard. As hard as he tried though, the words spilled out. "It was a power spell."

"Then you were instructed to come after Zoe."

"She was intended for the original sacrifice, after interrupting me at the cemetery."

"You kidnapped the wrong woman," Erik supplied.

"Piece of bad timing, that," Dale said ruefully. "Everything after the cemetery went to crap."

Erik walked closer, and Dale grew still. The revenant's skin was gray, and blue veins vividly stood out against his chalky skin. Dale's eyes rolled up, and his body grew taut. His eyes closed briefly.

When Dale stared at him, Erik knew Dale wasn't home. Someone else had taken over. Mammon.

Solid black seeped over the revenant's entire eye, and he spoke in Erik's ancient Armenian tongue, "Enough with the questions."

Demon Dale slid his glance toward the skeleton and ordered, "*Verjats'rets' nran.*"

End him.

Erik instantly turned and sent power toward the advancing skeleton, blocking its approach. Out of the corner of his vision, he watched Dale while concentrating on his attacker. He didn't want to spend too much time fighting the last skeleton. Dale could not get away, not if he wanted to keep Zoe safe and wanted to limit the new necromancer's power. Downing a nearly risen revenant and skeleton would certainly hinder the necromancer.

"*Aylevs kakhardakan,*" Erik shouted and sent his staff forward. His call to end the magic that enabled the skeleton's movements was answered. His earth magic was stronger than the visiting demon's. The leg bones holding the skeleton shook violently. The creature snapped its jaws at Erik, but as it tried to move forward, it crumbled into a loose heap of bones. A moment later, the bones disintegrated into a cloud of dust that covered everything, including him.

Erik turned back to Demon Dale. The solid black eyes told Erik; the demon still had control of the revenant's body. He decided to end this game, for he knew no more information would be given. He would cut his losses and leave no worse for the wear. Without fanfare, he uttered the spell to end the death that kept Dale Hicks's tied to the body, "*Avartel mahy.*"

Neither Dale nor the demon spoke as Erik's cross began to glow. He concentrated on working the spell around the room and into Dale's skin, and he ignored the radiant light that was emanating from his solar cross. He dared not take his eyes off Dale, while he performed the death magic. The revenant stumbled across the floor, his legs giving out underneath him, and attempted to grab onto a nearby table. Wordlessly it fell, and began to writhe on the ground. Its body shrunk in size, until a husk of a shell remained.

Erik continued to push the magic through, until he was certain Dale was truly dead. When he called back his magic, the light from his cross slowly dissipated. He stared at the figure at his feet, before he bent down and touched the clothes that housed Dale's shrunken body. No sign of life or magical death remained.

Ritual Of Blood

Dale was truly gone. His soul now belonged to Mammon, but he could no longer hurt a living person on earth.

He wouldn't feel sorry for the man. He made his decision, and he knew right from wrong. The lure of dark magic, with all its glory - power and corruption – was too strong for some. Erik scanned the area, making sure nothing could be traced back to him, including footprints. Once he was sure everything was in order, he quietly walked out of the building.

Calling Jenny, he instructed her to place an anonymous phone call reporting suspicious activity at the warehouse. As he walked to his car, he missed the lone figure in the distance, that watched him drive away.

Chapter 32

Zoe wasn't good at following directions. Right after Erik left, she thought about grabbing her car keys to follow him, but knew she'd reached her rescue limit. Nothing good would come about with her following behind like some tag-along six-year old. He was the expert. She would be fine here.

But an hour and a half later, she was ready to pull her hair out. During her brief time with Erik, she'd learned several things: she hated waiting, she needed something to drink, and she *really* hated waiting.

Located above the refrigerator, a mini-bar held bottled water, packs of crackers, cookies, and an expensive looking box of chocolates. To her dismay, there were no travel-sized bottles of alcohol. Did Erik already drink them, or were they never here in the first place? She tried to imagine Erik downing the little bottles, but the image didn't sit well with her.

It was possible that being on the Vatican team came with a "no libations" rule. There were probably a million rules he had to follow. A seven-hundred-year-old man probably got good at following rules. What other rules did he have to follow? He probably couldn't have fun or eat fast food. He was probably some stodgy old soul living in a god's body, she lamented.

But he could kiss. Boy, did he know how to kiss. What if he had taken a vow of celibacy? Her heart dropped at that. Surely, he wouldn't kiss her in such a … carnal way if his man bits were off limits.

With that depressing thought, she formed an idea on how to get alcohol. Poking her head out of the hotel room, she spotted a member of housekeeping passing by. "Excuse me," she began. "This might be a strange request." She stopped. What was she doing? She should *not* drink at a time like this. Erik was out there fighting dead revenants, necromancers, demons, and skeletons, while she considered her chances of getting wasted. "Oh, never mind."

The younger woman smiled. "What can I help with?"

Ah, screw it, her brain told her. "Do you have any of those tiny bottles of liquor?"

The housekeeper nodded, smiling widely. "I will be right back."

A couple of minutes later, a knock sounded at the door. Zoe checked the viewer and saw her new friend with her hands full of little bottles of alcohol. The women dumped her prize in Zoe's hands. "There you go," she said. "You and your man enjoy them." With a lascivious wink, the housekeeper departed, before she could set the record straight.

She stared after the women and wanted to shout, 'He's not my man,' but kept silent. She closed the door and took her booty to the table that once held the box of horrors and stacked them by style. She ended up with three bottles of rum, four vodkas, one bourbon, and two Fireballs.

Deciding fire was in her future, she choose the cinnamon flavored liquor. The red-hot whiskey nearly choked her to death on her first sip. Tears streamed down her cheeks, as she attempted to learn to breathe again. By the time she'd emptied the bottle, her skin felt molten hot and layers of clothing were coming off.

The more minutes passed, the tipsier she became. Zoe pointed the TV remote to find the right music station, while she reached for her second bottle of fiery goodness. Her body tingled, and a craving overtook her.

She was going to throw herself at Erik if he came back alive, she decided.

Ritual Of Blood

That thought drove her to down the second bottle in record time. Her eyes stung, and her throat had fire building inside. She stretched herself out on the couch. The smooth material caressed her legs. Her mind drifted to Erik. She tried to picture what he was going through, but only images from *Harry Potter* came to mind.

He didn't even have a wand! He had better not get himself killed, she thought desperately. She had no contact info for him. She couldn't call the Vatican and ask for the secret department that hunted down demons and their counterparts. The police here knew him by Agent Jordan Allen. They would probably be the first place to go, if something happened to Erik.

At that moment, she heard a scratching at the door. She sat up, and the world spun. Trying to stand without pitching face first onto the floor, she braced herself against the nearest chair. The door opened. Erik stepped through, and Zoe froze.

His hair fell over his brow. Grime covered him from head to foot, but otherwise he appeared unharmed. The first notes of a Vengaboys song blasted from the TV, with their 90's hit, "We Like to Party!"

Zoe's eyes grew wide when she heard the tune. The alcohol roared through her, and she swayed a bit. Completely forgetting Erik came directly from hunting demon spawn, she said wistfully, "I love this song. No one feels like partying anymore."

Erik narrowed his eyes and watched Zoe saunter over to him. Her lips parted, and her glassy eyes sparkled mischievously. In disbelief, he realized she was drunk.

His eyes took in several small bottles of liquor that sat empty on the table. His eyes found hers again. "While I was out, you were binge drinking?" A very small part of him found her sexy as she stood there, previously unseen parts of her seemingly on display. Her bare legs went up to a t-shirt that hardly covered the tops of her thighs.

She swayed and said, "Hey. You would have been doing that with or without me. I'm an add-on to your mission with the Vatican of churches." Zoe needed more to drink, so she reached for another bottle. "Yum, bourbon. I think, I think I like bourbon.

I can't remember." She shot him a wicked smile, before twisting off the lid. She tipped it up to her lips and prepared to down it. Hands reached and stole it from her. "Hey!" she cried as she lunged for the stolen bottle.

Erik set the bottle on the table before turning back to her. "No more drinking."

Scowling, she put her hands on her hips. "That's my drink. You can't take it away from me."

"No. I don't think you need anymore."

"Fine, then you drink it," Zoe challenged. Her eyes sparked mischievously.

"I'm not going to drink it."

"Either you drink it, or give it back to me. That bottle is not going to waste."

Erik continued to stand still; Zoe reached behind him to take the bottle. His grip stopped hers. They were so close he could smell cinnamon. Her eyes met his, and she breathed, "Oh, I forgot."

He was about to question what she forgot, but she lurched forward and planted her lips on his. She didn't care that he was covered in filth and other, unimaginable, things. Her hands clutched the edges of his jacket. It took Erik approximately three seconds to know what he should do.

He buried his hands in her hair and hauled her against him. His tongue touched her lips and elicited a small gasp from her. "Have you been thinking about me?" he growled against her mouth.

Zoe shivered at his tone. He sounded dangerous. He sounded exactly how she wanted him. "Yes," she confessed. "The drink gave me courage, but I had my mind made up before. I needed you to survive."

Erik pulled away from her mouth and sucked at the delicate spot on her neck. Her hips slammed into his, and she closed her eyes at the sensation. His hands lowered to cup her bottom, to hold her against him. She could feel his hardness, at the juncture of her thighs. Her hands helplessly held on.

"Why in God's name are you almost naked?" he panted against her neck. His tongue tickled a delicate spot, causing her to shiver against him.

She leaned back in his arms. "I got hot. It's very warm in here."

No doubt, he thought. The shots of Fireball must have hit the spot. He should buy a case the next chance he got and strategically place the bottles near Zoe, prompting her to remove her clothing more often. Erik paused in his thoughts. That would prove he was thinking about Zoe in a future way. He couldn't start a relationship with a woman from Ohio. His world was too different and too dangerous. She was too mortal.

Pulling her back into his arms, he captured her lips again as his hands moved over her hips. He didn't have the power in him to deny her, and for the life of him, he didn't want to.

Chapter 33

Zoe inwardly sighed as he reached for her. She was done with waiting. She was learning that life was too short, and if there was something she wanted, then she needed to go get it. She sank into his kiss, and he took her to depths she never knew existed.

Her hands ran up his shirt, and muscles rippled underneath. "Your shirt," she said against his mouth.

"What's wrong with my shirt?"

Her hands popped a button from its hole. "You're wearing it." Then another button came loose.

Erik smiled against her forehead. She was focusing on each button.

"Rip it," he encouraged.

Zoe's head lifted, and she stared at him with wide eyes. "I can't rip it. That wouldn't be –."

Erik didn't let her finish her sentence. He reached up, grabbed each side of his shirt, and pulled. The remaining six buttons flew through the air and bounced across the tile floor. Staring at her with a smirk, he shrugged off the shirt.

The only words that sprung to Zoe's mind were *He's mine.* That all-consuming thought took root, and she stepped forward to touch his beautiful chest. Old scars rippled across his muscles, telling of battles fought and won. Her fingers moved to his shoulders, then to his neck, and she pulled him in for another kiss.

His tongue glided across hers and stroked, causing her to

tremble in his arms. He wound his fingers through hers and gently pulled. He led them to his bedroom. "Are you sure this is what you want?"

"Yes," she nearly shouted. She didn't want anything more, than she wanted this. Her kiss told him so. She stepped into his body, and her ankle brushed against something hard. She pulled back to stare at his leg.

"My gun," Erik whispered, as he saw her confusion.

"Oh," she gulped. How could she possibly forget he was like a crime fighter against evil?

Quickly he bent down to unstrap his ankle holster. Laying the gun and its holder on the table, he turned back to Zoe and took her in his arms. His lips danced over hers, and her fingers trailed over his belt. Wasting no time, she worked the end free. Brushing her hands aside, he tore open his pants and hastily stepped out of them.

Next, he moved to lift her shirt over her head. "My God," he whispered against her skin. "You are extraordinary."

Laughing nervously, she bit gently on his shoulder, as he unhooked her bra and tugged off her underwear. They tumbled on the bed, and Erik rose over Zoe to stare down at her. He gently lowered his hips and rocked, sending waves of pleasure over her. Her knees widened to accommodate his entrance, but he pushed no further. She whimpered and pushed herself against him. The action only enflamed her body more.

Erik took her mouth in a hot kiss, and Zoe came undone. She wrapped her legs around him, in an effort to entice him to enter. He continued stroking across her, his cock sliding on her wet juices. He moaned quietly and tried to go slow. He didn't want to rush things, and he knew that as soon as he buried himself to the hilt inside her, there would be no going slow.

His intentions meant naught, as soon as she lifted her hips at the right moment to match his stroke. He entered her, swift and sure, and Zoe's breath hitched at the sensation. Her hands clutched at his hips. She threw back her head in a silent scream. He filled her completely, and with each gliding thrust, he pushed her to the edge of ecstasy.

Erik felt the need building inside, but he couldn't go without Zoe. He settled deeper against her and pushed his hips in a deep stroke. The tiny muscles gripped at his manhood, straining for more, and he gave it. A second later, she arched against him as she came. He felt his own release building, and he gave himself over to the sensations.

Zoe slowly came back to earth, as tremors in her legs eased. She didn't know how good a wizard he really was, but what he did to her body spoke volumes.

Erik moved beside her, his hands gently skimming the skin between her breasts. "Are you okay? I didn't hurt you, did I?"

She shook her head. "No, it was…" Wonderful? Earth shattering? The best thing ever? The answers could go on and on. "Really good." She wanted to pull the words back. How lame did that sound to a seven-hundred-year-old wizard, with a body of a god?

"Next time, I will be better."

Zoe laughed and asked incredulously, "Better? I can't imagine anything better than what I just experienced." Unless he meant better for him next time. *Yea, Zoe, keep shoving that foot deeper into your mouth!*

"It's been a while. I didn't give you my best."

She snuggled into his side, and he wrapped his arms protectively around her. "If that wasn't your best, I'm not sure I will be able to survive the next time."

Kissing her damp forehead, he told her, "You'll survive."

Sleep came swiftly to Zoe, and she fell asleep before she could form a coherent thought. Erik followed shortly after. He slept dreamlessly for the first time in decades.

Zoe awoke a while later, still tucked beside Erik and cautiously glanced at him. He smiled at her in the darkness. "I must have fallen asleep. I'm sorry."

"Don't be sorry. I fell asleep, too," he said as he wiped a stray lock of black hair from her cheek.

Now that she could think without exploding from lust, Zoe asked, "Is Dale… taken care of?" She didn't really know what Erik had to do, when dealing with Dale. Did he kill the man or arrest him and take him to church jail? Maybe he didn't get Dale.

Erik wrapped Zoe in his arms. "Dale won't bother anyone again."

"Did you kill him?" She couldn't help the shock that seeped out in her voice. She knew Erik had a job to do – capture the bad things – but the idea of him murdering someone, well, she should have thought about that.

"No," he told her. "Not in the traditional sense. Dale was already dead. He was animated with magic provided by the tutorials of the demon. I took away the magic."

Zoe had so many questions. "How did you learn magic?"

"I was adopted by a Knight Templar and –"

"Knight Templar?" she interrupted. "As in the knights that fought in the Crusades and hid gold?"

"Not everything you read about is true."

"What? The crusade part or the gold part?" Erik didn't answer, so she asked, "Is Erik your real name?"

"No, although I tried to stay as true to it as possible throughout the years. I was born Hurik Vardanyan."

"Ah, I see! Erik Vardan is very similar. So, how did you learn magic?"

His hands rubbed along her bare shoulder. "I'm not answering anymore, until you tell me about you."

Her smiling eyes met his. "You already know everything. I'm sure you were given a file about me. I'm wondering if it had my first boyfriend listed."

"I don't recall any intel on a first boyfriend."

"Really?" she said in mock surprise. "Nothing about Brian Ray and how we traded stickers?"

Erik laughed at the image of a young Zoe and some boy kissing over bartered stickers.

The sound of Erik's chortle caused Zoe's heart to beat faster. She realized he didn't laugh often. It was a rare delight, and it pleased

Ritual Of Blood

her that she caused it. "Yes. Unfortunately, we weren't destined to be together. I think he moved away. I can't remember anymore. What about your first girlfriend? Do you remember?"

Seven hundred years was a long time to hold memories. When Zoe thought about it, she didn't want him to remember his girlfriend from centuries ago. That would mean she truly withstood the test of time.

"I can't recall my first girlfriend. Once I started my studies with the church, I had no time."

"So," she prodded. "That must mean you were too busy learning magic."

"I didn't learn magic for many years. The opportunity was not afforded to everyone. You had to excel at your studies – in all areas."

"Which were?"

"You really want to hear me talk about this?" Erik asked, surprise in his tone.

She glared up at him through the darkness of his bedroom. "Yes, I'm sure! You are a walking piece of history! I'm sure you have been through so much. Tell me a little."

Erik narrowed his eyes at her cajoling. He'd never told anyone about himself outside of his contacts at the Vatican, but he found himself wanting to confide in her. He wasn't giving away state secrets. "I learned magic after decades of learning math, accounting, Latin, military strategy, philosophy, and religion."

"Didn't you know Latin already?"

"No. As a child, I spoke Armenian. The church taught me to read and write in various languages throughout the years."

Zoe grew quiet before asking, "Do you have any family left?"

His fingers stroked down her back. "I had no family when I was rescued from the town in Armenia. The Vatican and the people within have become my family."

"Do you like what you do?"

Readily nodding, Erik spoke, "Yes. I'm trying to level the playing field for humanity."

"How many demons are there?"

"There's no way of knowing. We only see the ones that reach out to humans, and that's only the small portion we know about. There could be untold numbers."

She shivered at his ominous words. "Do you ever get scared?"

"Yes. It's what keeps me motivated."

"Can you die?" Her voice trembled on the last word. She was in the bed of a seven-hundred-year-old wizard, who did the most exquisite things to her body, and she brings up the morbid thought of death? What was wrong with her? "I'm sorry. I don't think I want to know the answer to that."

"Yes, I can die," he told her simply.

Zoe let her hands move over his chest, but paused when he joined his hands with hers. Then he pulled their clasped fingers down his abdomen and lower. As soon as she brushed his manhood, his hips rocked up at the touch. He gasped at the sensation.

Chapter 34

"Would it be safe to say that I can go back to my apartment?" Zoe asked as she walked out of Erik's bedroom. She twisted her fingers nervously at her approach. She wasn't exactly embarrassed because she slept with him, but in the daylight, things were different.

Zoe's question was the same Erik asked himself earlier. He knew he couldn't keep her in his hotel forever. With Dale and his skeletons gone, she would be safe. Probably. He still had no idea who or where the necromancer was. It was possible the book made it to the hands of someone that went underground. New necromancers didn't always come out ready for blood. Some were cautious during the beginning stages.

But he didn't want to take any chances. "You need to stay here," he told her.

"But Dale is truly gone now, right? And his skeletons?"

He touched her shoulder. "I understand you are anxious to get back to some sort of normalcy," he conceded. "There is still the new necromancer to locate, and until I do, I want to make sure you are safe."

"The necromancer doesn't know who I am."

Erik's mouth formed a grim line. "Dale and the skeletons could have communicated details about you."

"That doesn't make any sense. Why would I still be a target? Dale only came after me because I saw him in the cemetery. I have nothing to do with the new guy!"

"Until I can be sure," he reiterated, "you are to stay put."

Zoe turned and flounced down on the couch with her arms crossed. "I'm going to die an old lady in this hotel room."

Smiling, Erik sat beside her. "You will not die an old lady in this hotel room."

Staring up at him, her breath caught. His eyes locked with hers. His hands rose to her jaw line, and he gently caressed her. "Do you do this a lot?" Zoe asked.

"What? Keep women locked up in hotel rooms?" He wanted to taste her lips again, but thought it might be too soon. Things happened last night, but he wondered if he should leave it at that. His body told him that wasn't possible.

"No." She scowled. "Do you sleep with women from your other cases? Please tell me you are not the Vatican's resident Lothario." Trying to block out images of him with other faceless lovers, she covered her face with her hands.

Erik reached for her hands and pulled them carefully away. "I do not seduce other women."

Narrowing her eyes, she said, "You might not have to seduce. I'm a prime example of that last night. I asked if you sleep with all the women you help."

With a swift move, he pulled Zoe up to her feet and against his body. Her hands flattened against his muscular chest, and he reveled in the rightness of it. "No," he growled a moment before he took her mouth in an all-consuming kiss. Her lips were supple under his, and she met him kiss for kiss, even sending her hands fluttering down his back. "I do *not* do this."

"Oh," she breathed.

Then his phone rang.

Zoe wanted to fall to her knees, scream, and cry at the unfairness in life. How dare they be interrupted when things were getting good? Instead, she stepped away to allow him space to answer the call.

"Agent Allen," he answered with a direct look at her.

She nearly snickered at the use of his alternate identity.

Ritual Of Blood

Pleased to be in his trust sphere, she tried to act disinterested in the conversation. On the inside, she was opposite.

"You did. Okay. I will be there as soon as possible. Can you send me the location?" Erik ended the call and turned to Zoe. "They found another body – or what is left of it – and believe it might be connected with Dale Hicks."

Wide eyed and amused, she said, "Imagine that, Interpol Agent Allen."

He stepped forward and kissed her quickly on the lips. "I have to go. Please stay here. Order food to be delivered this time, and do not leave this hotel for any reason."

"Okay. I promise to stay here. I have to catch up on work anyway. I know I always say this, but be careful."

His eyes took on an intent look, but he stayed silent as he gathered his coat and slipped it on. Before he walked out the door, he told her, "Thank you."

Zoe watched the door close quietly. She locked it behind him and headed to the bathroom to take a shower. When she was done, she turned on her computer and began to sort through dozens of emails, organizing them by priority levels. She worked from the easiest to the hardest, leaving the big reports for last. There was plenty to keep her busy until midnight and beyond, she mused. The first report she worked on took longer than expected, after she realized not all columns populated correctly.

Hours later, she stood to give herself a break and pulled a water bottle out of the stocked fridge. Thinking about Erik made her stomach flip, but she forced herself to think logically. A wizard from the Vatican probably wasn't looking for a girlfriend. She wasn't sure if he was even boyfriend material. With everything that's happened, she didn't really have the chance to get to know him. She didn't know what his favorite food was or his favorite movie. She didn't know if he'd ever had a wife… or three.

Okay, he could kiss, she'd give him that, and it was an important expectation.

He could definitely hold a job down. Yeah, didn't need to go further into that one.

Penny Pearson

A knock on the door interrupted her mental list. Her heart jumped up in her throat, until she realized it could be housekeeping. She had forgotten to put the Do Not Disturb sign on the doorknob. With a calming breath, she walked to the door and peeked into the hallway.

Susie stood on the other side of the door. Zoe was surprised at seeing her friend. Then worry shot through her. Something bad must have happened she thought, as she opened the door. "Susie? What are you doing here? Are you okay?"

Susie nodded as she stepped inside. Her eyes roamed the room quickly.

With a look of concern, Zoe asked, "Is everything okay?"

"Yes," Susie said lightly. "Everything is fine. I wanted to stop by and see how you are doing."

"I-I'm fine."

Both stood, staring at each other awkwardly.

"How is your mom?" Zoe asked, as she motioned Susie further inside the hotel. Glad that the box of relics was long gone, she gestured to the table. "Do you want to sit down?"

"No, Mom's doing fine, but I can't stay long." Susie craned her neck to look inside one of the bedrooms, Erik's room.

Zoe gritted her teeth at the view of rumpled sheets. "Did you need to speak with Agent Allen? He isn't here right now, but I can call him." The words sounded wrong to her ears. "How did you find me?" She couldn't help it. She didn't tell Susie she was staying at the hotel.

Waving her hand, she said, "It was the craziest thing, I was driving by and spotted your car in the parking lot. So I went to the front desk and asked them if you were staying here."

"But the front desk doesn't have my name," Zoe told her.

"Sure they do," Susie went on breezily. "How would I have found you if they hadn't given me your room number?"

Confusion shifted inside Zoe. She tilted her head to regard her friend. No other explanation for Susie's appearance came to mind. Susie seemed well, completely back to her confident self. Her blond hair glistened, and her makeup was flawless. "Are *you* okay?"

"Yes, never better. Have you by chance talked to Tiffany? She left me a message, but I haven't heard back from her. When was the last time you talked to her?"

"Oh, I talked to her a day or so ago. Well, I think. The days are blending. Let me check to see when I called her." Zoe turned to walk to her purse, to fish out her phone. Scrolling through the different menus, she pulled up Tiffany's contact info. "I talked to her Tuesday around 1pm."

Zoe stared in the distance, trying to place where she was during the phone call. Then, it came back to her. Erik had come with her to see Susie, after she was released from the hospital. They stopped to eat lunch before going out to Dale Hicks's house in the woods.

"It's been three days since I talked to her. When was the last time you did?" She turned to look at Susie and everything went blank.

Chapter 35

"**A**gent Allen!"

Erik nodded to Detective Williams when she pointed to where he was being summoned - into the next room. He knew his way around the warehouse, for he'd been there not a day earlier. Sergeant Vega stood beside a worktable in the main area. Erik stepped beside the police officer and waited for him to talk.

"We believe this might be Dale Hicks." Vega lowered his gaze to the floor and moved his boot in the direction indicated.

Vega certainly was direct and to the point. Erik narrowed his eyes and squatted next to the body.

Rumpled, tattered clothes covered a shrunken body. Emaciated skin stretched over Dale's face. His fingers were curved talons.

Erik nodded as he said, "From what I can remember of Mr. Hicks's face, I believe you might be correct." He needed to be confident in his delivery of facts, but not brash. His goal was for the police force to close their case quickly, but not provide too many unbacked theories. They needed to find their own conclusions to the death of Dale Hicks.

Vega handed a photo of Dale for comparison. A few seconds later, Erik confirmed the sergeant's suspicion. "Based on the decomposition, I can't be one hundred percent sure, but it looks like Dale Hicks."

A forensics officer neared and said, "We are going to start

prepping the body. We have an unidentified material we are processing, as well."

Erik glanced at the pile of blackened dust a few feet away. "Is that what you are talking about?"

The man nodded. "Yes, sir. We don't know what it is at this point. For the time being, we are treating it as potential hazardous and suggesting everyone steer clear, until we determine what exactly it is."

Nodding, Erik stayed quiet. He couldn't tell them it was the remains of a once-alive necromancer, who now served a demon in the afterlife. The same went for Dale. He mentally shook his head. Dale must be very unhappy with his bargain. Erik had surmised over his time researching, that the demon granted extra years on the life of those who served him. Dale should have been alive much longer, but with Zoe's surprise interference – on so many levels – the necromancer didn't last long in his revenant form. He certainly didn't last long enough to begin the phase of transitioning into a skeletal servant.

Dale's life of wielding deadly magic had been cut short. Erik was pleased that there was one less necromancer and three less skeletons walking the earth. He still needed to track down the Mammon's book to call this mission successful, but he would take every little win he could get.

"Come take a look at this," Vega called. He had stepped off to the side and bent to view something on a table. The sergeant didn't pick up the item. Fingerprints and other evidence might be on the object, and the sergeant knew better than to compromise his crime scene.

Following Vega's pointed finger, Erik peered down to a piece of paper. Written in ink, numbers and symbols were haphazardly recorded. The practical eye wouldn't have made out any rhyme or reason. But Erik knew what these were. Ancient symbols that some used as a way to communicate. Code was set up ages ago, as a way to pass messages without being detected. "Very interesting," he concluded, as he finished perusing the paper.

He studied Vega. "Have you seen anything like it before?"

Ritual Of Blood

Vega shook his head. "Damnedest thing I've seen. Looks like language out of tattoos."

Erik nodded. "I'm going to take a picture and send it to one of the labs at Interpol. We'll see if they can make heads or tails out of it." He placed his phone close to the paper and snapped a few pictures. He quickly sent the photos on the Jenny. "There," he said. "You can process as needed. Anything else unusual?"

The sergeant turned a full circle. "This doesn't make sense. This man," he pointed to what was left of Dale, "kills a young kid in a cemetery. He happens to be interrupted mid-killing by Zoe Hunt, who was on a Halloween scavenger hunt. A few days later, the same man, who probably meant to kidnap Miss Hunt, kidnaps the wrong woman, at Miss Hunt's apartment. That woman manages to call police, and we track her down, but the perp is dead."

Erik internally filled in some gaps, that he couldn't tell the sergeant, but agreed so far with the timeline of events.

"Then, said perp goes missing at the morgue, along with three skeletons that were found at his property. Hicks and skeletons remained unseen for a couple of days. Now we find ourselves here." Vega shook his head at Dale's form. "An abandoned warehouse with the same dead people. Now they are in a worse condition."

"I would have to agree," Erik pronounced, not offering further info, and he noted how Vega clenched his jaw. He wasn't here to make friends or to solve cases. As a Vatican-planted Interpol agent, he would be in the action, but not directly in charge of reporting or giving details to others, unless he deemed it necessary. His support role was ideal, in finding what he needed and getting out relatively easy.

A moment later, a text came through from Jenny. It said, "Bank accounts and balances. Also, locations of storage units. Still working on info."

Erik looked at Vega. "The research team came back saying the note seems like gibberish at this point. They will continue research. In the meantime, keep your team processing. We might get something helpful back."

Sighing deeply, the sergeant muttered something about

unhelpful foreigners and stalked out of the warehouse.

***

Zoe felt herself moving. She wasn't being carried or rolled. Her legs seemed to have a mind of their own. Nothing could be seen or heard. Only bright white surrounded her. But she was aware of her body operating around her, just not with her. Trying to gain control, she told herself to stop. That didn't work. Her body continued its trek.

She commanded her arms to lift. Nothing. She commanded her head to turn. Nothing. It was as if she were an automaton, controlled by someone unknown. Her brain rebelled at that logic. So, she tried again to make her body move under her own instructions. Head, legs, arms.

Nothing happened.

Terror clutched her chest.

She yelled, and then screamed when that didn't work.

Still nothing. Feeling as if she were on a runaway truck heading toward a steep curve, she begged her body to stop. She had no idea where she was heading. The last thing she remembered was talking with Susie at the hotel.

Hazy images flashed in front of her. A scuffle took place beside her, before blissful silence fell over her.

Zoe woke with a start, glad to be out of the clutches of the terrible nightmare she had. Her eyes adjusted to the bright lights above her, and she glanced around in confusion. White walls, clean and sterile looking, surrounded her. Her eyes scanned the room and caught sight of someone sitting on a chair in the far corner. They were slumped forward.

Zoe's hands were tied securely to the side of her chair. She pulled, trying to loosen the grip it held, but it didn't help. Her gaze tripped over a metal table that sat at the center of the room. Small items were strewn across the top, but Zoe couldn't make out what they were.

Ritual Of Blood

"Hello?" she called out hesitantly.

Nobody responded.

"Is anyone here?"

The person in the corner twitched slightly, but otherwise stayed still.

Zoe took a deep breath and screamed at the top of her lungs. Someone had to be near. She didn't think about her scream bringing the wrong people. She only wanted to find out what was happening, and why she had been taken. Suddenly someone grabbed her shoulder from behind.

She shrieked at the contact. Heart pounding, she swung around in her metal chair, as best she could.

Susie stood at the back of Zoe's chair. Relief flooded her at seeing her friend unharmed. "Susie! What happened? Did they take you, too?" Frantically searching her friend's face, she asked, "Where are they?"

Susie walked in front of her and headed to the other person in the room. She bent down and smoothed the person's hair back from her face, revealing a very familiar face.

Susie's mother sat slumped in the chair. Zoe's stomach lurched, as she realized they were all in a lot of trouble. Somehow, someone managed to kidnap her, Susie, and Susie's mom. But why? Who would do such a thing? "They took your mom, too? Is she okay?" she asked in a shaky breath. Her mind was still foggy, from whatever occurred before she woke.

Susie nodded and straightened. "Here, let me get your hands free." She stood beside Zoe and pulled against the duct tape wrapped around her wrists.

Grimacing at the pain that Susie caused, she stayed quiet. The longer she held still, the sooner she would be free. They would come up with a plan on getting out. "Did you see who took us?"

Ignoring Zoe's question, she concentrated on the tape. With one last hard yank, Susie looked up in triumph. "Whew. That was impossible to get loose. Here, I think your purse was thrown over in that corner." She walked over and grabbed a purse.

Bringing it to Zoe, she said, "We need your phone." Holding

the bag out, Susie shook it at her. "Hurry, I don't know how much time we have!"

The urgent tone got Zoe moving, and she quickly entered the pass code on her phone. Her fingers trembled, but she began to search for Erik's contact info. "Do you remember what happened at the hotel? Did you see who took us?" she asked again.

Susie snatched the phone from her fingers.

"Hey!" Zoe cried and reached to take it back. "What are you doing? We need that to call for help. Erik will find us!"

Susie paused a second, and then giggled girlishly, as she brandished the phone. "I'm just kidding." She smiled wickedly and waved a hand through the air. "I know exactly what happened to you. My helpers tied you too tightly."

Chapter 36

"What?" Zoe asked in disbelief. She must have misheard. "What did you say?" Standing now that she was free from the chair, she backed up until she hit the wall behind her. The hard surface provided a sense of reality she feared she was losing. She glanced around the room and took stock of any doors and windows.

One door. No windows. Susie came closer, and Zoe slipped sideways.

"You can't go anywhere," Susie informed her, as she read her actions. She glanced back down at the phone and pressed some buttons.

"You need to let me out of this room. You can't do this!"

"I did!" She fanned her hands out in front of her. "I did do this. You are here, aren't you?" Susie continued. "My earlier try didn't go as expected, but you are here now. Everything will be fine. I need your help with something."

Zoe shook her head, trying to fight at the words. A bad feeling welled inside her. "What is going on?"

At that moment, the door swung open and in walked Dale Hicks. "Hello, darling," he drawled. "I don't believe we've been formally introduced."

Panic shot through her, speeding up her heartbeat and causing her head to grow light.

Dale should have been dead! Erik had taken care of him

yesterday. She squinted in the low light of the room, trying to pick up some hint of duplicity. His features were never clear to her in all her encounters with him. The cemetery was too dark, and she was too shocked. The hospital parking lot encounter was too quick, and she had been injured.

Dale walked beside Susie and stood shoulder to shoulder with her. His face wore and expression of mock sadness. "She hasn't figured it out yet, has she?"

"Well," Susie piped up. Her eyes glinted merrily, as she shot Dale a teasing glance. "You didn't figure it out right away either."

Zoe watched Dale interact with Susie, as if they were old friends. Horror began to dawn on her. Tiny pieces of the puzzle tried to fall in place, but she didn't have the right connections yet.

Susie shrugged as she continued to talk to Dale, and she playfully slapped the phone against his arm. "Stop it. I'm in charge now."

"Give me my phone," Zoe ordered. If she were confident and showed no sign of weakness, she could possibly get out of this alive.

With eyes narrowed, Dale bit out, "You have no say here."

Susie continued to swipe through Zoe's phone, until she found what she wanted. "What's your Bitcoin password?"

"What?"

"Your password," Susie repeated, more slowly this time. "What is your password for Bitcoin?"

"I don't have Bitcoin."

Susie turned her eyes on Zoe and raised her eyebrows. "You do. We downloaded the apps together, remember?"

Zoe remembered that day. They giggled like little kids, remarking about getting on the government's list for spy activities. "No! I'm not going to tell you my password. I don't know what you are doing, but I won't be part of it."

Susie looked Zoe straight in the eyes as she stepped forward. The hard stare sent Zoe's stomach tumbling. "I'm going to ask you one more time. What is your password for Bitcoin?"

Zoe's chin rose a notch. "I'm not going to tell you."

Ritual Of Blood

Jumping forward with an exasperated look, Susie grabbed her hair and yanked hard. Strands of hair pulled out, and still she kept pulling. "You're going to tell me, or I will rip every strand out of your head"

Pain lit up instantly at Susie's harsh treatment, blurring Zoe's vision. She cried out and tried to pry the rough hands loose from her hair.

Dale broke in, "Hey, hey, hey. Calm down." He stepped in to separate Susie from Zoe. He bent to check their captive for severe injuries, before turning to glare at Susie. "You can't manhandle your way into everything. Sometimes it takes sugar to get what you want."

Zoe snarled at Dale's words. There would be no sugar. She'd let them tear her hair out before she gave them what they wanted. Watching Dale remove the hat from his head, he turned away from her, and Zoe saw the giant meaty gaping hole in the back of his head.

She must have gasped, for he turned around and smiled at her. "I see you've caught sight of my grievous wound." He glanced at Susie – a look that promised retribution – and said, "Sometimes you don't know what resides in the deepest recesses of the heart."

"Enough philosophizing!" Susie stormed in front of Zoe. "What's your password?" This time she grabbed her fingers and twisted brutally.

It took only a second of pressure until Zoe felt her finger pop. She screamed in pain.

"Now!" Susie commanded. Any trace of compassion was completely eradicated from her gaze. Zoe's hand was still in her grip, and she began to bend the broken finger back further.

She screamed, trying to pull her hand from Susie's grasp, but she refused to relinquish it. Susie pulled again and lights flickered in Zoe's vision. The pain was unbearable. Her brave face didn't hold up in the line of attack. "Firefly2003 with a capital F," Zoe gasped out as tears blinded her.

Susie released her finger, as she tapped the password in Zoe's phone.

Stepping away from the duo, she cradled her hand against her chest. A quick look told her the finger had been broken, considering its awkward angle. Her hand began to throb, and her skin grew clammy. Zoe briefly closed her eyes, breathing in slow and deep, in an effort to fight of the urge to pass out from the pain.

"You have to hurry," Dale instructed Susie. "You need to be in and out as quickly as possible if you want to avoid detection."

"I got it. You don't have to treat me like a novice."

He glared at her. His grayish skin shining in the light. "You *are* a novice."

While they bickered, Zoe cautiously, and very slowly, moved to the open door. If she could get out of the room, she might be able to make a run for it. She had to time it right if she wanted to get a jump on them. Without wasting another second, she sprinted to the door.

"Hey!"

"She's running!"

Zoe didn't glance back to see if they chased after her. She only looked ahead and ran as fast as she could. Darting out the door, she made a quick adjustment in stride to move down the hallway. Ceiling lights illuminated her path, and she pressed forward. In high school, she ran cross country. She wasn't a sprinter.

But today, she was Flo-Jo, the faster sprinter of all time.

Unfortunately, fast didn't always win the game. Not when it came to animated skeletons. Two jumped out and clothes lined her. The impact and the reverse force sent her feet up and forward, while her upper body flew backward. The force of the fall knocked the air out of her, but she rolled over as quickly as she could to get to her feet again.

Then pain in her head and her broken finger lessened, and then was forgotten as she peeked behind her to see Dale striding toward her. Staggering to her feet, she lunged forward, but he caught her easily and dragged her back to the small room. Zoe kicked and flung herself in his arms. He was unmoved. As he dragged her through the opening, she screamed for help.

"Wow," Dale said in amusement. "You've got a set of pipes

on you." Flinging her from him, he gently rubbed his hears. "Your screams hurt my newly dead eardrums."

Zoe narrowed her eyes and screamed again as loudly as she could. That earned a cuff to the side of the head.

"Enough playing around," Susie said with rolled her eyes as she watched the pair reenter the room. "Tie her back up again. We got the money."

Zoe kicked at Dale as he herded her to the chair, then she reached to grab the chair to swing it at him, but it was stuck to the floor. He laughed evilly. She hit at his hands, but he held onto her with superhuman strength and easily pushed her down. He held his free hand out, and a skeleton was by his side immediately, handing him a roll of duct tape.

"How did you get me from the hotel?" Zoe rasped. Adrenaline slowly drained the energy from her.

Susie looked up from the phone and smirked. "The same way I was taken from your parking lot. Dale dubbed it zombie dust. I don't really like to think about what it is exactly. All I know is, it works if you need someone mobile, yet completely out of it. Zombie dust is really the best description."

"How could you do this? He kidnapped you!" Then she turned to Dale. "What did you do to her? You must have brainwashed her."

Dale shrugged, as innocent as could be. "Out of my hands. Once I died, my freewill flew the coop."

"Erik will find me," Zoe vowed. "You can't think you'll get away with this."

"Ah, yes, but I thought he was Agent Jordan Allen or something like that, according to the business card he left on your table. There is definitely a tale to be told."

"He's the white wizard," Dale filled in.

Susie threw him impatient look. "You idiot. I knew that. You've been drilling the white wizard spiel in my head since the first lesson. Yeah, yeah, I know he's a wizard. I was going for effect. It's really no fun if I have to explain everything." She shot him another look before pressing the cell phone. Holding the button for several seconds, she remarked, "Really, Dale, you are going to have to keep up if you want to continue to hang with me. There, the phone is rebooting. I only need to get the memory card and battery, in case there is some sort of homing beacon on it."

"Why are you doing this?" Zoe asked again. She sounded like a broken record, but she was trying to understand. Her mind wasn't connecting the pieces.

"You would never understand," Susie sneered.

Zoe had no idea Susie even had one evil bone in her body, but it seemed this new Susie, one she didn't recognize, was alien to her. The Susie she knew could be snide at times, but Zoe never heard, and certainly not seen, her threaten to harm anyone. So, why had Susie joined with Dale – whom, by the way, should be *totally* dead now? "Try me," she said smartly, refusing to be bullied by her friend. "Help me understand why you are doing this. Because it makes no sense."

"Factory re-install is complete," Susie said triumphantly, ignoring Zoe. Wrestling with the back of the cell phone, Susie finally managed to open the cover. She pulled the battery out and dug for the memory card. "We have the money, and now her phone can't be traced."

Dale stepped up. His grey face slack with emotion. "You don't have much time. Even though you destroyed the phone, that doesn't give you all the time in the world."

Zoe didn't like the sound of that.

"Have the skeletons destroy this. Can they do that?"

"Don't you know what they can do?" Dale asked.

Shaking her head, she said defensively, "I have only been doing this for less than a week. You haven't been the most astute teacher. You were off doing, whatever it was you were doing. I haven't had time to read the fine print. That book isn't easy to understand!"

Fine print. It took a moment for Zoe to realize Susie had the demon's book. Suddenly everything made sense. Zoe felt as if she'd run straight into a brick wall.

Susie walked to her mother. She bent down and put a hand

on her knee. "Mom," she whispered.

The rest of the conversation couldn't be overheard, even though Zoe tried to strain hard to her Susie's words. Susie nodded to Dale and motioned her to follow him, when she had finished talking with her mother.

Chapter 37

At the station, Erik sat at an empty desk, waiting for results from forensics. The DNA tests were expected to confirm the identity of the corpse in the morgue and match it to Dale Hicks. He leaned forward to compare prints, from different crime scenes.

Dale's prints were found at his apartment in town, the house in the woods, and at the warehouse. Other markers were picked up at the warehouse, but Erik didn't know the last time the building had been in use, so he expected miscellaneous prints.

He sat back, thinking about the case. The necromancer he had come to Ohio for was now dead, the book was missing, and no whereabouts on a new necromancer was known. As he pondered his luck, his phone rang.

Before he greeted Jenny, she said, "Zoe's phone has gone off."

"What do you mean *gone off?*"

"Her phone has been taken off-line."

Dread slammed through him. He was on his feet and heading to the door. "Do you know where she was last time you got a hit?"

"No," she told him, her voice laced with apologetic tones. "The last I got was at the hotel."

"Damn it," Erik swore. He knew Zoe wouldn't have left the hotel. Surely not. Doubts crept up, but he pushed them away. She wouldn't have left.

Almost out of the door with the phone pressed against his

ear, Vega stopped him.

"Agent Allen, a second please."

Erik shook his head, his mind still reeling from the news. It was possible her phone battery died, and he was overreacting. "Get me something, Jenny," he told her before disconnecting. He turned to Sergeant Vega. "Something has come up."

"You'll want to hear this." Vega did his own scowling. "Forensics reports the corpse at the warehouse doesn't match Dale Hicks's previous DNA samples."

"What?" Disbelief sharpened his words.

Vega shook his head, clearly stumped. "They say there is no match."

"That can't be possible."

"We jumped to conclusions at the warehouse, before tests to positively confirm identity returned. It isn't Dale Hicks."

That couldn't be possible. He had talked with and put an end to Dale yesterday. "You need to run the tests again."

"We did," Vega shot back, his eyes flashing. "Is there a reason you are so sure this was Dale Hicks?"

Erik gritted out, "No." His head hurt as worry overcame him. Zoe was in trouble. He could feel it.

"Do you have any information to share?" the sergeant asked.

"No." He couldn't let the police become involved. They weren't prepared to handle magical warfare. Dale on the loose again complicated things, but didn't make his plan impossible. He had an idea on how to find Zoe, but it wasn't a good one.

***

Left alone, Zoe tried to find an opening to escape from the room, but she had no luck. There was only one door, and the solid metal wouldn't budge. Glancing at Susie's mom, she slowly approached her.

"Mrs. Monroe?"

Susie's mom slowly lifted her chin and met Zoe's eyes. Pain and confusion filled the woman's gaze. Gently touching her shoulder, she asked, "Do you know why Susie is doing this?"

Mary Monroe squeezed her eyes closed, as if trying to block out a disturbing vision. She shook her head, and whispered, "No. I don't remember getting here. I don't know what she is doing." Her hand raised to rub the brittle skin beside her eye. Small, red and blue veins dotted the side of her face.

Zoe got a sick feeling. Mrs. Monroe didn't look good. "Do you need to lie down? I'm sure I can get something together for you." As she said the words, she searched for blankets or something soft to make a bed, but nothing was in the room, other than their chairs. "This isn't right," she mumbled angrily.

"Zoe, don't blame Susie."

Zoe grew still at Mary's words. Did Susie's mom know everything Susie had done? Because Zoe was getting a feeling that wasn't possible. There would be no way Mary would be sitting here, asking her not to blame Susie for their predicament if she knew.

Susie had the demon's book.

Granted, she hadn't seen the book with her own eyes, but it explained how she was working with Dale and controlling the skeletons. She thought back to what Erik had told her. Some people were drawn to the book because it offered them things. It certainly offered Susie something. The question was what was Susie going to do next?

They kidnapped her from the hotel and brought her to…

She didn't know where she was. Erik would never be able to find her. Her phone had been destroyed, so locating her was probably out of the question. She had to come up with a plan on her own. She eyed Mary. Maybe she could use Susie's mom as leverage to get out. She didn't want to take her as a hostage, but if left with no other option; she might have to do just that.

Then she really asked herself if she could hurt Susie's mom, and the answer was no. She couldn't do it. Walking around the room, she noted every crack in the wall. There were no windows, so she couldn't break her way out.

She could surprise them when they came for her. If she stood off to the side of the door, she might be able to get the jump on them. She'd battled a skeleton once, and even though, she didn't soundly defeat it, she still managed to hold it at bay. Until Erik arrived.

Zoe shook her head. Relying on someone else to come save her was pure folly. If she wanted saved, she had to be the one to do it. Another glance around gave her an idea. The legs on her abandoned chair would be a help, she realized. Trotting to the metal chair, she tipped it over and bent one of the legs. At first, nothing happened, but a minute later, she could feel it give slightly.

The leg slowly began to breakdown, and Zoe worked it back and forth, trying to break it free of the body of the chair. With a sharp snap, she had a weapon in her hand. Setting it down, she began to work on the other legs. If she had four weapons, she might be able to get somewhere. Carefully, she eased two of the metal legs inside the back of her waistband and tightly palmed the other two.

With a deep breath, she walked to the door and pounded and kicked on it as furiously as she could. She screamed at the top of her lungs, until her voice became hoarse. Finally, when she heard the lock slide, she eased behind the door, making it hard for anyone to locate her. They would have to walk inside to find her. The door flew open, but Zoe easily caught it and slammed it forward. A dull-white skeleton stumbled into the room, knocked off-balance.

Zoe silently jumped forward and brought the chair leg down on its head. The creature fell to the ground, but instantly tried to regain its feet. Glancing at the doorway, she noted the no other skeletons were nearby. She stepped over the skeleton, bent, and tried to pull the head off. Bony hands wrapped around her arm, as the skeleton struggled against her. She gritted her teeth and pulled harder. A loud pop filled the room, as the head flew from her hands to roll across the floor.

Staring wide-eyed as the rocking head, she pushed at the now still body that clung onto her legs. She continued to stare at the head, hoping it wouldn't somehow magically reconnect with its other parts.

Susie's mother made a sound in the corner, pulling her

attention away from the decapitated skeleton.

Mary's eyes were wild, and she sneered at Zoe. "You cannot undo my daughter's work!" Her suddenly compassionate nature gone. It was as if a wild creature took her place.

Zoe's time ran out. Before Mary could sound the alarm, she clutched her makeshift weapon and ran from the room. She didn't bother with grabbing her purse; it would only slow her down. Her life depended on her quick action and quick wits. She raced down the hallways in a sense of déjà vu. This time her escape would work, she vowed. Her legs pounded down the empty corridor, as she made her way to a door at the end of the hall.

She spotted an emergency exit with relief. Running as fast as she could, she silently made her way toward freedom. Right when she touched the door handle, someone grabbed her roughly around the waist and swung her around. She cried out as she saw Dale sneering at her.

He grabbed her arm and began to pull her with him.

"No!" she screamed. "Let me go!" She pulled back, trying to stop him. When that didn't work, she punched at him. Nothing slowed him down. Then, she let herself drop onto the floor. Her dead weight barely distracted him. Dale held onto her arm and pulled harder, dragging her roughly across the floor. She jerked back against his grip, and he lost his hold.

Instantly, she jumped to her feet again, but didn't make it three strides, before Dale captured her again.

"You're making this more difficult than needed," he growled into her ear.

The smell of decaying flesh hit her nose, and she knew, this time, it wasn't because of her paranormal-sensing nose. He smelled like decay, because he was decaying. She shivered and pulled as far away as she was able. If only she knew magic, she lamented. She might have been able to blind him or make herself invisible, so he'd never find her. "Why would I make this easier on you?" Zoe shot back bitterly.

"Because if we like you, we will kill you quickly."

Chapter 38

Erik pulled the storage-shed door open. As it rose, he stared inside at the contents. Boxes piled high in neat stacks, and a lone clipboard sat on a table next to the entrance. The workers hired by the Vatican to ready all valuables for shipment to Italy, had worked diligently on their task. He picked up the board and glanced at the inventory form. He searched through the neatly typed list to find what he needed. Glancing at the boxes again, he noted each were numbered at the top corner.

It was possible he was going to go to Hell, for what he was about to do.

The Vatican hired personal contractors, to organize what Erik collected throughout his time tracking down the various necromancers and revenants. This storage unit would house everything he deemed important, while he was in Ohio. Most of the boxes consisted of the books he had found in Dale Hicks's house, in the woods. They were the pile he made invisible to the police during his first visit, therefore, he couldn't simply release the spell and not cause mass confusion. He had to keep things consistent. They hadn't seen the pile of books. It needed to stay that way.

He found the box he needed and unearthed it. He set it on a larger box near an open area and stood back to regard the container. He had a bad feeling about this. In fact, in his entire existence, he'd never attempted what he was about to do. Erik spotted a light switch toward the front of the unit. He turned the light on and closed the door, blocking out any spectators that might come by.

He pulled out his phone and dialed Jenny.

"Any news?" she asked by way of greeting.

Nearly smiling at her eagerness to help Zoe, he told her, "No. Not yet, but I do need your help." He waited for Jenny to chime in her acceptance and continued, "Can you get me Marc's phone number?"

Jenny was silent for a moment. His cell phone chirped. "There is his number. What else can I do?"

"That's it. For now."

"Be careful. You've never asked for anyone's number, when you're on a job."

"I want to run something by him first," Erik explained. "I have to go."

He hung up with a quick goodbye and dialed the number Jenny had sent. Marc Brinnon was a fellow wizard and in the midst of his own case. Dubbed the Tracker, the wizard was three-hundred or so years younger than Erik, but an equal when it came to magic. They both worked for the Vatican, but Marc worked on the Bathory Recovery and Detainment team or Team BRaD, as some liked to call it.

Marc answered on the third ring. "Hello, Erik."

"Marc," he greeted.

"Has something happened?"

Erik regarded the box. *Had something happened?* He laughed harshly. "You can say that." Pinching the bridge of his nose, he squeezed his eyes shut. He was contemplating doing something so foolish the Vatican could disavow him.

"Where are you?"

"I'm in Ohio, tracking a necromancer. Where are you?" Erik questioned.

"Michigan. I've only been here a few days. It's been quiet. Nothing has come up to make me think Erzabet is nearby."

"Do you know who the new target is?"

Marc sighed. "No. The Countess's bloodline is getting bigger with each passing year, making this almost impossible to locate the next host."

Therein lie the difference between the two men. Marc was charged with finding a particular spirit that jumped bodies. The younger wizard had been locating Erzabet Bathory's victims, and confining them, in hopes of stopping the serial killer since the early 1500's.

One case from beginning to end.

For Marc, it was personal.

Erik didn't have a similar story. A Knight Templar and his tutors at the Vatican showed him the possibilities of a new life. For him, it was a career. One he loved and took very seriously, but he'd not lost a loved one to evil as Marc had.

"You'll get her soon," Erik assured his friend. "I want to get your opinion on something and ask for help." Erik gave Marc a quick explanation of Dale and Zoe. He concluded with, "I'm thinking of using Dale's Hand of Glory to track Zoe."

"What?" Marc's voice cracked with disapproval and disbelief.

Erik expected the burst of incredulity. He would have the same reaction if Marc had told him the news. The Hand of Glory was pure dark magic. Dale used Zoe's blood from her injury at the cemetery on the first night, to feed the object to aid in locating her. If he can tap into the same power – the same spell – he could find her.

"There has to be another way," Marc stated.

"I would be open to any suggestion," Erik told him, his voice serious. "I know what could happen, and I know it's not good. I don't have time for the research team to come up with nothing."

"Erik," he began. "You are inviting the powers you took a vow to protect against."

"I understand." And he did.

There was a moment of silence on the phone for a good fifteen seconds, as if Marc were racking his brain for an alternative that wouldn't lead to soul damnation. "Is the Hand of Glory with you?"

Erik glanced at the box. "Yes. It's right in front of me."

"Okay," Marc said slowly. "How can I help?"

"After I use the Hand, I won't be able to access my magic. I need a clock of invisibility spell. Do you think you can work on one for me?"

"Yeah. How long will you be without magic?"

Erik grimaced. "I don't know for sure. I'm thinking it might have something to do with how long I have to use the Hand of Glory. If I can locate Zoe quickly, I should be good within the hour."

"You are doing this for a girl?" Marc asked, skepticism threading through his tone.

"I can't let her die."

"But you could lose your soul," he argued. "I'm pretty sure a girl isn't worth that."

Erik realized he was more than willing to risk his soul, if it saved Zoe. If he could pull this off, it was possible to surprise Dale in the process and finally put a stop to this leg of his journey: one less revenant serving the demon. At this point, he was beginning to understand Marc's predicament. As time went by, if he didn't collect enough manuscripts from the demon, more were released into the world, thus creating more soldiers. An almost impossible task, similar to Erzabet's multiplying relatives.

So, his feelings for Zoe distracted him from his goal, but his entire being told him there was no other way. She meant too much to him. "I know this isn't rational, but since the moment I met her, rational doesn't apply. She's been taken, and I can't let her be hurt."

Marc snorted into the phone. "God deliver me from the foolery of love."

"At the moment, I need God's help to deliver Zoe into my arms. Save your request until later. I don't have much time. Can I rely on you to perform the spell for me?"

"Yes. Hang on and let me get the correct items."

Erik heard Marc set down his cell phone. Pressing the speaker button, he rose and walked to open the box that contained the Hand of Glory. He pulled on the packing tape to reveal the Hand. A leathery brown appendage lay inside with bony fingers spread wide.

Ritual Of Blood

Dread marched over his skin, a testimony to the danger the hand represented. This artifact offered other opportunities that were hard to resist. It wasn't his first encounter with a Hand of Glory. He'd been alive, and chasing things that go bump in the night, for too long to not encounter this specific relic.

His grip was steady, as he reached to pull out the hand. The leather warmed instantly to his touch, as if reacting to his own magic. He pulled his shields up to block any dark magic, until he was ready. Erik didn't want to take the chance of prolonged exposure. For when he started the spell, all his white magic would be lost. His soul was secure, he knew, but if he tarried too long, he could lose his magic forever.

Flecks of blood, Zoe's blood from the cemetery, decorated the palm of the withered hand. Erik wondered briefly about the owner of the missing hand. The hand was so aged, it seemed to be centuries old, perhaps as old as him. Unease flared again. Magic that old could push him past a point of no return.

"Okay," Marc's voice echoed through the speaker on the phone. "Are you ready to conduct the spell, or do you need to get things in order?" There was a pause. "Are you sure there is no other way?"

Erik shook his head, even though Marc couldn't see him. "No. I've thought of every possibility. They all lead to this eventuality."

"Have you run your idea past the monsignor?"

"No." End of discussion. He knew what the monsignor would say.

With a heavy sigh, Marc capitulated. "Okay, then. Let's do this."

The location spell was simple. There had been a candle attached to the Hand of Glory, presumably when Dale used the relic to locate Zoe, before the botched kidnapping event. The candle, relic and words uttered would cause the hand to tune into his request: the location of Zoe.

Then Marc's invisibility spell would come into play.

"Once I've completed the spell for the Hand of Glory to locate Zoe, you'll need to start working on the concealment spell immediately."

"Do you have a driver on standby?"

"Yes." Erik had texted Jennifer back with his location and ETA of his expected driver. He would be waiting outside to take him where the hand led them.

"Are you bringing some sort of protection with you?"

"Do you mean other than my winning personality?"

"Exactly."

"I have my gun and a ceremonial knife or two." Erik patted the blades tucked inside his jacket. His gun was tucked into his ankle holster. He was going to corner Dale in his own den. There would be violence, and he would be prepared. "I'm covered. We need to hurry. By my calculations, I have no more than four hours to find her. The moon will set around 1 a.m."

"It's a waning gibbous moon."

"Not a lot of power during this phase, but if they attempt a sacrifice at the exact moment the moon sets, they could get a boost," Erik mused.

"The demon will be happy," Marc supplied.

"I can't have that." He turned toward the Hand of Glory, took a deep breath to clear his mind, and began the incantation.

A dark force flowed into Erik the moment he began the spell to utilize the relic. He felt his own magic fall back, slowly draining from his body, until there was nothing left other than the Hand of Glory's spell. The years of praying and worshiping his god caused his body to shudder at the invasion. Another deep breath forced his own defenses down, allowing room for the dark magic of the Hand of Glory to seep inside. Hot liquid flowed over his arms and into his fingers. Scorching fire crawled up his neck, over his jaw, and proceeded to burn his eyes.

Marc said over the phone, "Erik, are you alright? Are you still with me?"

"Yes." He didn't know how long he would be himself, though. The dark magic flowed stronger, rushing through his veins. He briefly wondered if he made things worse, by joining the opposing team.

Chapter 39

I t took five minutes for Erik to gain control of the horrible thoughts rummaging around his head. Once the Hand of Glory's power settled within him, he felt his body still. Carefully he moved his fingers and, when they responded, he worked on moving his legs. He felt almost normal, if one discounted the barely controlled rage that seemed to be lying in wait to rush forward and take over everything.

His mind grew cloudy, and he lost track of where he was, what he was doing. *Get Zoe.* The thought brought him back to reality. He had a plan. "Marc, I'm ready for the concealment spell."

Marc wasted no time and began the incantation in Latin. Each wizard had their own language of comfort when conducting spell work. Erik was fluent in Latin; therefore, knew the words his fellow wizard spoke. The spell was short, and his body disappeared from sight. He turned his hands over to check for any sign of distortion, but his body stayed invisible.

"We're good," Erik confirmed.

"I will be on stand-by when you need me again."

"Thank you and I appreciate your help."

Marc snorted. "Thank me after you get out of this alive."

"Will do," Erik murmured. "I have to go."

"Be careful."

Erik slipped his phone into this jacket pocket, while he clutched the Hand of Glory in front of him and headed to the door. Parked in the middle of stored boats and yachts, his ride was waiting for him. If the driver was surprised at the passenger door opening and closing, seemingly under its own volition, he gave no indication.

"Mr. Vardan," the driver acknowledged the empty space beside him.

"Jim. Nice to see you again."

"Can't really say the same," Jim Meeks stated, sarcasm dripping from his words. "Since I can't really, see *you*."

Erik settled into the seat and held the Hand of Glory in front of him. He pushed at the volatile power inside him and murmured in Armenian, "Show me the way." Zoe's blood on the hand would drive the spell, feeding it until her location was revealed.

***

For more than an hour, no one came to see Zoe or Susie's mother. Mary sat in the corner, wilting slowly against blankets spread out. The woman's eyes closed, and she slumped over. She had known Susie and her mother for years. Pain made people do strange things. Zoe believed it was the pain that made Mary act the way she did earlier. All those years trumped the way they acted today, so Zoe called out for help.

She didn't know if Mary had passed out or was dying, but she didn't want to sit quietly, while Susie's mother breathed her last breath. The woman Zoe knew would never condone the way she was being treated, and that was the woman Zoe intended to save.

The door opened and another skeleton stared at her.

How many of these damn things are running around? Two or three, probably. She didn't know if the skeleton she'd managed to decapitate in her earlier escape attempt survived, but obviously more were running around.

She thought about the demon's book. Susie had it the entire time. Disbelief continued to cloud her thoughts. If she could get a hold of the book and get it to Erik, there would be one less problem for the Vatican. There would also be one less necromancer and revenant, if they managed to take the book.

The skeleton began to close the door without coming in. Zoe pointed to Mary, who continued to slump sideways, and said, "She's sick. She needs help."

Without any sound, the creature fell back and closed the door. Yelling after it, Zoe continued to call for help. Minutes passed, but no one came. Zoe rose from her spot and crossed the room, closer to Mary.

"Mary? Can you hear me?"

She showed no signs of awareness.

Zoe bent and touched Mary's bare wrist. The woman's skin was freezing. Quickly walking to the door, she pounded on it.

This time the door opened, and Dale stuck his head in to scowl at her. "What is your problem? Are you that eager to be a sacrifice?"

Gulping at Dale's words, she shook her head as she cradled her hand. The finger continued to pulse ceaselessly. She pointed at Mary with her free hand. "I think she might be dying."

Dale shrugged. "Happens every day."

"But not to me!"

He raised his scraggily brow. "Well, today will be your lucky day."

Zoe didn't like those ominous words. "Can't you at least tell Susie? She might want to do something for her mother."

He shrugged again, then turned and left. Zoe stood for a moment before reaching out to try the door handle. Was it possible he forgot to lock the door behind him? Disappointment welled inside, when the handle resisted her attempt.

The same moment the door opened quickly, knocking Zoe back. Susie rushed over to her mother. "Mom," she knelt to check her vital signs.

Zoe waited in the back of the room, watchful of the exit, but Dale must have known she'd try to escape again. With arms crossed, he stepped in the middle of the doorway. Trying another tactic, she told Susie, "I think your mom needs a hospital. She doesn't look well."

Susie's head whipped around to pin her, with an anguished glare. "Of course, she doesn't look well! She has cancer! She's dying." She bent to whisper something into her mother's ear, then called out, "Help me get her out of here."

Dale didn't move a muscle.

Susie rose slowly and crossed the room, to stand before the revenant. "That is an order. You serve me."

Something flickered across Dale's dead face – something Zoe couldn't put into words. Anger, hate, despair, resolution – all rolled into a single look. He stayed still for a second longer, before crossing to Zoe and her mother. Bending, he picked her up.

Excitement raced through Zoe. The door stood unguarded. Dale's hands were full. Susie's attention was focused elsewhere. She might have a chance this time, but before she could move, Dale called out, "Necromancer, you need to guard your exit. Unless you want a third attempt at escape, and after that, it just gets embarrassing."

Two skeletons filled the door. Zoe sneered at the pair. If only she could get her hands on them, she'd pop their heads off, like the other one. Then her finger reminded her of its injured state. Her index finger was twice its normal size and a deep purple bruise crept forth over the entire length. She needed to make a splint to limit motion.

As Susie passed Zoe, she shook her head. "You need to accept what's going to happen."

"Never!" Zoe shot back. She wasn't going to be bullied. If she were going to die, she would try to be brave. "Erik will find me, and I'm pretty sure now that you are the new necromancer, you are his number one priority."

"He hasn't had any luck so far. I'm not too concerned about that."

Zoe knew differently. Erik would find her. She only hoped it would be in time.

Everyone cleared out of the room, leaving Zoe behind. She glanced around. Other than the single chair, a large blanket laying rumpled in the corner. The blanket could be used, if she could tear it into small strips, to help make a splint for her finger. She walked over and tried her hand at tearing fabric.

A few minutes later, she had her hand swathed in ripped strips of fabric. The blanket tore easily, and Zoe tried not to shudder at the hard, smelly material. At least her finger was protected.

Suddenly the door opened, and Dale walked inside. Wordlessly he ushered her toward the door.

Chapter 40

Zoe sent Dale a questioning glance and silently pushed her in front of him. They walked down the brightly lit hallway, before maneuvering her into another room. This room had a wooden large table at the center. Several chairs and a rolling table accompanied it. The scent of bleach and something ominous filled Zoe's nostrils. A large box about six feet long nestled against a corner.

After Erik told her about how she can now smell different kinds of magic, good and bad, she knew something wrong had happened in this room. She stopped in her tracks when Dale continued to push her. When she refused to move, he shoved her so hard, that she stumbled forward and slammed into the table.

Her finger stung at the treatment, but Dale simply reached down and swiped her legs out from underneath her. With a frightened cry, she fell onto the chair. Dale roughly wrapped her hands with duct tape, in front of her. He stomped out without a word. Her body shuddered; at the realization they were going to go through with the ritual killing.

Somehow, this nightmare had come full circle back to her and the killer. It wouldn't be Dale this time. It would be Susie and wouldn't be an innocent bystander. She would be the victim. Her heart would end up in a relic box somewhere. Her stomach revolted at the thought, and she pushed herself to her feet. Walking to the large box, she struggled to break her hands loose from the tape, but nothing helped. She attempted to rub the tape across the lid of the box, but the top was too smooth. Nothing loosened her bonds.

Curious to see if anything helpful could be found within the box, she lifted the lid. A blue plastic tarp was folded inside, so she bent to lift it out of the way. As she raised the plastic, a scream tore from her lips. Tiffany stared sightlessly up at her. Zoe fell to the floor, and the lid slammed shut.

Shaking her head with a sob, she scooted away from the horror trapped inside the container. Tiffany was dead. Susie killed her. The facts repeated themselves over and over in her head. She didn't hear the door opening, but Susie's voice startled her.

"I see you couldn't stop being so curious." Susie walked over and peeked inside the box. She grimaced and let the lid slam closed.

Tears fell down Zoe's cheeks. "Why, Susie?" She felt broken inside. Up until now, she thought of things as strange and only slightly dangerous. Seeing Tiffany's body, one of her friends, dead by Susie's hand suddenly made her feel ill. "How could you do this?" Zoe stared up at Susie with tear-filled eyes.

"I told you once I would do anything for my mother. She needs me. Now I found a way to help her."

"But I thought we were friends," Zoe said. The shock began to take its toll on her. Her blurred vision made it hard to focus on Susie.

The newest necromancer hopped up, to sit on the box that contained Tiffany. She kicked her feet like a child and smiled serenely. "We are friends."

Zoe shook her head. "Friends don't kill friends."

"You are my friend. If you didn't mean anything to me, you wouldn't be worth anything to me."

Susie's cryptic words sank in, as Erik's words from earlier made the connection. *My guess is once upon a time, Dale stumbled across a ritual that helped him. Maybe it was money, fame, health.*

Health.

Susie chose this path of death because she wanted to help her mother. "Susie, you have to know this isn't right. Whatever was promised, you can't be sure it will come to light. You committed murder. You killed Tiffany in cold blood."

"I needed Tiffany. Just like I need you." She glanced at her watch. "I don't have time to chat right now. I have to get my things in order for the ceremony." Susie slid off the box and knocked on the lid before coming to stand over Zoe. "You are going to help my mom. I'm sorry it has to be this way, but it's the only option left."

Zoe didn't have a chance to retort. Susie was out the door in an instant, slamming the door behind her. Slowly rising to her feet, she glanced around the room again. She had to escape because if she failed, she would be dead. With tied hands, she pushed against the walls, ran her fingers over any crevice she could get, and desperately hoped for a bone tossed her way. She completed a trip around the room with nothing to aid in her escape. Still, she refused to give up. There had to be a way out.

A quiet murmur of a sound echoed around the room. Her body stilled. Then, another soft noise as metal screeched slowly. Zoe stepped back, while watching where the disruption originated: the door. Alarm rocked her body when the door opened, but no one was there. Her rooted feet didn't move. "Hello?" she called uncertainly.

Still no one appeared. A whisper of a sound reached her. "Zoe."

Her rattled nerves couldn't comprehend what was happening. The door still remained open.

"Zoe, it's me."

Startled, she squeaked, "Erik?" Her heart threatened to jump out of her chest.

He nodded, but realized she couldn't see him. "Yes. Stay quiet. I'm going to get you out of here."

"You have to hurry," Zoe whispered. "I don't have much time." So many things tumbled in her head, that she wanted to tell him. He gripped her hand, and she nearly melted at the contact. Against the odds, Erik managed to find her.

Voices converged outside the door. With a pull, Erik moved to the door and stuck his head out, to see how many were coming.

All of them.

He cursed. "We're going to have to run for it." Realizing he was going to have to lose his concealment spell, if he wanted Zoe to have a good visual on him if they were separated, he dialed Marc on his phone. "I'm ready."

Hundreds of miles away, Marc released the spell. "Good luck." The line went dead.

"That's not something you see every day."

Erik focused on Zoe. Her shock expression belied her calm statement. Taking her bound hands again, he said, "We're going to have to move fast."

Zoe nodded in understanding. Right, move fast. She could do that. She was at his side, as they raced out the open door. Susie's angered cry reached her, as they rushed down the hallway. Adrenaline pushed her faster, to keep up with Erik.

As they ran, she asked breathlessly, "Why don't you use your magic to zap them?"

"I don't have any magic at the moment."

"What?" she exclaimed. With a quick glance behind her, she saw they had a good lead on Susie and the others. "What happened?" The door was within reach.

They both hit the door at the same. Zoe backed off, since her hands were not at their most helpful. In horror, she watched as Erik attempted to turn the knob. It wouldn't budge. He tried again, but nothing worked. They were locked inside.

A harsh laugh greeted them, as they turned to watch Susie, Dale, and the skeletons saunter toward them, as if they were enjoying themselves. "You honestly didn't think the building wouldn't be spelled, did you?" Susie cast Zoe and Erik a disappointed lip pucker. "Take them back to the room."

The skeletons grabbed Zoe's arm and hauled her back down the hallway. "No!" She tried to pull away, but the creatures were too strong. She peered over her shoulder. Erik struggled with the remaining skeleton, having no better luck.

Shock wasn't an emotion that happened to him often – if at all. But he was shocked to find out Susan Monroe was the necromancer. It should have occurred to him something nefarious happened, at the house the night Dale died. Susie played such a convincing victim; he never stopped to look closely at the signs that were there. Hell, he had even been in her house!

"Wizard," Dale called. "How is it the door didn't drop you to the floor? The spell we used was to paralyze any white magic."

Erik refused to offer up information, on his momentarily – he hoped – diminished magical supply. Better to keep them guessing, than to fess up to a complete lack of defense. Once in the room, Dale divested him of both his blades. The ankle holster remained undetected for the moment. The skeleton pushed him into the chair and stood by his side, like a skeletal watchdog.

Watching Dale direct Zoe to the table, Erik's stomach hit the floor; when he realized they were prepping her for the sacrifice. Susie was the last to enter the room.

The smug smile on Susie's face made Zoe furious. "You have no right to do this!" Her seething words had no effect. "You killed Tiffany, and for what? Do you seriously think murdering people is going to give your mom more years to live? If you do, you are insane."

Susie's smile slowly faded as she stared at Zoe. For a moment, she thought her friend had come back, and then the nightmare would be over. But she neared Zoe and roughly pushed her back onto the table.

The hard wood bit into her shoulders. She struggled against Susie's grip. Looking down, she grabbed Zoe's bandaged finger and bent it backward. White-hot pain seared through her veins, and she cried out.

"Insane?" Zoe's eyes flashed. She pointed at Dale. "I killed him." She continued to bend Zoe's finger. "I beat him with a rock. And he's walking now!"

Zoe was beyond listening. Every particle in her body focused on the pain. Vomit surged up her throat and she gagged.

Quickly letting go, Susie stepped away and sneered at her. "You'd never have survived if he took you instead of me." She leaned down and whispered, "That man is the walking dead. With more power, I can save my mom."

"Tiffany's life didn't seem to help," Zoe gasped, as she cradled her hand to her chest. She didn't try to rise from the table, so she followed Susie's movements with her eyes.

Flinging herself around, Susie stood in front of Erik. She ran a finger down his chest and stared at Zoe. "I miscalculated how deep I needed to cut, in order to remove a beating heart. It won't happen with you, Zoe."

Chapter 41

"You can't expect to get away with this. The police will know something. They probably already figured out that people around you are suddenly turning up dead. I wouldn't be surprised if they aren't on their way right now."

Another smile. "You're right. We need to hurry." With a wave to Dale, Susie walked to the door. An instant later, they left the room, leaving their sentient guards.

Zoe let out a shaky sigh. Her eyes found Erik's. "You're not nervous," she remarked, uncaring that the skeleton stood over her.

"I've been in worse situations."

"Of course you have. Have your compatriots fared as well as you?"

Warmth filled his eyes. "Compatriots?"

Nodding, she leaned up on her elbows. "Other people that have been with you, have they survived, too?"

"For the most part." He wouldn't tell her about the time a demon decapitated several of his helpers in 1810. "I'm usually pretty safe to be around."

Zoe caught his wry humor and held onto it. She felt something bubble up inside her. Something dearly wanted to get out, and no matter how hard she tried to tamp it down it grew stronger. There wasn't much time, so she blurted, "I love you."

Erik blinked at her confession. For a moment, shock robbed him of speech. She loved him? Was that possible? No one had ever loved him. He never let anyone close enough to grow to love him. Yet, somehow, Zoe came into his life and brought all her impossibilities.

Zoe took his silence as a denial. "I'm sorry, I shouldn't have said anything, but since I'm going to die, I wanted you to know. I don't expect you to return the feelings." She eyed the nearby skeleton and had to wonder if the thing could hear. It didn't have any ears, so how could he? It didn't matter, though. She told Erik she loved him. She had amazing sex with a wizard from the Vatican, and she'd fallen in love. If she was going to die, at least she'd lived a little.

"You aren't going to die."

She raised her bound hands. "I'm on a table waiting to be sacrificed, while being guarded by a walking skeleton. My chances of survival are very low. And you don't need to love me back. I'm not that needy. Actually, after this I won't need much."

Erik snorted at her dry humor. He wouldn't let her die. Not after her admission that she loved him. He needed Dale to come back. He could overpower the revenant and keep the skeletons at bay. They were nearly impossible to destroy, but he could keep them occupied. Attempting a flare spell, his body didn't respond and sat magically quiet. He cursed under his breath. He'd hoped his power would return right away, after discarding the Hand of Glory.

"Can you do magic now?" Zoe asked, heedless of the skeleton. "No."

"Why? What happened?"

"I used a magical item, that stripped me of my powers."

Zoe didn't like the sound of that. "Why did you do that?"

"To find you."

"Oh. Then you must like me a little."

Erik almost snorted at her comment. He never imagined being trapped in a building discussing his budding love life. "I do," he admitted. "But we need to get out of here."

Looking at the unmoving skeleton, she asked in a whisper, "Can they hear us?"

The skeleton turned its head minimally, an apparent indication that it could hear just fine.

"I think you have your answer." Erik concentrated again, trying to find the smallest edge to his magic, in an attempt to pull it toward him.

The door burst open. Dale strode inside, carrying a rolled-up case, and placed himself near Erik. Susie cradled in a large book, holding it to her chest. Its jagged edges told of various additions to the work. The worn leather cover was engraved with strange symbols.

Her eyes met Erik's, and she mouthed to him, *is that the book?* Erik nodded once.

Susie set the book down on the table next to Zoe. A rotten odor floated toward Zoe.

Her mind raced. Maybe she could grab the book and... The errant thought shot through her brain, but another part of her whispered caution. Hadn't she already been captured at least four times? Her track record wasn't that good.

"Dale, bring my mom here. You'll have to help her. She's not able to walk." Susie ordered, as she held her hand out to him. Dale handed her the case, before walking out to retrieve Mary Monroe.

Susie laid the case next to the book, and Zoe watched in fear as she unwrapped it to reveal a set of knives. The blades gleamed menacingly. Bright red nail polish glittered off the surface, as Susie chose a knife and teased it in front of Zoe. Finished with her display of malice, Susie turned to the book and leafed through the pages.

As the pages turned, the parchment crinkled, sending small dust particles into the air. In silence, Susie continued to rifle through the book. Mary appeared in the doorway, looking frail and sickly, for a moment, Zoe felt guilty.

Then she remembered Susie was going to kill her, so her mom could live. The guilt slid away. "Please, Mrs. Monroe! You can't let Susie do this!"

The woman stared at her. Her face drawn in pain. "I can't do this anymore." She touched the side of her head. "The pain. I want it to stop. Susie says she can make it stop."

"Come on, Mom." Susie led her mother to the box in the

corner and motioned for her to sit on it. She came back to Zoe. "Nice try, but she deserves this peace."

Erik spoke for the first time. "Who is going to give you peace?"

Slowly looking up at Erik, Susie shrugged.

Seeing a hint of uncertainty, he continued, "You cannot keep killing without repercussions. Time runs out. Dale can attest to that. Your skeletons can attest to that. Eventually you will be called upon to pay the price, and I think you have no idea what awaits you."

The look of uncertainty was replaced with anger. "I don't need your lecture, *wizard*." A strange look came over her, before she crossed the floor to whisper in Dale's ear. He looked at Erik and shrugged. "I can run a truth spell on him, like he did on your imposter at the warehouse," she told Dale.

"Could work, but if I were you, I'd stay the course. You've been bade to sacrifice her. Finish the task."

Susie pouted a moment. "Fine. But we keep him bound while I do research. What if all the power he has would come to me?"

Dale wisely stayed quiet.

Approaching Zoe, Susie took the knife in hand and began to cut open her shirt. She cried out at the sensation of the knife point grazing her collarbone. Zoe turned her head away from Susie and instantly locked onto Erik's. Her body began to shake in fear, but Erik continued to stare at her.

Then she noticed he wiggled his foot back and forth.

Confusion at his movements held her still for a moment. What the heck was he doing? Why would he shake his foot at her like that, when she was about to die? A flash of silver caught her attention.

Suddenly comprehension slammed into her. The gun! His gun had never been detected. She thought about her options. A few minutes later, she still had no idea what to do. But when Susie leaned over the demon's book and began to read, Zoe panicked. The knife was poised over her skin.

Without thought, Zoe bucked up against the knife. She never

felt it slice into her skin, because she was instantly rolling toward Erik. Her momentum sent her body off the table. She moved her bound hands to grab the gun strapped to Erik's ankle. She fumbled with sliding her index finger into the trigger ring. She was right-handed, but Susie had broken that finger and it was utterly useless.

She heard a shriek behind her. Turning quickly around, she pointed the gun at Susie and pulled the trigger without thought. Susie screamed again and dove for the spell book.

Loudly shouting, Susie tried to continue reading the spell, "Bring the edges of reality to me!"

Zoe scanned the room frantically and spotted Dale. He cowered against the wall, and she aimed the gun at him. She pulled the trigger and missed. Realizing his time was up; Dale took one last look around and ran for the door.

"Dale!" Susie screamed. "Get back here!"

Dale didn't answer. He disappeared from sight.

A skeleton reached for Zoe, but Erik leaped toward it, knocking them both to the ground. As the two wrestled, Zoe took aim at Susie again. She fired a shot, but Susie only glared angrily at her and continued to read from the book. Struggling to rise, Zoe walked toward Susie.

"You won't ruin this! I've worked too hard! Oh, Mammon, hear me. I give you this sacrifice."

Chapter 42

The same moment Susie leapt for Zoe, with the knife above her head, a strange light shot through the room. Zoe held her hands up to protect herself from the plunging knife and tried to scoot backward. As they struggled, the air distorted and shimmered. Zoe watched in horrified fascination, as a large hole opened in the air next to Susie. The light burned Zoe's eyes, and the most terrifying noise penetrated the room.

Erik leapt forward and yanked her away from the opening circle. The screams within didn't dissipate. Encircling Zoe in his arms, he distanced them further away from the portal. He'd seen a few in his lifetime, and he didn't want her near what was coming. Mammon had put up with enough apparently. At that moment, Susie stopped to stare at the hole. A giant creature rushed in, grabbed Susie, and fell back into the portal.

Instantly, the room grew quiet of all screams and only a lingering scent of something that made Zoe's stomach clench remained. She leaned her head back against Erik's shoulder. The silence left behind, after the shrieking was painful.

Zoe sat for a moment and tried to process what happened. "What. Was. That?"

"That would have been Mammon. He doesn't usually get involved with his servants, but Dale and Susie really messed things up. Mammon must have decided enough was enough."

Erik's arms tightened around her. Zoe closed her eyes and let herself breathe deeply. She was safe. She didn't die. Erik didn't die. "Skeletons!" She quickly looked around, but the room was empty, except for the demon's book and Mrs. Monroe. The woman's body was still on the box that held Tiffany.

Motioning for her to stay where she was, Erik checked on Susie's mom. "She's alive. Barely, but there is a pulse."

Zoe gazed at the women. Would she wake up and remember any of this? Erik stood beside her, and he gathered her unhurt hand gently in his.

"Dale ran away," Zoe stated. "What will happen to him?"

Quirking his mouth, Erik shrugged. "I'm guessing he won't be an issue much longer. With the necromancer no longer here, no one is feeding him power. He won't last the hour. I have a team in route, so they will pick up his trail."

"Were you surprised to find him alive?"

Erik nodded. "Yeah, but not as much as finding out that Susie was the new necromancer."

Shaking her head in wonder, Zoe said, "She did it all for her mom. I'm not saying she was in the right. She did kill Tiffany and the imposter that resembled you. But in her head, she thought her decisions were the best, for the health of her mother." Zoe glanced at Mrs. Monroe once more. The woman would be devastated to learn her daughter was dead.

Zoe's skin had gone pale and clammy, and her eyes had taken on a faraway look. He knew shock was setting in. Erik maneuvered Zoe to one of the chairs and waited for her to sit down before calling Jenny. "Can you call a team to my location? I need some time, before the police get here. And I need a transport for one."

Transport for one? Zoe worried he was going to send her away. She wouldn't let that happen. She told him she loved him! But part of her argued he was doing his job, and his job was over. The bad guys caught, book in his possession, another crisis averted. She watched him pace a few steps away, as he talked on his phone, and she glanced around the room again.

Something whispered in the back of her mind. The book sat on the table, seemingly harmless. But Zoe knew better. She knew it was calling for its new owner. It was reaching out for anyone who would listen. "Erik."

He turned to her.

With a finger pointing in the direction of the book, she told him, "You need to get that book."

He cast a quick glance, between the book and her before nodding. "Okay," Erik spoke into the phone. "I will be back to the office soon." After hanging up, he walked to stand beside Zoe. They both stared at the book. "Did you hear it?"

"Yes. I'm not tempted, but I heard it. Can you hear it?"

He shook his head. "No, but my magic has returned."

"How did you lose your magic?"

Erik reached for Zoe's unhurt hand and linked his fingers through hers. "I used the Hand of Glory to find you."

"That was a stupid thing to do!"

He laughed. Then leaning down, he cupped her jaw. She closed her eyes at his touch, and he told her, "Yes, it was stupid, but I would do it again. I couldn't bear the thought of Dale hurting you." He touched her lips with his, and her sigh told him everything he needed to know. His mouth covered hers, in a deep kiss that told her how much she meant to him.

She raised her hands to his chest and held on to him, as he pulled her closer to his body. He tasted of spice and smelled of leather, and she welcomed it, reveled in it.

"I love you."

He spoke the words this time. Zoe pulled back and sent him a beaming smile. "Hey! You said you loved me, and you weren't even under the threat of death!"

Smiling, he whispered against her mouth, "I love you. Threat of death or no."

Her arms looped around his shoulders. Careful not to disturb her broken finder, she pulled him back down to her lips. "We could be a paranormal team. I could go with you, when you're searching for more of the demons' books. Maybe I can learn some magic. I do have my special nose."

For once in his life, the idea of someone by his side felt *right*.

Before he could comment on her plans, sounds of new arrivals floated down the hall. Bracing her at his side, he turned to the door and scanned out his power to create a shield. He would take no chances on her safety.

"Erik!" Jim Meeks's voice sounded, on the other side of the door.

"In here," he shouted. He turned to Zoe. "He's my driver. There will be more people here in a few minutes." Glancing down at her cradled hand, he gently raised it to get a closer look at the damage.

Zoe's index finger rested at an awkward angle. Swollen to more than twice its normal size, her finger showed an impressive array of bruising. His eyes met hers. "This is going to sound ridiculous, but does it hurt?"

She nodded. "Yes, and if you say you are going to set it, I will punch you in the face."

"No," a voice came from behind, startling them. "He's not going to set it. I will."

Both turned to watch Dr. Blackwell walk into the room. The older woman smiled at them and motioned Zoe back toward the chair. "I see you are still with us, Miss Hunt."

"Yes," Zoe said with a smile.

"Hmm. Nasty break." She looked up at Erik. "I would recommend an x-ray at the hospital for this. I'm assuming you can take her to a hospital now?"

The admonishing look Dr. Blackwell sent Erik echoed her thoughts, on her first visit with Zoe. The woman did get hurt a bit. He nodded in the affirmative. "Yes. The hospital is a viable option now."

Dr. Blackwell sniffed. "This man sweeps in every once in a while, sometimes leaving a trail of injured, sometimes not."

Zoe frowned at Erik. "You said your compatriots weren't usually injured."

"*Compatriots*," Erik corrected. "You are not a compatriot."

Stomach filling with butterflies at his husky words, Zoe stared up at him.

Ritual Of Blood

Dr. Blackwell stepped away, patted Zoe on the shoulder and glared at Erik. "Don't mess this up," she muttered as she walked away.

Erik gathered Zoe into his arms once more. "I love your bright spirit; I love that you push me to do more. You are not a compatriot. You have somehow become my life. I've wondered this earth for more than seven hundred years, and I've never found someone like you." His eyes met hers. "I cannot tell the future. I don't know what it holds, but I want to ask you to share it with me."

Zoe's heart stopped at his words, and all she could think to say was, "Really?"

He leaned down and kissed her. "Yes, really. Share the future with me, and we'll see what trouble we can get into."

She loved the sound of that and agreed with every fiber of her being. She took his hand in hers, as they walked out of the room that she was meant to die in, and walked out to start a new adventure.

Epilogue

Zoe stared at the buildings surrounding her and reached for Erik's hand. "I've never seen anything like this," she breathed in wonder.

"It has changed much over the years."

"You saw it all, didn't you?"

"For the most part, yes. The Vatican has grown into a city, but it's been home."

The brisk breeze blew Zoe's bangs into her eyes, and she shook her head to dislodge them. Erik reached over and patted them down. His warm gaze heated her better than any furnace. After looking her fill, she glanced back down at the tourist map. So many artifacts and famous structures, she didn't know where to start.

But Erik did. He took her hand and led her into the museum. From there, they took an elevator that was flagged as *Employees Only*. Zoe hefted the tote she carried more securely over her shoulder.

The book was getting heavy, but she refused to relinquish it. For some reason, she felt as if she needed to bring the demon's book herself. She had no doubt Erik was capable. It was his job after all, but to her, this was her mission. When Susie's mom passed away two days after the kidnapping, Zoe knew she had to see the book delivered to the Vatican's vaults.

Erik had spoken of the paranormal treasures housed within the walls of the Vatican's storage unit. The book would find its rightful place alongside numerous other spell books. They walked down a long brightly lit hallway, until they stopped at a door. Erik pushed it open, and a slim man sat at a desk. He smiled up at them, as they walked in.

"Erik, good to have you back. Did you bring me something to store?"

"Yes. My partner, Zoe, has a book for you to catalog."

The man looked at her in keen interest, and then Zoe realized he was waiting for her to give him the book. She glanced at Erik. When he nodded in encouragement, she handed the tote to the man.

"Excellent! This one is by Mammon's disciples, correct?"

"Yes," Zoe confirmed.

"It'll be in good hands."

Erik guided Zoe out of the office. "He will take excellent care of the book. He's insanely fastidious."

A huge wave of relief washed over her, at the delivery of the book. It felt as if a chapter in her life had been closed, and she was ready for something new and even more exciting. Erik would bring the new and exciting and she would be right by his side.

As they walked along the hall, she heard a whisper reach out to her. At first, her stomach dropped, thinking it was the demon's book. But Erik glanced at her.

"It's nothing," he said.

It didn't sound like nothing. Then, the sound came again. "Please. Please let me out."

"Erik, someone needs help," Zoe gasped.

He shook his head and nodded at a door they passed. "That's exactly what she wants," he told her cryptically. "Come, let's head back upstairs and enjoy some of the sights. Tomorrow will be soon enough for work. Tonight, I'm going to show you exactly how far I've come, with the language of love."

She laughed. "I'm sorry, I don't speak French."

Erik pulled her body into his. "I will speak it for you." He bent his head and captured her lips. "The world is at your fingertips."

Zoe leaned up and whispered, "I'm not asking for the world.

Ritual Of Blood

I only want you."

Their heated kiss lit the fires within. Taking her hand, they headed out of the basement of the Vatican and into the rest of their lives…

ABOUT THE AUTHOR

Penny Pearson lives in southern Indiana with her husband, young daughter, two quarter horses, two rescued dogs, and two grey barn cats. The love of writing has always been with her. At a young age, she began to pen stories, and found she liked to write about unexplained beings having the chance at love.

Please visit Penny's website to learn more:

www.ParanormallyWeird.com

Continue the adventure in the next book of the Wizards of the Vatican Series, *Bequest of Blood*! Available now in print and eBook editions!

CONNECT WITH SEVENTH STAR PRESS!

Join our email list at: https://www.seventhstarpress.com/ssp-enewsletter/

Support our work on Patreon: http://www.patreon.com/seventhstarpress

Facebook: http://www.facebook.com/seventhstarpress

Twitter: http://www.twitter.com/7thStarPress

Instagram: http://www.instagram.com/7thStarpress